# MR. MONK
# IS OPEN FOR BUSINESS

Center Point
Large Print

Also by Hy Conrad and available from
Center Point Large Print:

The Monk Series
  *Mr. Monk Helps Himself*
  *Mr. Monk Gets on Board*

**This Large Print Book carries the
Seal of Approval of N.A.V.H.**

# MR. MONK
## IS OPEN FOR BUSINESS

## HY CONRAD

Based on the USA Network television
series created by Andy Breckman

CENTER POINT LARGE PRINT
THORNDIKE, MAINE

This Center Point Large Print edition
is published in the year 2015 by arrangement with
New American Library, an imprint of Penguin Publishing
Group, a division of Penguin Random House LLC.

The text of this Large Print edition is unabridged.
In other aspects, this book may vary from the original edition.
Printed in the United States of America on permanent paper.
Set in 16-point Times New Roman type.

ISBN: 978-1-62899-720-0

Library of Congress Cataloging-in-Publication Data

Conrad, Hy.
Mr. Monk is open for business / Hy Conrad ; based on the USA
Network television series created by Andy Breckman. — Center Point
Large Print edition.
        pages cm
Summary: "Monk and Natalie are hired to find a disgruntled employee
who came into work and started shooting, killing three coworkers and
leaving a female hostage severely wounded. But the more he and Natalie
try to track down the assailant, the more he seems to have disappeared
from existence altogether"—Provided by publisher.
        ISBN 978-1-62899-720-0 (library binding : alk. paper)
        1. Monk, Adrian (Fictitious character)—Fiction.
        2. Private investigators—Fiction.
        3. Obsessive-compulsive disorder—Fiction.
        4. Murder—Investigation—Fiction. 5. Large type books.
        I. Breckman, Andy. II. Monk (Television program) III. Title.
PS3553.O5166M83 2015
813'.54—dc23
                                                    2015023886

To Key West,
my end-of-the-road paradise

# AUTHOR'S NOTE AND ACKNOWLEDGMENTS

One question a mystery writer always gets asked: Do you work from a detailed outline or just make it up as you go? The answer, of course, is yes.

This particular book began with a search through my old *Monk* files, looking for unused nuggets. A nugget, according to Andy Breckman, our beloved showrunner, is the central twist or cool idea around which you build a mystery. For *Monk*, we used to put them all on a corkboard and give them names. For instance, one we called Coat Check, in which a killer leaves something incriminating in his coat pocket, then loses the coat to a disorganized coat-check girl. By season three, we'd figured out how to use that one.

Anyway, in my old files, undisturbed for years, lay two of my favorites. I mashed them together—artistically—and made sure they could play well with the concept of Monk and Natalie's opening a detective agency. At that point I had a beginning (the mystery setup) and an end (the big twist) all outlined. That was it.

As you might imagine, the first thirty pages are great fun to write and the last thirty pages are a dream. What comes in between is the maddening challenge—and the great reward. Characters you thought would be one-paragraph sidebars become main players. Monk and Natalie find a way to make the story personal. Little red herrings become comedy gold. And, with luck, it all meshes into something you couldn't have foreseen, even if you'd spent a month writing a detailed outline.

I'd like to thank a few people here. First, my literary agent, Allison Cohen. We were thrown together when I switched TV agents. But she's proven to be an invaluable partner and a tireless supporter. Laura Fazio at Penguin is my new soul mate, even though we've never met. Lee Goldberg continues to be a generous booster of the *Monk* series. Finally I need to thank Andy Breckman, who called me up in 2002, said, "Hey, do you want a job?" and changed my life.

# MR. MONK
## IS OPEN FOR BUSINESS

# I

# MR. MONK AND THE EMPTY OFFICE

"So, you're not telling me anything about the murder?"

"I didn't say there was a murder, Monk."

"No murder?" Adrian Monk's hands were poised in front of his face as he moved across the room from left to right, his head tipping slowly from side to side to catch all the angles. He let his hands fall. "Okay. What are we doing here?"

"I was hoping you could tell us." Captain Stottlemeyer's upper lip moved and his mustache twitched. That was his tell, an unconscious sign that he was enjoying himself. Monk must have caught it. Monk can catch every detail, dozens of them at once—it's uncanny—except when he chooses not to. Then he can be as thick as a brick.

"I want you to have a clear mind," added the captain.

We were in a storefront office in a tiny strip mall, about halfway between Monk's Pine Street apartment and my bungalow in a neighborhood called Noe Valley. There were no signs on the front windows and next to nothing inside the

11

building space to indicate its occupant. But that wouldn't be a problem for Monk.

He threw the captain a sideways glance, then continued. I've seen him do this hundreds of times. He walks into a room full of CSIs and cops and at least one corpse. Five minutes later, he has the whole thing figured out: victim, murderer, and motive. This time he had less to go on. There were no CSIs with little tidbits of information to throw his way, no corpse, and only one cop, his oldest and only male friend this side of New Jersey, Leland Stottlemeyer.

I actually knew more about this case than Monk did, but that wasn't because I'm brilliant. I'm just Natalie Teeger, a San Francisco single mom who got talked into being Monk's assistant, keeping him focused and functioning, and trying to keep half the people he meets from strangling him to death.

Being joined at the hip with one of the world's top detectives must have rubbed off, because I am now Monk's full partner in our own agency. Technically, I'm Monk's boss, since I'm the one who studied and got my California PI license. I'm a decent investigator, but I know the business would be nothing without Monk. So does everyone else.

"This space has been recently rented." Monk's nose was just far enough away from the front window so that no germs could make the death-defying leap onto his skin. Germs are just one of his many phobias. I would say countless, except he actually does count them.

"There are traces of tape glue set at diagonals eighteen inches apart, twelve inches high, which is the standard size of a mass-produced For Rent sign. The wood flooring is new. But there's a half inch of standard white tile in the corner, suggesting this was an inexpensive food establishment." He pointed across the room. "The row of two-hundred-and-twenty-volt outlets on that wall confirms my theory, as does the tiny shred of lettuce on the welcome mat, which has not been replaced. Or cleaned properly. This used to be a sandwich shop."

"That's all well and good," said Stottlemeyer. "What about now?"

"I'm getting to that." Monk walked over to a pair of identical desks.

I knew how his mind was working. At least I thought I did. The desks were equally spaced, with identical, ergonomically designed office chairs, everything brand-new and spotless. A pair of perfectly aligned picture hooks along one wall showed that someone was planning to mount something, probably artwork, but hadn't gotten around to it. Another picture hook was behind one of the desks. I could tell from Monk's body language that there were other things he was seeing that I wasn't.

"This place was recently rented by a woman, about five foot five, according to the height of her chair. The other chair hasn't been adjusted from its delivery height, so her partner hasn't yet sat down. They are equal partners in this business. She's working hard to establish this. You can tell from the symmetry and sameness of the furnishings. But the picture hook behind her desk is perfectly placed to show off a diploma, so I assume she's the boss."

"Anything you can tell us about the man?" Stottlemeyer asked, his mustache twitching. I would mention this to him at some point, but noticing the captain's twitch can sometimes come in handy.

"The man," Monk repeated. "Since he's not been here, I know very little—except that he's over fifty, under six feet, and has a healthy obsession with neatness and order. You can see how the woman tried to arrange things symmetrically for his sake but didn't succeed. In fact, she's a slob."

A slob? Well, that was a little insulting.

"They intend to run a service business." He turned slowly in a circle and focused on a pair of chairs and a coffee table facing the two desks. "Not a travel agency, since there's only a setup for one group of clients at a time. Not an insurance office. Not a tax preparer. Not a . . ."

"How about a detective agency?" I asked. I couldn't resist.

"No, not a detective agency. This is the wrong neighborhood. And I'm familiar with the other licensed detectives in San Francisco. They all have offices already."

"Maybe these detectives are new to town," I suggested.

"No, if they were new, they wouldn't have picked this location."

"You mean a residential location halfway between your apartment and Natalie's house?" Stottlemeyer finally allowed himself a full-blown smile. "Seems like the perfect location for a couple of detectives I know. What do you think?"

"I don't know what you're talking about."

"Yes, you do, Monk."

"Ta-da!" I opened my arms wide in a symbolic air hug. Nearly all hugs with Monk are air hugs. "Surprise, Adrian!" It was almost a squeal. "This is it. Our new office. Monk and Teeger, Consulting Detectives. The sign goes up tomorrow. But I couldn't resist trying to surprise you."

"Congratulations," said Stottlemeyer. "Now you're a real business. No more people calling me when they want to find you, or clients knocking their dirty fists on your door. Next thing you know, you'll have a Web site."

"I've been planning this for months," I said. "When you and Luther were away last week, I knew it was the right time."

"She was afraid if she told you in the normal

way, you'd make a fuss," said Stottlemeyer with a chuckle. "But it's the right thing, buddy. Trust me."

"Did we surprise you?"

In case you're wondering if I'm somehow omitting Monk's reaction to all of this, I'm not. He just stood in the middle of the office—our new office—like a statue.

"So, when did you know?" I asked. "When you said the woman was a slob, I figured you must have known by then."

"Known what?" Monk finally mumbled. "I'm sorry. I was distracted by the pigeon in the parking space beside the captain's front-left tire. It's gone now."

"This is our office," I said again.

"We don't have an office," said Monk. "But the people here are somewhat similar, I'll grant you. What a coincidence."

"No, this is us."

"No," he said with a shake of the head. "The clues don't add up. But I can see how you'd make that mistake."

"How can it be a mistake, Adrian? I rented it."

"Oh, Natalie, Natalie. You have so much to learn about the science of deduction." Monk turned to the captain. His frown was thoughtful and puzzled. "It's a tricky problem, Leland. I can see why you brought me in. I'll mull over the evidence and get back to you."

And with that he was scurrying out the door, leaving Stottlemeyer and me just staring at each other. "Denial?" I said.

"Big-time. I think he knew the second he walked in. But there's a part of him that thinks if he doesn't admit it, it won't be true."

Yes. I knew that part of Monk well. About two years ago, he had traveled alone from Summit, New Jersey, where we'd been working on a case, back home to San Francisco. I was still in Summit, and I remember getting a frantic call that night. Monk was in front of his apartment door on a phone borrowed from Mrs. Worth, his next-door neighbor. "Natalie, I looked all through my luggage. I can't find my house keys."

"Yes, Mr. Monk. I was waiting for your call." I called him Mr. Monk in those days. "Your keys are here on my kitchen counter, right beside your set of backup keys. Not to worry. I'll send them both to you by FedEx. Meanwhile, your landlord, Mr. Mugabi, has an extra set, right?"

"No, no," he shouted. "I can't call Mr. Mugabi. He doesn't like me. Oh, wait a minute. I didn't check the side pouch on my suitcase. Let me check."

"The keys are not in your side pouch," I insisted, raising my voice and pronouncing each word. "I'm looking right at them."

"No, I think they're in the side pouch. Just a minute."

He kept me on the line for another hour, with Mrs. Worth patiently waiting to get her phone back, before he finally admitted that his keys might not be hiding in his luggage. That is the power of Adrian Monk's denial.

"He'll come around," Stottlemeyer said, patting me on the shoulder. "I don't know any other detective who doesn't have an office."

I let the captain try to reassure me some more. Then he said his good-byes and left. The next few minutes I spent unpacking a box of office supplies I'd been keeping in a closet. I took a satisfying minute to hang my PI license on the wall behind my desk, making sure it was nice and straight. "Damn right I'm the boss," I said, but I know I didn't sound convincing.

I had just locked the front door of Monk and Teeger and set the alarm when I noticed a black Lincoln sedan parked by the pawnshop at the far side of the strip mall. It was Luther Washington's car, the pride of his small fleet of limousines. I could see Luther, large and lean, sitting behind the wheel.

As I approached, Luther rolled down the window. As usual, he was in a dark suit, although I noticed this one was rumpled, with a tear in the vest pocket. His driver's cap was missing and it looked like he hadn't shaved in days. I was afraid to ask. So I asked a simpler question. "Where's Adrian?"

"I made him walk home. It'll be good for him."

"You mean for his health?"

"Yeah." Luther looked steely-eyed and taut.

I had been expecting this moment. I was surprised it had taken so long. Luther is a big guy, an African-American with close-cropped hair, probably in his early thirties. He is smart, even-tempered, unfailingly polite, and hard to argue with. I knew it was only a matter of time. "How was your cross-country trip?"

"How do you think it was?"

There had been a point in my relationship with Monk, a relationship previously defined by my being available every waking moment as his assistant and confidante and chauffeur, when I had stopped being so available. He had solved this problem by buying Luther's car service company and using Luther as his backup chauffeur. Luther had never asked if I thought this was a good idea. It takes a certain personality to be at this man's beck and call.

"I think we stopped at every car wash between here and New Jersey," added Luther. "The same ones on the way back. Plus he made me drive ten miles below the speed limit, which is actually more dangerous. And that's not even counting what happened during our few wonderful days in Summit."

"Was there a murder?" I asked.

"Yes, there was a murder. How did you know?"

"It's an easy bet. And how did Monk do with Ellen? Did he apologize and make up?"

That had been the whole reason for Monk's making this coast-to-coast odyssey and dragging Luther along, to visit his ex-girlfriend, Ellen, and try to repair the damage.

"You're going to need to buy me a drink to hear this story," said Luther. "Several drinks."

# 2

## MR. MONK'S ROAD TRIP

I know I've mentioned Summit, New Jersey, more than once already. Monk, Summit, and I have this checkered past that may need a little explaining.

For quite a few years, Captain Stottlemeyer's second-in-command was Lieutenant Randy Disher, a sweet, enthusiastic officer, a hard worker, and a loyal, good friend. Those who don't know him well might claim that Randy lacks a certain intellectual strength. Those who do know him well would agree. Randy isn't the sharpest nail in the toolbox. That was why it was a bit of a shock for everyone when Randy was offered the job of police chief in the picture-postcard town of Summit, less than an hour outside of Manhattan.

What clinched the job offer for Randy was that Sharona Fleming lived nearby. Sharona had been my predecessor, a registered nurse who'd been Monk's sidekick before I came into the picture. She and Randy had had this big-time flirting thing going on during their years together. No crime scene was complete without the two of them bantering back and forth. Now, on Sharona's home turf, they quickly graduated to living together. So far we haven't gotten any wedding invitations.

In the past year or two, Monk and I have spent time in Summit. And that's where Monk met Ellen Morse. Ellen is tall and blond, and she was infinitely kind when it came to dealing with Monk's quirks. She eventually opened up a San Francisco branch of her store, just so that she could spend more time with him. It had been Monk's first serious relationship since the death of his wife, Trudy, so many years ago. But it didn't work out. Apparently even Ellen has her limits.

"The woman owns this store called Poop," Luther said. He was sitting in my living room, working on his second glass of cabernet and looked like he might need another. "I kid you not. Everything in there is made of animal poop: furniture, artwork, stationery, coffee beans retrieved from the poop of some kind of Vietnamese weasel. The weasel eats the coffee beans. . . ."

"An Indonesian civet," I explained. "And the result is the most expensive coffee in the world. It's wonderful. Ellen's shop is a lot of fun."

"Well, that makes it all right," Luther said with a note of sarcasm. "I can see why the San Francisco branch went out of business."

"Actually, the main reason she closed it was to get away from Monk and me. We weren't very nice to her toward the end."

"I know, I know. Mr. Monk told me the story a hundred times. It's a very long drive when you go under the speed limit and stop at all the car washes." Luther still called him Mr. Monk.

Two weeks ago, when Monk had made the decision to go cross-country to try to rewin Ellen's affections, it probably struck Luther as a romantic thing to do for the man who'd bought his company and was now his boss. "What could go wrong?" Those were Luther's actual words as they pulled away from the curb in front of Monk's apartment building on a bright Monday morning.

A lot, to answer his question.

Monk and I have done a few road trips. I know all about the food requirements, the need for bottles of Fiji Water at regular intervals, the backseat driving, the fear of bridges, not to mention tunnels, the long silences followed by the endless repetition of the same story over and over. "So tell me about the murder," I said.

Luther took another long swig and I was right there to refill his glass. "Do you know the TV show *Master Chef*?"

"I do indeed," I told him. "It's a favorite."

When Luther and Monk finally turned off I-78 and headed down Springfield Avenue, the town of Summit had just experienced its first murder since—well, since the last time Monk came to town. Don't ask me for the logic. It's just the way things happen.

This particular murder started when the Union County Red Cross came up with an idea for a fund-raiser. Six local celebrities would compete for two weekends in a cooking contest called Summit Chef. The Channel Eight weatherman had volunteered to show off his cooking skills, as had the Chamber of Commerce president, Kathy Enbrel, and the recently elected mayor, Charlie Cates, to name half of them.

The competition started out friendly enough, but by the time weekend two approached, an angry rivalry was brewing between Mayor Cates and Kathy Enbrel, whom everyone thought had big political ambitions and wanted to go on the record as being better than Charlie at everything.

"Don't tell me Kathy was killed and Monk arrested the mayor." I know I shouldn't have been jumping ahead, but I couldn't help it. Monk has this habit of pointing at the most important person and saying, "You did it," whether it's a TV star or a business magnate or a ship's captain—which has happened twice if you include submarine captains.

"Half-right," Luther said. "Kathy was killed. But Mr. Monk didn't arrest the mayor. Randy Disher had already done that."

"Yikes. Poor Randy. Hold on." I stopped his story long enough to go into the kitchen and uncork a second bottle of the California cab. We would be needing it.

The murder had taken place Saturday afternoon in the kitchen of the Grand Summit, an old grand dame of a hotel that I knew well. This was the prep area for the final cook-off, which was taking place that evening in the ballroom.

The rules of the competition were strict. Each contestant had to cook from a mystery box of ingredients chosen by the judges and kept hidden in the walk-in cooler. No one could see the ingredients ahead of time or do any advance prep work.

Police Chief Disher was acting as head judge. And when he walked into the kitchen an hour before showtime, Kathy was already there, lying in the doorway to the cooler. She was a short woman, maybe five foot even, almost enveloped in a large white apron. At least the apron used to be white. It was now covered in sprays of blood. Or blood spatter, as Monk kept calling it.

It didn't take Randy long to piece together the sequence of events. One of the amateur chefs had sneaked into the kitchen to peek at the mystery boxes and get some sort of advantage. Another chef was also in there. Or maybe the second one followed the first one in. It didn't really matter, according to Randy. The two competing chefs began arguing about rules and about cheating. Tempers flared. And a carving knife wound up in Kathy Enbrel's stomach, ending the fight forever.

By the time Monk and Luther had checked into the Grand Summit, it was all anyone was talking about. Chief Disher, who had filled in as the mayor of Summit for a short spell, arrested Mayor Cates on very little evidence except motive, a bruise on Cates' arm—which Cates said came from a fall on the stairs at home—and the fact that the mayor didn't have a verifiable alibi.

"The whole town was ready to string Randy from their cute little bell tower," Luther said. He held up his empty glass, but I was rationing his intake. I wasn't sure if alcohol was good or bad for someone suffering from post-traumatic stress. "The town finally had a good mayor," Luther went on, waving his glass at me. "Everyone liked him. And then this friend of yours arrests him for murder."

When Randy and Sharona found out about Monk's visit, they were over the moon. "You can prove me right," Randy had said with all of his customary self-confidence. "The mayor's prints were in the walk-in cooler—along with everyone else's, sure. But he had a key to the kitchen—along with all the other cooks, sure. And he had no alibi, although no one else has a good alibi, either. But, hey, he did have that bruise, am I right? Prove it, Monk. I'm counting on you." Luther's impersonation of Chief Disher wasn't perfect, but I could almost hear Randy saying those words.

"But Randy was wrong," I said.

"How do you know?" Luther asked. He had given up waving his glass.

"Because Randy and Monk never agree on a killer. Never ever. Monk is almost always right and Randy . . . Well, Randy is Randy."

This turned out to be true. Monk spent a few hours interviewing suspects and looking at photographs. He walked around the Grand Summit, holding up his hands like a movie director, and reviewed the video from the first weekend, where every one of the cooks seemed to be taking the contest very seriously.

Finally he had the five surviving chefs line up in the ballroom, all dressed in their white aprons with the custom-designed logos. "It was like some old movie," said Luther. "He lines them up. Then he walks back and forth and talks. And then he points and says, 'You're guilty because you're wearing the wrong apron.'"

"The wrong apron?"

Luther sipped from his empty glass. "It was the TV weatherman, Adam Morse. He's this tall guy. But Monk kept pointing out how short his apron was and how this made him the killer."

I mulled this over and came to my own deduction. I asked a few more questions just to make sure. "There were only six custom-made aprons? No more?" Yes. "Did the aprons come in different sizes? Small, medium, and large?" Yes. "Were the aprons kept in the kitchen in between the two weekend contests?" Yes, at each contestant's station. How did I know?

For those of you who haven't spent years watching Monk's every move and trying to figure out how he thinks, I'll give you the solution. The rest of you have probably figured it out and can skip the next few paragraphs.

Adam Morse, explained Monk to Chief Disher and Sharona and a handful of other bystanders, had been the one to sneak into the kitchen and take a peek in the mystery box. He had put on his apron, an extra large, and began doing a little prep work.

At some point, Kathy Enbrel walked in. Monk didn't know what happened between them. He's not a mind reader. But they both had a lot to lose from any scandal. Kathy was a woman with political ambition and Adam's career was based on being the lovable, community-minded weatherman.

After Kathy's fateful encounter with the carving knife, Adam realized he had a second problem. His extra-large apron was covered in Kathy's blood. These were specially made aprons, one for each player. There was no way he could clean the apron in time, if at all. And for him to tell everyone that he had lost it would look suspicious, especially since the aprons were kept with the other supplies in the locked kitchen.

Adam's only way out was to trade aprons with his victim. He put his large bloodstained apron on Kathy and put her clean small one at his station. Monk had basically figured it out from the moment he saw the photo of Kathy in the huge bloody apron.

Giving Monk credit where it's due, this was something I never would have come up with. He clocked the unusual size of her apron and that the blood was in a spatter pattern, which is different from the way blood looks when it oozes out of a wound. But once Luther told me about Monk's pointing a finger at the man in the small apron, it wasn't hard.

"Well, that doesn't sound like a horrible weekend," I said. "Solving a murder. Getting Randy off the hook. Sounds pretty good."

"I didn't tell you about Ellen," said Luther.

"Oh yeah." After all, this had been the whole reason for the trip. "Was Ellen around for this? Did she see how Monk's obsession can be a good thing?"

"Not so much. When we first showed up, before we even got involved, Mr. Monk went over to Ellen's and tried to apologize. He was persuasive. The man really likes her. Ellen's brother was there and he did his best to talk Ellen into giving Mr. Monk a second chance."

"That's good," I said, but I had a feeling it wasn't. "Does Ellen listen to her brother?"

"Ellen loves her brother. Ellen and Adam Morse are very close."

"Adam Morse?" I wanted to make sure I heard

it right. "As in Ellen's brother is the weatherman Adam Morse? As in Monk wound up arresting Ellen's brother for murder?"

"Yep. Now, where's my wine?"

# 3

## MR. MONK GOES TO WORK

When I didn't hear from Monk, I didn't worry. I waited until the next day, then tracked him down. He wasn't in his apartment. Captain Stottlemeyer hadn't heard from him. And Luther swore that he wouldn't be taking him anywhere, not until Luther had had time to recover from the long, tearful drive home. But I was a real detective now, full of deduction skills. Monk had just been rejected by the only woman he'd had any romantic feelings for since the death of his wife. Even nondetectives could figure this one out.

It was around midmorning when I arrived in Colma, a pretty little town just south of the city where the dead outnumber the living by about a thousand to one. I don't mean brain-dead or boring. I mean physically dead in the ground.

The city of San Francisco stopped building cemeteries more than a hundred years ago because things were getting crowded. The city fathers even went as far as digging up old graves and moving the bodies. You would think that after reclaiming all this land, parking might be a little easier in San Francisco, but it's not. Colma, not far from Daly City, wound up as the epicenter of the new funeral industry.

I've never known how Monk finds his way out here. My two guesses are a very clean bus or teleportation. Either one. But long before Luther came on the payroll, this had been Monk's go-to place whenever he had something to discuss with the one woman who completely understood him.

Trudy's resting place is in Greenlawn Memorial Park, just south of Woodlawn Memorial Park, a scene of artificial rolling hills and hundred-year-old trees, all very well maintained. I know how to get to the grave site by heart, without checking the little row markers. But all I had to do on most occasions was listen for the sound of a clarinet.

Monk is not a great musician, although he does claim to have almost played in a jam session with Willie Nelson, whatever that means. How can you almost play in a jam session? But Trudy must have liked his playing.

I found him, as usual, sitting cross-legged on a blanket on the grass in front of a simple headstone—TRUDY ANNE MONK, 1962–1997, BELOVED WIFE AND DAUGHTER. He was playing the old love ballad "Till There Was You." There were more than a few squeaks coming out of his reed instrument, so I assumed he hadn't made the trip for a while and was out of practice.

Monk and Trudy met in college. Their seven years of marriage was the only true happiness

Monk had ever known. Her unconditional love soothed his obsessive nature and made him almost forget his phobias. And then she was murdered by a car bomb and things got ten times worse than they'd been before.

"Someone will love you again, Adrian. It's not over." He looked up, not at all surprised to see me. "Luther told me everything."

"Did he tell you that Ellen was right? That I'm not worthy of being loved?"

"Did Ellen say that?"

"Not in so many words. She said she hated my guts and never wanted to see me again."

"Well, you did send her brother away."

"It's not my fault. The truth is the truth. Did she want someone innocent going to jail instead of her murderous brother?"

"Is that how you explained it to her?"

"I tried. I sent Luther into her poop shop to explain for me. I sent him in four times, until she slapped him and he wouldn't go in again. The woman is stubborn."

"You'll find someone else. I promise."

"Who?" he demanded. "No woman is going to put up with me. From all reports, I'm pretty impossible. Am I impossible, Natalie?"

"Nothing's impossible. But you can be difficult. When the right woman comes along, you'll want to be a better person for her. You'll be kinder, more considerate. It'll come naturally."

Monk placed the cap back on his clarinet mouthpiece. "I took Ellen for granted," he admitted. "Not to mention the whole killer-brother thing. I can see that was the wrong strategy."

"Just leave yourself open. Love will come when you least expect it."

"I don't expect it now."

"You see? You're halfway there."

"So if I'm not expecting it, it should be here, right? Of course, now I'm expecting it. That's the trouble with phrases like that. I'll always be expecting it and so it won't come. Ever. Thanks a lot."

I smiled. "You know what will make you feel better? Getting settled in your new office. It'll be like a new beginning."

"What new office?" said Monk, blinking and trying to look perplexed. "Oh, you mean that case yesterday in the strip mall."

"Give it up, Adrian. You're not fooling anyone."

Monk reluctantly accepted my ride back into the city. He didn't jump out of the car as I pulled into the strip mall, which I counted as progress. The sign company had been by this morning and the tastefully scripted black letters welcomed us from the front window: MONK & TEEGER. The second line was smaller and in red. CONSULTING DETECTIVES. It looked pretty cool, I have to say.

Monk got out of the car and stared, arms folded

across his chest. "You tried this once before, you know."

"I know. But this will be different."

We *had* tried this once before. Several years ago, I took it upon myself to open up an office in a storefront not unlike this one. I was tired of seeing less talented PIs making a lot of money and us just scraping by. This was back when Monk was our only consultant. I couldn't even call us private investigators at the time since neither of us was licensed. The experience did not go well.

"I hate being on display like a monkey in a window. And I hate sitting around the office and having no one show up."

"Well, if no one shows up, you won't be on display in the window. First problem solved."

"I wasn't through," said Monk. "I hate risk, especially financial risk like monthly bills. I hate not having any authority when I interview suspects. I hate not having Lieutenant Devlin to do police stuff that we don't have the resources for. And I hate risk again, especially physical risk like not having the police around to back me up. I hate meeting new people. . . ."

"Are you working your way up to ten reasons?" I had to ask.

"I'm actually working my way up to a hundred. I hate being in the vicinity of a pawnshop and a Laundromat both. The one is a breeding ground for the crime, the other a breeding ground for—"

"Adrian," I pleaded, then took a deep breath and leaned back against the side of my old Subaru. "I know how you hate change. But things change. We can't make a living just on police work and by hoping for the occasional reward to bring us into the black. I worked long and hard to become a private investigator. You encouraged me—as much as you're capable of encouraging any change. I studied how to run a business. I've made connections. And we can't run a business out of your living room, especially when you refuse to open the door half the time or you make the clients wear plastic booties."

"Are you working your way up to a hundred reasons?"

"I have one more." I stared him in the eyes. "At this moment, do you really want to have another woman mad at you? Huh?"

"Good point."

And this was enough to propel him through the door. Just inside on an end table were an ice bucket and a bottle of nonalcoholic champagne—sparkling wine I suppose is the correct term—dropped off by our friend Tony Rassigio, proud owner of the only restaurant Monk will patronize. Beside the bucket were two glasses wrapped in cellophane.

I gently blocked the door with my body and set about unwrapping the foil and popping the cork. While Monk was busy retrieving the cork and placing it in a wastebasket, I removed the cellophane and filled the glasses.

"To Monk and Teeger," I said, handing him a glass and proposing a toast. "To a new chapter in our lives."

"I'd prefer if you didn't use the word *new*. New is only good when it means shiny and untouched by human hands." But Monk accepted the glass and clinked it with mine. He actually took a sip to seal the deal.

"Natalie? What are you doing?" The voice wasn't Monk's. It came from a woman standing right outside the door I was blocking. She did not sound pleased.

"Daniela. Hello."

The woman was Daniela Grace, a wealthy, thin, well-put-together woman of indeterminate age. Monk and I had met Daniela on a business cruise we'd taken not long ago. She was the senior partner in the law firm of Grace, Winters, and Weingart. She was also, through a mix-up that was only partly Monk's fault, my Alcoholics Anonymous sponsor, even though I don't have a drinking problem. I really don't. I just go to an occasional meeting to keep Daniela happy. It's a long story.

"Natalie? Is that champagne?"

"It's nonalcoholic," I blurted out. "Check the label."

She actually put on a pair of reading glasses and

did just that. Her tone eased and she smiled. "Thank goodness."

Thank goodness is right. I'd gone back and forth about using real champagne. But Monk isn't much of a drinker—or a celebrator. "You came just in time for our grand opening," I said. "Really more of a soft opening, since no one else is here."

"I'm not staying long," said Monk to our guest. "You can drive me home."

Daniela ignored him. "I didn't come to check up on you, Natalie. I read about your new business in the *Pennysaver* and I wanted to see for myself."

"You pick up the *Pennysaver*?" I asked.

"Heavens no. But my gardener does. So . . ." I made way for her in the doorway and Daniela stepped inside. "It seems you're the real deal after all." She nodded in approval. "You never know. People will have a nice business card or a brochure. Then you show up and they're running it out of their garage or some such."

"My living room," Monk corrected her.

She continued to ignore him, which was fine. "You're officially open for business, then?"

"Yes," I lied. I was actually planning a grand opening in a week or two—with Evites and a new Facebook page and maybe balloons. This was better. "Is there something we can help you with?"

"I hope so. A client of mine has been arrested for capital murder. A very sweet man, if that doesn't sound too odd. He was apprehended by the highway patrol, who found him dragging a dead man, a drug dealer, into a vacant lot at two in the morning. The victim had been shot in the head. There was no weapon found. There was, however, a shovel at my client's feet, which doesn't help our case."

Interesting. "What does your client say happened?" I asked.

"That's the problem, dear. He won't say anything. He's clammed up, to use the vernacular. The man is ready to be convicted without saying a word in his defense. It's hopeless."

"Nothing is hopeless," said Monk. "Except my love life. That's hopeless."

# 4

## MR. MONK AND
## THE KINDRED SPIRIT

I have to admit I was stoked. We hadn't even opened and already we had a client. The right kind of client, too: an influential lawyer with a puzzling case. On our drive out to the jail, I played around with catchphrases. "M and T. Your solution for all things mysterious." Hmm, maybe not. I didn't want it sounding trivial, like we were going to find your lost car keys or figure out why your cat stopped eating the Meow Mix.

The murder had not taken place in San Francisco, but in a commuter town to the south. Our client was residing in the San Mateo County jail, a white, two-story industrial-looking complex right off the Bayshore Freeway. I must have driven past it a hundred times and just assumed it was a warehouse. Inside, it was like any other detention center, especially the interview rooms, which are the same the world over—square spaces with a bolted-down table and nonbolted chairs, metal doors, one-way mirrors, plus microphones and cameras. For a consultation with a lawyer, the microphones would be off.

Henry Pickler was waiting for us. He was slight

and pale and in his thirties. In my opinion, he was not the type to be caught dragging a murdered drug dealer through a field. If I hadn't known better, I might have thought he was part of the jail's cleaning staff. That was mainly because he was cleaning the room.

When Monk, Daniela, and I walked in, he had already borrowed a handkerchief from his guard and was wiping down the steel table. "You never know who was here last," Henry explained, and scrubbed harder to make up for the lack of any disinfectant. I knew exactly what Monk was going to say.

"This man is innocent," he said in my ear, then brought out his own handkerchief and a little spray bottle of Formula 410, with a custom-made label. I'm not sure if he's actually added anything to the ingredients of Formula 409, or if he just feels better having it in a bottle with an even number. I never get a straight answer, except that it's better this way.

Monk has worked with OCD suspects in the past, and he always starts out believing in their innocence. What it often means isn't innocence, just that they're better at cleaning up after.

Daniela and I stood by as Monk and Henry finished polishing the table and arranging the four chairs. As soon as they let us sit, Daniela made the introductions. Neither man volunteered to shake hands.

"I got to know Henry through his wife," Daniela explained. "Becky worked for me. Well, three days a week. She was my house cleaner."

"Married to a house cleaner," Monk said. "Sweet deal."

"Not as romantic as it sounds," sniffed Henry. "She wasn't very good."

Monk's face fell. "I'm sorry. So many people call themselves professionals when they don't remotely have the skills."

"I wouldn't let the woman near a vacuum, not in my house."

"Excuse me," I said. "You talk about your wife in the past tense. Did she walk out on you, Henry?"

"How did you know? Are you spying on me?"

"I'm a good guesser."

"She did," Henry admitted with a sigh. "And for no reason. I was just trying to show her the correct way to floss. Becky didn't always floss. She lied to her dentist about it. One minute I'm giving her a flossing tutorial, the next she has a bag packed and is walking out the door. After five years of marriage."

She lasted five years? I thought.

"This woman is going to get gum disease, mark my word," Monk predicted. "Was she still living with you when the incident happened? The incident in the vacant lot?"

"No. Becky left me eight months ago."

"The dead man was connected to drug trafficking," Monk said. We'd both read the report. "Does your wife have any drug connections? Untidy people often have drug connections. That's been my experience."

Henry chuckled. "Becky was raised in a Dutch farming community in Iowa. She wouldn't know a drug dealer if she tripped over one."

"Tripped over one?" I asked. That was an interesting choice of phrase. "How about you, Henry? Would you know a drug dealer if you tripped over one?"

Henry turned to face the wall. "I'm not answering any questions."

"So what were you doing in a vacant lot at two a.m. with a corpse and a shovel?" I asked.

"That lot is part of my property. I can be out there whenever I want."

"And why were you there at two a.m.?"

"Two twelve to be exact. I mean, no comment."

I softened my tone, drew my chair a little closer, and tried to sound reasonable. "I'm sure it's not your fault, whatever happened. Did you get involved with drugs somehow? Do you owe them money? If they were threatening you, it could be called self-defense."

"No comment."

Daniela rolled her eyes. "See what I've been dealing with. Henry, dear, if you don't explain what happened, you could be convicted of murder. Whatever you're hiding, it can't be worse than murder."

I could go on and re-create the next few minutes of this one-sided conversation, but it wouldn't be helpful. This was all there was to learn from Henry Pickler. He himself called the meeting short, preferring, I guess, the company of his domestically abusive cellmate (accused) to that of his lawyer and the two private investigators who were trying their best to help.

We watched a guard lead him out. Then Daniela asked the other guard if we could use the room for another few minutes. "As long as we have a clean table," she asked, "and the microphones are still turned off." We were told we had fifteen minutes, the rest of our allotted time, until they needed the room.

"I need to know this." Monk paused, waiting until the guard left and the door closed behind him. "Why did you employ a terrible house cleaner?"

"Henry's wife? She wasn't terrible. She was hardworking and reliable, and she didn't steal."

"I could say the same for Natalie. But I wouldn't let her clean."

"Okay, guys," I interrupted. "Let's stay focused. Henry must be protecting someone."

"I thought of that," said Daniela. "But he's pretty much a loner. He works from home as a Web site designer. His one phone call after his arrest was to me, the only lawyer he remotely knew. According to the jail records, no one else has come to visit. Henry is an only child. His parents died a decade or so ago and left him a sizable inheritance, which is frankly the only reason I'm continuing to represent him and bill his hours."

"So, he's willing to pay for a top-notch lawyer," said Monk. "And yet he won't explain what happened. Where's the logic in that? Spending money for help and then refusing it?"

"That's why you're here," Daniela said. "The inexplicable. Isn't that your specialty?"

"Did we really say that?" Monk asked.

"You did. It's in the brochure you gave me on the ship."

"Did we mean it? I'm not sure we meant it."

"We meant it," I assured Daniela. "How about Henry's wife? I know they're separated. But could he be protecting her?"

Daniela shook her head. "Becky hasn't been back. We've traded e-mails a few times and I follow her on Facebook. She's living in the Seattle area. Don't tell Henry, but I think she's seeing someone."

Monk grunted at the news and shifted his shoulders. I could see him mentally changing gears. "Okay, what about the victim?"

Daniela reached down into her yellow leather Gucci handbag and pulled out a manila file folder. "Esteban Rivera. A legal immigrant from

Guatemala, twenty-six. From his DEA sheet, we know he was a small-time street pusher—crack, weed, meth—working North Beach for the Mexican cartel."

It was fascinating to hear Daniela Grace using a little street lingo. She had the look and manners of an upscale real estate broker showing off a Nob Hill condo. I had to remind myself that this matron was a top-notch defense attorney.

"North Beach?" Monk said, making a face. "That's Lucarelli territory. What are the Mexicans doing selling drugs in North Beach?"

"Trying to get a foothold," said Daniela. "If this murder had occurred on an inner-city street corner, it would be a textbook turf hit; the Lucarellis sending a message with a nine-millimeter shell delivered at close range. There was a similar example last year. Also the Lucarellis. Suspected to be the Lucarellis, I should say. They were investigated. No one was arrested."

"Had the body been moved?" I asked. "Maybe he'd been killed elsewhere and dumped in the lot."

"The M.E. says it hadn't been moved, except by my client. The body was also newly killed. Less than half an hour before Henry was caught."

"The Lucarelli mob wouldn't move the body," Monk said. "They'd shoot him on his street corner and leave the body there as a message."

"We're acquaintances of Salvatore Lucarelli,"

I mentioned, in an effort at full disclosure.

"More than acquaintances," said Daniela. "I've done my homework, people. You cleared him of a murder charge."

Monk twitched his shoulders. "On that occasion Lucarelli was innocent—even though he happens to be a killer and a mobster. None of that is my fault."

"Well, you can start from that angle. Talk to Lucarelli. If you find out who really killed Rivera, we won't have to get anything out of our uncooperative client." Daniela handed me the file folder. "The forensic report's in there, along with the M.E. report and the officers' statements."

I transferred the folder into its new home—not a Gucci handbag but a PBS tote. "I'll send over the paperwork."

"Your standard rates are fine. It's the client's money. The more I charge the stubborn little man, the better I'll feel. Oh, one more thing." In a reflex move, she eyed one of the cameras in the corner of the room. "You already know this, but I just want to make it clear. No offense."

I was intrigued. "What?"

"Working for a lawyer is different from working for the police."

"What did I tell you?" Monk muttered under his breath. "Another reason."

"Your job is not to broadcast Henry's secret, whatever it is, or get him convicted of some other

47

crime. It's to serve his best interests. Right now that involves finding out what he's hiding and why. That may or may not involve the police."

"Another reason not to be in business," muttered Monk a little louder.

"You're not saying we should let a crime go unreported?" I asked.

"Not exactly," said Daniela. "But any information you garner as my agent, paid for by our client, is private. It's to be used to further our client's case. That's not just my policy. It's the law."

A few minutes later, Monk and I were in the jail's parking lot, getting into my old but clean Subaru. "If you want to dissolve this PI thing, I'm okay with that," said Monk. "No harm, no foul."

"We are not dissolving the business."

"So it's fine to work for an unethical lawyer?"

"Daniela is very ethical. And law-abiding. She came to us, needing to find an alibi for an uncooperative client. What she does with that information is her call, not ours."

"We're no longer on the side of the angels, Natalie."

"When angels hire us, then we'll be on their side."

"I'm serious. We could be helping Pickler get away with murder."

"What murder? You just said he was innocent."

"That was based on personal hygiene, which is not infallible."

"Look, if this goes to trial, Daniela will have to turn over all of our hard evidence, whatever we find, to the DA's office. That's also the law."

"I'm not comfortable with this."

"You're not comfortable with anything. Do you want to hear my theory?" I asked.

"Not really."

"I think our client is Walter White."

"He's Henry Pickler. Don't you even listen?"

"No, I mean from *Breaking Bad*. And before you ask, that's a TV show. It's about this very smart, obsessive chemistry teacher who is dying from cancer. He becomes a meth cook and gets involved with the Mexican drug cartel. Before long, Walter White is shaving his head and killing people, but no one suspects for the longest time because he's such a quiet, peaceful guy."

"There are three things wrong with your theory, Natalie."

"I know. Henry isn't a chemistry teacher, doesn't have cancer, and didn't shave his head. But doesn't this account for the fact that he won't tell us anything? He really did kill Rivera over drugs but can't tell us why because that would endanger his whole drug operation."

"Do they really make TV shows about teachers turning into meth cooks?"

"Yes, Adrian. It was very popular."

"Hmm." He cocked his head and shrugged. "Well, as long as they didn't show the bad guys cooking meth. Because then people would learn how to make it and that would be wrong."

"Of course," I lied. "TV executives are decent, moral people. They would never show things like that."

# 5

# MR. MONK GOES TO THE BARBER

My partner has gone through nine barbers since I've known him. Three of them he fired, complete with pink slips and exit interviews that carefully detailed the reasons for their termination. Of the six he liked and went back to twice a week for trims, one retired at the age of thirty-two; two moved out of state; one had a nervous breakdown; one took out a restraining order; and one vanished so thoroughly even Monk couldn't find him. I personally think the man enrolled in some witness protection program set up for service people who've worked for Monk.

He has since taken to being his own barber, snipping exactly one hundred hairs a day as part of his morning routine. If you want to know how he remembers which hairs he's cut and which ones he hasn't, he divides them into sections and numbers them. I've seen the diagram.

All of this is to say that we rarely step into a barbershop. The one exception is Albert's in North Beach, nestled on a side street between Telegraph Hill and the Financial District. It's a homey Italian establishment run by Albert himself, a half-blind haircutter with shaky hands and a twitch. But you have to walk through Albert's in order to get to the social club in the back. That's where you can almost always find Salvatore Lucarelli, godfather of the crime family bearing his name.

Salvatore was there that afternoon when Monk borrowed a broom by the front door and swept his way through a layer of fallen hair to get to the back room. Usually this place is off-limits to law enforcement. But the mob makes an exception for Monk.

The back door was closed, and I made sure to knock and wait. It's never good to go around opening doors in a Mafia establishment, just in case there's something you don't want to see. One of the don's nephews came and ushered us in.

"My friends," Salvatore said in a raspy voice, looking up from his desk. He swung off his reading glasses and moved aside a ledger. It wasn't necessary. I didn't want to get anywhere near that ledger. "Always a pleasure to see Adrian Monk and his pretty little assistant."

You know how it is when something hits you the wrong way—even a simple phrase. "I am not his pretty little assistant," said I. "Not any-more."

"Nonsense," said Sal. "I think you're very pretty. Aging well. You should learn how to take a compliment, Natalie."

"Pretty is not a compliment," I argued. "It's a way of belittling me and I don't appreciate it."

"Hey, I don't belittle women, lady. I put 'em on a pedestal."

"Mr. Lucarelli," Monk said, holding up his hands. "She didn't mean anything. Honest." The alleged mobster was one of the few people Monk called mister.

Today seemed to be a relatively slow day. A few associates hovered around the air hockey table, which had replaced the pool table when the boss had decided his guys needed a little more cardio. Fat Tony switched off the table and strolled over to join his uncle at the rolltop desk. By the time we got there, he had rolled it all the way closed.

"I assume this is not a social call," said Fat Tony. As usual, he was munching a carrot, just about the only piece of food I've seen him eat since he'd gone vegan about ten years ago. At one point they say he weighed more than three hundred pounds. Now he was well under two hundred, almost skinny. The only thing Fat Tony hadn't been able to shed was the nickname. The same was also the case with Vinny the Schnozz, a mobster with a deviated septum who had undergone an operation back in the nineties and now had a nose smaller than Zac Efron's. The mob likes its traditions.

"Adrian and Natalie are our friends," Sal

reminded his nephew. "They've kept me out of jail more times than my best lawyer."

"That's because you weren't guilty," said Monk. "But the law of averages is working against you."

Sal chuckled. "Never heard of that law." He leaned back and laced his fingers across his belly. "Let me guess what this is about. That Rivera fellow working for the Menendez cartel. The cops have been here twice, even though they got a suspect in custody who don't deny a thing. I'm thinking we should all leave well enough alone, don't you?"

"Afraid not," said Monk. He looked a lot more confident than I felt. "We represent that suspect, Henry Pickler. He's a clean, upstanding citizen who, based on his hygiene alone, couldn't be a killer. Probably not."

"Represent him?" asked Sal. "What does that mean?"

"Let me explain." I cleared my throat and stood a little taller. Then I explained—how I was now a licensed private investigator and how we were actively seeking cases from the public. I was even brazen enough to walk around the air hockey table and hand out business cards. All of the associates took a card, which seemed to provide them with amusement.

"Natalie Teeger, CPI," said Fat Tony. Everyone there knew the initials: Certified Professional Investigator. "That's rich."

I had prepared myself for reactions like this, but you're never really prepared. "Is it rich because I'm a female private eye or because I'm Monk's boss?"

"Both," said Fat Tony. "Plus you're sweet Natalie who drives him around and hands out wipes. That makes it three ways funny, like a humor trifecta." The others chuckled along, including Uncle Sal.

I had only a second to decide how to push back. I went with cool and hard. "Glad you're amused. But I didn't come here to tell jokes. I came to ask questions."

"Ask away," said Sal himself. His tone was as condescending as his nephew's. "By the way, how's your beautiful daughter? Julie, right?"

"Julie is fine," I said, refusing to be intimidated—or at least refusing to show it. "We know you have an ongoing dispute with the Menendez drug cartel."

"Whoa, lady. You don't know no such thing," said Sal. "And out of respect for our friend Adrian, I'm not going to have anyone frisked for a wire."

"Thank you," said Monk. "I owe you." He so hates being frisked.

"I will save the lovely Natalie time by saying the Lucarellis have Mexican relations who we don't always see eye to eye with and who can get a little unruly at times. You know how it is with families."

55

It was my turn. "We also know one of your employees was killed in Daly City last week, shot in the head, just the way Esteban Rivera was shot in the head two days ago."

Salvatore stretched his hands across his belly and cracked his knuckles. "I'm a retired cement contractor, Miss Teeger. I don't have employees. As for this Mr. Rivera . . . His body, according to what the police tell me, was found in Millbrae, well south of the city. Is that a hotbed of activity for this Menendez cartel you speak of?"

"No, it's not," I had to admit.

"But it is near the home of your client, Mr. Pickler, who was found with the man's body and a shovel if I'm not mistaken."

"You're not . . . mistaken, that is. But the last place Mr. Rivera was seen alive was here in North Beach, your territory. He was standing on the corner of Bay and Mason, like he did on most nights. A witness saw him approaching a dark sedan and lean in the front passenger window. A few seconds later Rivera got into the backseat."

"Did this witness get a license number or recognize anyone?" asked Salvatore.

"No," I had to admit again.

"Did the witness say Rivera got in against his will?"

"No."

Salvatore grunted. "Adrian, my friend, will you

please explain to your little boss how the rules of evidence work?"

In a perfect world, Monk would have my back in a situation like this. Seeing me surrounded by a pride of smirking gangsters, he'd be able to forget his phobias and his aversion to the mob, and be supportive. In a perfect world, he would have stepped up and found a way to put these guys in their place. What happened next might not have been perfect, but it was darn near close.

"I think my boss is right." He said it in a loud, clear voice.

"Ooh," Fat Tony said. "So she is your boss."

"Yes," said Monk. "Technically. Tell me, Tony. Why did you get a new gun?"

"What?" Fat Tony's hand reached toward his shoulder holster, easily visible under his blue Windbreaker.

Monk pointed from across the room. "That pancake holster is made for a nine-millimeter Beretta. I know because that's what you usually carry. That holster doesn't quite fit your new gun, which, if I'm not mistaken, is a Smith and Wesson Chief's Special. They make them a little shorter than the Berettas. It's starting to annoy you, the loose fit. I can tell by the way you've been moving your left arm."

Fat Tony eyed the offending holster, then zipped his Windbreaker halfway up. He dropped both arms to his side. "The way I'm moving my left?"

"You hug it a little closer to your side than the other arm. It's been bothering me since we walked in. In a while, you'll get bothered enough yourself to go buy a holster that fits. After all, you've only had the gun for a day or so."

Salvatore grunted. "Tony, is this true?"

"The gun's new, yeah. But I got a permit. I got a whole slew of permits."

Monk continued. "My guess is your nine-millimeter Beretta's at the bottom of the bay where no one will ever be able to do ballistics and connect it to Esteban Rivera's murder, which happened to be committed with just such a nine millimeter. I'm sure my boss saw the same thing. Didn't you, boss?" Mob or no mob, how I wish I'd had a microphone on me at that moment.

"Uh, yes," I replied.

"So, yes, I could explain the rules of evidence to Natalie. But I think she understands them pretty well."

"Tony, Tony," said his uncle, shaking his head. "Your Beretta? That was a Christmas present."

For the next ten seconds, you could have heard a pin drop. Not a snicker, not a snort. That was probably why we all noticed the sirens at the same moment.

They were far away but coming closer. Fast. The two-tone wail of police sirens. Not an ambulance. The room grew even tenser as the vehicles turned onto a nearby street, probably

Filbert. A few hands eased their way toward shoulder holsters, including the ill-fitting one under Fat Tony's arm. Glances flew back and forth, looking for some sort of signal from the man in charge. The tension eased a little as the sirens continued wailing down Filbert, then, one by one, cut out. Whatever it was, it was nearby and bad. But it wasn't us.

We were still all glued in place when the door from the barbershop flew open. Old Albert stood in the frame. "There's something happening. I think over on Stockton. Something big."

Fat Tony grabbed the remote from the lip of the air hockey table and clicked on the TV hanging from a wall mount in the corner. He began to change channels, surfing to find some breaking news. It didn't take long. Every local station was interrupting its regular programming.

"We're trying to get the details now in this recently developing story," said a young, nervous-looking reporter across the street from a down-town warehouse. You could see him still adjusting his microphone and earpiece. The echo of a gunshot made him jump and sent him edging closer to the local ABC mobile unit. "According to what we've been able to learn, a lone shooter has entered an office building in downtown San Francisco and begun firing. At least three people are believed to have been killed so far."

Godfather Sal sighed and threw up his hands.

"What's this world coming to, huh? It's enough to make you despair for humanity."

Fat Tony agreed. "A regular breakdown of society. Why aren't you guys there?" he asked, pointing to the screen. "I thought you two worked every big police case. Captain Stumblebum should be giving you a call any second."

"Stottlemeyer," Monk corrected him without getting the joke. "And this isn't our kind of case."

"Are you sure?" said Tony. "It's a better use of your time than harassing a bunch of citizens for no reason."

"I'm sure," Monk confirmed. "I don't do SWAT teams or shootouts. Not my thing, and the captain knows it. I can't imagine a set of circumstances that would turn a workplace shooting like this into the kind of case that could use my skills. . . ."

It was just then, exactly on cue, like the punch line in a bad sitcom, that my phone rang. Monk stopped. Everyone stopped as I pulled it out and checked the display.

"Captain Stumblebum?" Fat Tony guessed. "That him?"

"Um . . . Maybe." I swiped the screen and held it to my ear. "Hello. Captain?"

# 6

## MR. MONK AND THE SHOOTER

By the time we arrived on the scene, quite a lot had already happened.

A full block of Stockton Street had been cordoned off, with a SWAT team suited up and making its way into place. The center of the action was a three-story warehouse, currently the focus of dozens of riflescopes and binoculars and, from a greater distance, cameras from the TV affiliates. Captain Stottlemeyer had taken up a position behind a barricade of black-and-whites, which was where we found him.

The building was the U.S. headquarters of East Decorative Imports, an importer of high-end statues and pottery and religious trappings from the Far East. If you've ever been to a Zen center or a trendy spa, then you know the kind of things they supply. The first two floors made up the company's warehouse, while the third floor, the center of the SWAT team's attention, housed the showroom and offices.

"Someone's alive in there with a phone," Stottlemeyer said as we settled in beside him, our heads popping over one of the hoods. "As far as she knows, it's a single shooter. One of the employees. Wyatt Noone by name. We did a quick check and he fits the profile. Mid-thirties, Caucasian, a loner, no local family. It seems that he came in this morning with a shotgun and started firing. We don't yet know the cause."

"How many are in the building?" I asked. Monk was paying attention even though he was busy wiping down the driver's side door with a handful of antiseptic wipes.

"All the office staff," said the captain. "Four plus the shooter. The warehouse doesn't open until midafternoon. Maybe it's got something to do with local time in Japan or wherever the company is based. The good news is the warehouse workers aren't here. It could be a lot worse."

"You say there's someone still alive?" I asked.

"The office assistant, Sarabeth Willow. We think she's hiding out in the second-floor warehouse space. Nine-one-one patched her through to me. I told her not to call, to find somewhere safe, then text us her location. That'll make it safer for her when the SWAT team goes in."

"Why am I here?" Monk asked. He had finished with the door and was reaching up to do the rearview mirror.

"Devlin is coordinating site access. Normally that's a SWAT function. But she was here early and jumped right in, flashing her homicide badge and filling in where needed. I think she misses this kind of action."

"Are you worried about her?" Monk asked, forgetting for a moment the smudged mirror. He raised his eyes over the hood and found Lieutenant Devlin, the only woman I know who looks even better in a Kevlar vest, not that there are many women wearing them. She was at the building's main entrance, sharing a few words with a team member on the door. Then she made her way around to the alley to check another access point.

"Devlin's a pro," said Stottlemeyer. "But yeah. Anything off protocol is a worry. That's why I need your eyes, Monk. She's family."

Lieutenant Amy Devlin is the captain's number two, having replaced Randy Disher after he'd gone off to run the show in Summit. She is tall and muscularly thin, which I found a bit intimidating at first. Her hair is the kind of shiny, spiky mess that always looked different and probably took more time to arrange in the morning than my dirty-blond locks. Devlin had taken some getting used to, just the way Monk had taken some getting used to for her. But Captain Stottlemeyer was right. She was family.

The transceiver on the shoulder of Stottlemeyer's tactical vest started to squawk. "Movement, movement," came a male voice. "Second floor, northeast corner. Shooters, wait for confirmation." It sounded like the SWAT team commander.

The captain lunged for his binoculars and trained them on the corner window. I could see it, too: a medium-sized figure with a bald or shaved head, apparently male, in a dark sweatshirt, flitting back and forth across the window. In his right hand, hanging by his side was what looked like a shotgun. In a second, Stottlemeyer was comparing him to an image on his smartphone. "Looks like our guy," he said, pushing a button and leaning into his transceiver. He handed the binoculars off to Monk. "Here."

"Thanks, Captain."

Stottlemeyer heaved a sigh. "Don't clean them. Use them."

"Oh, okay." Monk put away his wipes and gingerly lifted the lenses within an inch of his eyes. That's as close as they would get.

"Take your shot," crackled a voice.

We all waited, eyes focused on the window, ears tuned for the sound of gunfire. But the figure in the window stepped back into the shadows and within half a second the shot was lost. Curses sputtered over the transceiver from at least three sources.

Stottlemeyer's phone pinged. "Sarabeth, good for you," he muttered. But his face fell as he read the text message. *Shot bad hiding help.*

The captain relayed the information and somewhere on the other end a decision was made. Four or five SWAT team members scrambled around the edges of the building. And out of the half dozen voices crackling over the transceiver, Devlin's was the only female, as gruff and decisive as the others, guiding the officers to the entry points and barking out last-second information.

A lot of things were said and done over the next few minutes. Honestly, I have no idea how these people do it. I felt so helpless, hunched behind the police cruiser, staring at the captain's transceiver. Helpless, but a little grateful that I didn't have to be a part of it.

The first floor, consisting of the loading dock and lower warehouse, was soon cleared. One body, no shooter. The teams positioned themselves at the two opposite stairwells and started the second-floor assault at the same moment. Outside, officers were in place at every possible exit and sniper rifles had their scopes trained on the roof.

"We got her," a voice shouted. "She's alive." All of us couldn't help giving a little cheer. Even Monk clapped his hands and grunted in approval.

Someone shouted back. "Stay put until clear. He's still in there."

"Second floor clear," came another voice. And then the teams repeated the process for the third-floor assault.

"Be careful," I said into the transceiver. I felt

instantly foolish but I really couldn't help myself. Whatever danger remained had to be on the top floor. Not to mention the confusion and carnage.

We were in radio silence for what seemed like forever. Everyone was staring at the three-story building, listening for shots. The door to the roof opened and two SWAT members emerged, scanning for an escape route that hadn't been used.

"Two more down," came the next voice from inside. "Both dead."

"What about the shooter?" Captain Stottlemeyer and the SWAT team commander said it almost in unison.

"No shooter. Send in the EMTs. Our survivor looks critical."

"No," the SWAT commander barked back. "Stay locked down. Do another sweep."

"Did it twice. He's not here."

"How can he not be there?" Stottlemeyer shouted. "We saw him."

"He must have gotten through." A little angrier this time. "We know what we're doing. He's gone."

"Keep locked down," the commander ordered. "We'll send in an evac team for the survivor."

Stottlemeyer kept staring at the radio on his vest, then finally clicked it off. "This isn't good."

"Of course it's not good," I said. "How could he have escaped?"

"No, I mean, it's really not good. Devlin was in charge of site access. She's not SWAT trained."

"Are you saying she let the shooter slip through?" I shook my head. "Amy wouldn't make a mistake like that."

"It doesn't matter," said Monk. "When something like this happens, they always look at procedure. Anything out of place, that's what gets the blame." He was right. Sometimes I forget that he was a cop and knows how the system works. "Devlin will be getting the blame."

# 7

## MR. MONK ON THE REBOUND

Less than an hour later, the four of us were at work in the building.

At first glance, the lower two floors of East Decorative Imports were a funhouse of eerie delights. Or perhaps a nightmare. That was what it must have been for Sarabeth Willow, when the lights were off and the place was encased in shadows while a fellow employee, out of his mind with homicidal rage, stalked her through the warehouse.

Buddhas of all shapes and sizes congregated in groups, like gently smiling juries. Multi-limbed gods from India danced in place, entertaining the rows of fat, elephant-headed boys. Wooden crates, still unopened from their long voyages, stood guarding the corners. The more valuable items— at least I supposed they were—sat inside locked cages: jewel-encrusted daggers, golden masks, and more Buddhas. Hundreds of them. Everyone seems to love a good Buddha.

"It would be easy to miss something in this mess," Monk observed. It was a little hard to understand him, possibly due to the gas mask he'd borrowed from the hazmat van the SWAT team had brought along. To protect from dust, you know. Asian dust, which carried all sorts of exotic, incurable diseases, at least in his mind.

"We kept the place locked down," said Lieutenant Devlin, "until the whole building was searched. Except for the survivor and the EMTs, of course." She shook her head in disgust. "How'd I let myself get into this?"

Monk was tilting his head from side to side. The warehouse was giving him plenty to frame. Then slowly he followed some invisible trail, invisible to normal humans, and wound up in a cubbyhole made from two crates and a massive teak chandelier, set in a loose triangle. "This is where she hid from him," he said. "Where they found her." With the gas mask on, he sounded like an adenoidal Darth Vader.

"That's right," Devlin said in a surprisingly cooperative tone. Her usual reaction to my partner was to be caustic and impatient. She generally saw him as the captain's human, dysfunctional cheat sheet, a way for him to close cases that she her-self could solve, given some more time and manpower. But in this particular case, with her professional reputation on the line, she was playing nice. Monk didn't seem to notice the difference.

He spent a minute framing Sarabeth's hidey-hole—the blood, the moved crates, the angles of view—then walked straight to the stairwell on the other side. The captain, the lieutenant, and I followed. As soon as the door to the warehouse was closed, as soon as we were safely separated from the world of Asian dust, Monk removed his mask.

"You guys are going to need vaccinations, you know. Cholera, hepatitis A and B, Japanese encephalitis. The federal government needs to do a better job of regulating the entry of foreign particles. They're like microscopic terrorists."

"And yet billions of Asians live with Asian dust every day," I pointed out.

"But you're not Asian, are you? So you really need those vaccinations. I'm saying this as a friend who will have to spend time around you and watch you die horrible deaths."

"We'll take our chances," said the captain. He pointed. "What can you tell us about this?"

Just inside the door, on the landing leading down to the first floor, was a pile of men's clothing: a dark blue sweatshirt and tan Dockers slacks, with a pair of brown loafers on top, as if to hold it all in place.

"Nothing's been touched," Stottlemeyer said. "And that goes for you, Monk. No straightening out the clothes."

"What about the button?" Monk asked. I hadn't seen it until he pointed it out, a broken black button on the edge of the first step going down.

"It's been examined and photographed," said Devlin. "It's consistent with the buttons used on the EMT uniforms. That's the department's working theory. But that's not how he got away, I swear."

The department's working theory—based on Wyatt Noone's clothing in the stairwell, his vanishing act from a secure building, and the broken button—was that he had escaped in the flurry of EMTs leaving the site with the stabilized survivor. According to this theory, Noone had it all carefully planned—to injure his last victim instead of killing her. He knew her evacuation would be a top priority, even with the rest of the building shut down.

"Four EMTs entered the building and four left," Devlin insisted. "I was there. No one on the medical team saw anyone extra. They would have been the first to notice."

"Not if they were all focused on treating the victim," said Stottlemeyer. "He could have slipped out right behind them."

"But he didn't," said Devlin. "At least . . . At least I don't think so. I couldn't have made a mistake like that."

Monk was reaching out for the shoes. But I have eyes in the back of my head, and I grabbed his arm. "I wasn't going to touch," he said, insulted at the thought. "I'm just wondering why they're on top."

"What do you mean?" I asked.

"I mean you normally take off your shoes first, so they would be at the bottom of this unruly mess, not the top. And . . ." Monk cocked his head to the right. "And why would he change shoes in the first place? If this was his plan, then he'd already be wearing the right shoes, probably even the right pants. And the broken button? That's too much of a coincidence. The button was planted for us to find."

Stottlemeyer did an identical cock of the head. "You're saying this is a setup, Monk? That Noone didn't leave this way? He just wants us to think he did?"

"Why would he do that?" Devlin asked. She thought for a moment, then almost gasped. "You think he's still in the building."

"It's worth checking out," said Stottlemeyer, reaching for his transceiver. "The man used to work here. He could know of a place we haven't checked, just waiting for our security to loosen up."

"Then it's not my fault," said Devlin. "He didn't get past me. He couldn't have." And she allowed herself a half smile, her first in quite a while.

Devlin stayed behind at East Decorative Imports, heading up nearly a precinct of officers. If Noone was in the building, she was going to track him down. Another half dozen cops were assigned to the suspect's friends and background, in case he had somehow made it out.

Meanwhile, Stottlemeyer, Monk, and I made our way to San Francisco General, where Sarabeth Willow had been stabilized and was strong enough to talk, at least for a few minutes at a time. She was in one of the few private rooms in the ICU, more for her security than the severity of her injuries. She'd been shot twice, a grazing wound to the left shoulder, and a more serious shot in the abdomen.

"Are they really dead?" Sarabeth asked. "All of them?"

"Everyone," Monk answered. "Except you. You were lucky."

Lucky seemed an inadequate word to describe her situation. Or maybe it was just the wrong word. The office assistant looked to be the kind who always wore a smile, remembered your anniversary, and brought in cupcakes with candles for your birthday. She would probably never be the same.

"Do you have any idea why Mr. Noone did this?" said the captain. "Was there trouble at work? Did he seem unstable?" He had turned on a digital recorder. I was taking notes. Monk, being Monk, didn't need either.

Sarabeth was middle-aged, a little taller than average, one of the efficient, nurturing breed who used to be labeled secretaries but kept half the offices in America up and running. She was probably more attractive than I gave her credit for. You can't be looking your best when you've been through hell and just been pumped up with three pints of blood. I did notice she wasn't wearing a wedding ring.

"Wyatt's been our financial officer for about a year." Her voice was raspy and swallowing seemed difficult. "Before that we did without one, until the bookkeeping got too much. He seemed good. Everyone liked him, although he kept to himself. Not much of a sharer, if you know . . ."

"What happened this morning?" Stottlemeyer asked.

She swallowed again. A second later, Monk was there, holding a cup of water to her lips, adjusting the bendy straw at a ninety-degree angle. I've rarely seen him do anything like this. He's not what you would call a caregiver.

"Thanks," she said, trying to smile. "This morning Wyatt was late. Maybe eleven? I was at my desk and the sun was coming through the front windows, so I could barely see."

"He was backlit," Monk suggested.

"That's right. Not that I was paying close attention. I thought he was carrying an umbrella, which is silly. It's been so dry."

"He was carrying the shotgun," Monk said.

"I know that now." Sarabeth took another sip. "He went right in the back, to Mel's office. Didn't

74

say a word. Next thing I know there was a gunshot. Very loud. I didn't know what was going on."

Sarabeth paused again and took her time. After the first shot, she said, Mel had come running out of his office, holding his bloody shoulder and screaming. If Mel had tried to escape through the front, things might have been different. Sarabeth might not have survived. But Mel ran toward the back, perhaps thinking about the fire escape and the stairs. Two more shots followed, one right after the other.

Sarabeth and the other woman in the office both placed 911 calls from their cell phones. But Katrina's call was cut short by a gunshot into her head, all of it recorded by the city's emergency-response system.

When Caleb, the last victim, came running into the reception area, Sarabeth was under her desk. She peeked around the corner to see the young, heavyset man wasting precious seconds pushing the elevator button. Then he headed for the stairwell, just a few yards in front of Wyatt who was striding after him, pulling hot shells from the shotgun and reloading. Caleb's body was later found on the first level, a gaping, bloody hole in his back, just yards from the loading dock exit.

All this time, Sarabeth's phone was open to 911 and the dispatcher stayed with her as she took the rear stairs. The sound of rushing footsteps from below made her stop at the second-floor landing. But she wasn't quite in time. The first shot hit her in the shoulder. The second shot caught her in the stomach. Her weight pushed open the iron door, and she collapsed into floor two, the upper level of the warehouse.

"I don't know why he didn't come in then," Sarabeth said. Her energy was fading and we wouldn't have much longer to question her, not this time.

"He was reloading," said Captain Stottlemeyer. "We recovered shells on that landing."

"Thank God," said Sarabeth. "I bolted the door as best I could, then tried to find someplace safe."

The place she found to collapse and wait for death was just feet from the door. The two angled crates and the teak chandelier she pulled in behind her blended perfectly with her modest brown blouse and made her nearly invisible.

"He must have really wanted you dead," said Monk as gently as you could possibly say those words.

"Me?" said Sarabeth. "What do you mean?"

"I mean Noone could have escaped. He knew the SWAT team was coming. Yet he took the time to shoot through the door and search the warehouse. We saw him through the windows, scouring the place. Why do you think he did that?"

"He was waiting to escape with the EMTs,"

said Sarabeth. "That's what they told me." I wasn't surprised she'd already heard this theory. People love to gossip, even doctors and nurses.

"That's a faulty theory," Monk said. "We had a top-notch officer on the door. That's not how Noone escaped." It was nice to hear him defending Devlin. "He probably did want you dead. Why did he want you dead?"

Sarabeth didn't have an answer. "Why does a crazy person do anything? I was always nice to Wyatt. We never had an argument."

Stottlemeyer frowned. "Are you saying Miss Willow was the main target?"

"No," said Monk. "If she was the target, he wouldn't have left her till last. But maybe he needed all four of them. He attacked when the warehouse workers were gone. Just the four office workers. Do you know anything that could help us?"

Sarabeth shivered. "If I did, I would tell you. Honest."

Monk nodded and didn't press his point. Instead, he turned to the rest of us. "Miss Willow needs some rest," he said. "We should leave."

"Call me Sarabeth."

"Sarabeth. Can I come back?"

"Please," she said, and reached out to squeeze his hand. "They were all my friends. Please catch him."

"I will," said Monk, and squeezed back. I reached

in my bag for a wipe, but he didn't seem to want it.

"What was that about?" I asked five minutes later. Captain Stottlemeyer had just said good-bye and left us standing on the third level of the hospital parking garage. "And don't act all innocent. You know what I mean."

Monk wanted to get in the car and end the discussion. But I wouldn't beep him in. "Sarabeth's been through a lot," he said. "It's called empathy."

"I know what empathy is. I'm just surprised you do."

"Do you think she likes me?"

"Likes you?" I was in shock. "Since when do you care if people like you? If you cared, my world would be so much easier."

"I noticed she was trembling when I spoke to her. That means she likes me, right?"

"It means she's got an arm wound and a stomach wound and is in intensive care."

"You're a very cynical woman."

I digested this for a moment, then took a moist wipe from my bag. I held it out. "Wipe."

"What?"

"The spot where she squeezed your hand. Wipe it off." It was half an offer, half an experiment.

He shrugged his shoulder and cricked his head. "That's okay. I don't have to."

"Oh my God. You like her. You want to go out with her."

"No," he said, following it with a hearty laugh.

"Not until she's out of intensive care. According to her background, she's single, divorced for about three years now, although she kept her husband's last name. Women. Who can understand them? Not me."

"Adrian. Since when do you go trolling the hospital wards for dates?"

"Sarabeth is not a troll."

"No, troll has a different meaning. She's very attractive, I guess."

"Attractive? The woman is a babe."

"Since when do you use the word *babe?*" I didn't know what to think. On the one hand, I was surprised and reassured that Monk was keeping his heart open to another relationship. On the other hand . . . "Adrian, Ellen dumped you just a week ago. I think you're on the rebound."

"Yes. Isn't it wonderful?"

"No, the rebound isn't wonderful. The rebound's a bad thing."

"Natalie, you're mistaken."

"No, I'm not. The rebound means you're not thinking clearly. It means you're liking someone just because you feel abandoned."

"Natalie, Natalie." He clucked his tongue. "I wish you could hear yourself."

"I can hear myself fine."

"Well, this is just one of those times when we're going to have to agree to agree that you don't know what the heck you're talking about."

# 8

## MR. MONK GOES TO WORK

"Adrian is almost sure it was Fat Tony who killed Rivera, not our client." I was practically shouting into the phone. "After our visit with the Lucarellis, he's ninety-one percent sure." I was making that number up, but I assumed I was close to the actual one. Even though Monk was less than ten yards away, I knew he couldn't hear me above the noise. "We're working under that assumption."

On the other end of the line, Daniela Grace was also shouting. "Did you say Brad Doney?"

"No. Fat Tony—like obese. Our next step is to check into the Menendez cartel, to see if there's a connection between them and Henry Pickler. There has to be some reason why our client was burying the body."

"Natalie, what's that racket?"

I'd been expecting her to ask. "It's the cleaning staff. They're vacuuming."

"Can't you have them vacuum after hours, like a normal office?"

"You know how it is. Cleanliness is next to godliness. It's also next to impossible with Adrian."

"You're next to where?" she asked.

"Impossible."

"You're right. This is impossible. We'll talk later, after your cleaners leave."

"Yes," I said. "Don't worry. We're working on your case. It's all we think about."

We shouted our good-byes. Then I hung up and took a deep breath. "Adrian! Stop it!" I shouted it loud enough this time to get his attention.

Monk reached around to his side and switched off the HEPA filter backpack vacuum cleaner. He took off his noise-canceling earmuffs. "Why are you shouting? I assume you were shouting. Otherwise I wouldn't have been able to hear you."

It was shaping up to be a long day.

I had arrived at his apartment around nine thirty, expecting a fight or a barrage of excuses, perhaps a bout of Japanese encephalitis left over from yesterday in the warehouse. Instead, he was uncomplaining and ready to go. He even had Spam sandwiches packed for both of us in matching white paper bags. (Monk actually buys brown paper bags, then bleaches them himself. And irons them.)

By ten we were at the strip mall, opening our storefront right on time, the words MONK & TEEGER gleaming on the glass. Once again I postponed even thinking about a grand opening. At some point we would have to host an event, with dozens of potential clients and TV cameras and maybe a politician or two. But not now. There was too much going on.

Monk stood in the shop doorway, inspecting the interior with an eagle eye. I wasn't worried. I had spent most of the previous evening there, making sure everything about Monk and Teeger was perfect. Then I'd set the alarm, just in case some sloppy vandal decided to break in during the night and rearrange the paper clip trays.

For the first half hour, I escorted him around, explaining everything from the coffeemaker to the phone system to the proper way to greet the walk-in clientele, which was for him to sit there and say as little as possible.

After the orientation, he settled himself at his desk and methodically began to review the file that Lieutenant Devlin had dropped off for the Noone triple murder. I was quite proud of him—and of myself for thinking through all the possibilities. That was just minutes before Luther showed up, dropping off the HEPA filter backpack vacuum cleaner and the noise-canceling earmuffs.

"You're doing this to annoy me, aren't you?"

"No, I'm not. This place is filthy."

"Filthy?" I pointed to the machine's clear plastic canister. "You've been vacuuming for an hour and how much have you cleaned?" I eyed the contents. "Maybe half an ounce of dust. Max."

"Half an ounce?" Monk looked aghast. "I think I'm going to vomit."

"No, you're not." I kept my voice controlled. "You're going to put that contraption in the closet and get back to work. If you're good all day and behave yourself, then maybe I'll let you do a little dusting before we leave. Maybe."

Monk met my gaze, worked out the percentages of just how angry I was, and did as he was told. I took the extra precaution of locking the cleaning closet.

"I did do it to annoy you," he admitted. "That was wrong, Natalie. The office is very clean and well-ordered, and I appreciate everything you've done to make our agency a going concern. This feels like a real, grown-up business. And I don't know anyone else who would do what you've done for me. Thank you."

It was actually quite touching and just what I needed to hear. "Thank you, Adrian."

"This is going to be great," he said, trying to convince us both.

"I appreciate your openness to change. I know you're trying."

"Good. Can I dust now?"

"No."

Around noon, we had our Spam sandwiches—rectangular slices of meat on rectangular slices of bread with the crusts cut off and rectangular-cut leaves of lettuce. I'd never eaten Spam before thanks to Anita, the family cook who would never let us eat anything out of a can. The only thing I knew was the urban legend that it tastes like human flesh. Spam is actually not bad, although I can't confirm or deny that it tastes like flesh.

We were washing down the sandwiches with our bottles of Fiji Water when Lieutenant Devlin walked in. She looked around, congratulated us on our new business, and took a moment to inspect my shiny, new PI license on the wall. Despite her smile, an unusual expression for her, I could see the worry in her eyes.

"I just happened to be in the neighborhood," she said.

"In this neighborhood?" Monk asked. "Why were you in this neighborhood?"

"Just happened to be."

"Why?" Monk insisted.

"Can't I be in the neighborhood?"

"First off, it's a terrible neighborhood, with a pawnshop and a Laundromat in the same complex. Second, you live on the other side of town, if I'm not mistaken. The precinct house is twelve blocks in your direction, so this is on your way to nowhere." He pointed outside. "Third, I can see the GPS suctioned onto your windshield, which you only do when you're trying to find an address. Otherwise it's in your glove box."

"Maybe I wasn't in the neighborhood."

"There used to be a decent sandwich shop here,"

Monk allowed. "That's what I heard. But it went out of business and someone rented the space for a seedy detective agency—no offense."

"I made a special trip. Okay? You caught me." Devlin lowered her lanky frame into the client chair, facing our desks and spaced perfectly evenly between them. The first person to ever sit there, I noted. "The Noone investigation isn't going well."

Devlin had been working nonstop with nothing to show for it. Despite an exhaustive search, the suspect had not been in the building and his escape route was still presumed to have been with the EMTs. That placed the blame squarely on her narrow shoulders.

"Anyone can make a mistake," I said, trying to console her.

"I didn't make a mistake. But that's not the worst part."

Monk nodded. "The worst part is that you volunteered to be the lead investigator and you're coming up blank. No trace. Like he vanished from the face of the earth."

"How did you know?"

"The file you dropped off this morning." He indicated the document, centered on his otherwise polished desk. "You're listed first on the cover sheet, indicating you're the lead investigator."

"I mean how did you know we're coming up blank?"

"Because of his name."

"His name?" It's amazing how, after all these years of my seeing him work, Monk can still surprise me. "How can you know anything from his name?"

My partner retrieved the folder and pulled out a page torn from a notepad. *Torn* may be too strong a word; *surgically removed*. I'd seen him writing on it this morning and hadn't given it much thought. At the top, he'd printed the name, *Wyatt S. Noone*. And below, in the same, eerily perfect hand were variations of the syllables. *Wyatt is no one. Why it is no one. Why? It is no one. Wyatt's snow one.*

"The last one's a reach." Monk was looking over my shoulder. "But the others all amount to the same thing, a play on words."

"You're saying . . . It's a fake name?" asked Devlin. Why had the two of us not seen this? It had been right there in front of us.

"Totally fake," said Monk. "The man was having fun, rubbing our noses in it. I'm betting that everything about Mr. No One is fabricated."

"Except the fact that he worked at an import company for a year," I said, "and murdered three people."

"Well, now it makes sense," said Devlin. "The man's address is a post office box. He doesn't have a driver's license. His social belongs to a dead guy in Pasadena, which wasn't a problem for him since Wyatt—whatever his name is—didn't file tax returns."

"How about fingerprints?" I asked.

"He had the foresight to wipe down his office, so we're dusting the rest of the third floor. But we're not holding out much hope. One good thing, Wyatt does show up on a few Facebook posts, office functions with the other EDI employees, so at least we have some photos."

"How did he get hired?" I asked. "Didn't anyone at the office check his references?"

"I'll get right on it," said the lieutenant. She took out her smartphone and began texting something to someone. "And let's keep this quiet. I'll tell the captain about our man without a past. But we should keep it out of public knowledge—and far away from the press."

"He must have left some trace," I said. Personally, I couldn't imagine being off the grid for more than a week. "The man slept somewhere. He must have done something for relaxation or social interaction. Or food. No one can stay invisible."

"No one?" Monk asked with half a devilish grin. "As in Noone?"

"As in nobody," I insisted. "Take Sarabeth. She worked with Noone every day. She must have talked with him about things, noticed things about him."

"Luckily she survived," said Devlin.

"That's a good approach," Monk said. His face brightened. "We need to interview Sarabeth again. Several more times. I'm thinking ten. Ten's a good number."

If Devlin had any inkling about Monk's enthusiasm for Sarabeth Willow, she didn't let it show. "Does that mean you're continuing on the case?" Her shoulders relaxed. "I was afraid, since you opened a real agency, you might not have time."

"We'll make the time," I said. "As it happens, we have a big case. A mob murder with a wealthy client somehow involved. Very puzzling."

"It's nothing," Monk said. "Inconsequential. I can finish it in a day."

"You can finish it in a day?" I asked.

"That's a figure of speech. I meant the Sarabeth case is more important."

"Good to hear," said the lieutenant. "And . . ." Her voice hesitated. "I know the department is cutting back. If they can't cover all your expenses or you have to put in extra hours, I don't want you skimping. I have some savings of my own."

"You would pay?" Monk said. "Your own actual money?"

"This is important to me."

It was an amazing offer to come out of Devlin's mouth. In all the time I'd known her, she'd never once hinted that Monk's skills might be essential. To her, he was a mental trickster who somehow jumped to the right conclusions a day before she would have gotten there herself. Now suddenly she was a believer. I guess my old Lutheran minister was right. There are no atheists in a foxhole.

"That's a generous offer, Amy," I said. "But we don't want your money."

"Speak for yourself," said Monk. "I need to pay the rent on this dump."

"I'm speaking for myself and you. We are not taking her money. She's family. As close to family as a couple of misfits can have."

"Thanks," said Devlin before Monk could object again. "I'll make sure you get paid. The thing with the fake name? I would have caught that, but not for a day or two. Meanwhile, he's getting away."

"We're on it," I said, and shook her hand to seal the deal. I shook an extra time on behalf of my partner.

"I so appreciate it," said Devlin. "Now I have to get back to the station."

"The big question here is why," said Monk, almost to himself.

"To work on the case. Although I can stay if you need me. Just tell me what to do."

"No. I mean why would this man create a fake identity, spend a year working as an accountant— not a very exciting or lucrative job—and then shoot up an office full of coworkers? He must have had a good reason."

# 9

## MR. MONK AND THE THEORY

I made one more call to Daniela Grace after my staff of cleaners had stopped their racket and Lieutenant Devlin had gone back to her job of tracking down No One.

I assured our lawyer that we were focusing our laserlike brilliance on Henry Pickler but, to be honest, his case had plummeted to the bottom of our pile of two. It's hard to get passionate about a client who would rather stay cooped up than give the police a plausible explanation. On the top of the pile we had an office shooting with three dead and the beginnings of a nationwide manhunt for a man who didn't exist.

To add to this case's appeal, I had a No One theory of my own that I was nurturing. I talked it over with Monk on our way to San Francisco General.

"I think this whole mass murder is just . . ."

"You're wrong," said Monk. He was clutching his seat belt, as usual and checking all the mirrors—passenger, driver's rearview—in a seamless rotation.

"I haven't said anything. How can I be wrong?"

"You said mass murder. You're wrong. According to the FBI, a mass murder has four or more victims with no cooling-off period between the homicides. The bureau is very strict about these things. Mr. Noone might have intended for this to be a mass murder but luckily it's just a triple homicide."

"Just a triple homicide? How about massacre? Can I say massacre?"

"You can, but it's not very accurate."

"Fine. Triple homicide. Can I go on? I have a theory."

Monk turned his head from the passenger rearview and stared at my profile. "First Walter White, the drug lord, now this? Is this what it's going to be? You coming up with theories? I'm all in favor of a partnership. But I'm not sure that includes you having theories."

"It does. It's in our corporation bylaws. Section two, paragraph three. Want to read it?"

"Can I amend the bylaws before hearing your theory? Then I won't have to hear your theory."

"No. You're going to listen."

"I don't even think we have bylaws."

"My theory is that the murders were collateral, not part of his original plan. Wyatt Noone went to a lot of trouble setting up his identity. He took a midlevel accounting job just to make ends meet and stay below the radar. Meanwhile, he was working on something big."

"Big like what?"

"An assassination or espionage or corporate espionage. Maybe a massive bank heist where the fictitious Noone would need to disappear at a moment's notice. But then his coworkers got suspicious. They began to find out things. Noone had to change gears and kill them before the plan fell apart, whatever it was."

"He could be a terrorist." Monk shuddered. "You know how much I hate terror."

"And his job, working for an import company? Maybe that's part of the terrorism. Or the assassination. Something he had to import into the country."

Monk made a face I've rarely seen him make, curving his lower lip into a frown and opening his eyes a little wider. It meant, hmm, not bad. Very rare.

"Why didn't Sarabeth tell us about this?"

"Maybe she didn't know; just the others. Or maybe it's something she doesn't realize she knows. But this accounts for him taking the extra time in the warehouse to try to kill her. He had to kill them all."

"It's not your worst idea," he said grudgingly.

"High praise."

"It means I'll need to have many long talks with Sarabeth to figure out what— Yield, yield, yield! Don't you see the sign? Signs have meanings."

I didn't even have to look. "That's a yield sign for the merging lane."

"No, it's for everybody. Everybody has to yield, all the time." And with that, he white-knuckled his grip on the seat belt and stayed silent for the rest of the ride.

Sarabeth was still in the private ICU, although technically her improved condition placed her out of intensive care. A burly, confident SFPD patrolman sat in a chair outside her door. On our way in, Monk asked to check his sidearm to make sure it was fully loaded. "You can't be too careful." The officer replied that if Monk continued this nonsense, he would have to take action and the sidearm would no longer be fully loaded. I liked this guy.

The office assistant was looking better. Three pints of blood had done their job, improving her color dramatically. A nurse, she said, had come in earlier to wash her hair. It was still slightly wet. The style was short, a pageboy that ended just below her ears with bangs that were now swept to the sides. The color was reddish brown. Truth to tell, she was probably my age, not much older.

"You're looking better today." Sarabeth was actually the one who said that to Monk. As I said, she was the nurturing sort.

"Thanks," said Monk. "I started using a face scrub." He settled into the chair next to the bed. I stood a few feet away with a pen and a notepad.

"Sarabeth, we need you to tell us everything you know about Wyatt Noone."

"The police should know more than I do."

"We don't. That's why we need your help."

There didn't seem to be much to tell. A little more than a year ago, the four office employees had complained to the parent company in Japan about their workloads. They'd been hoping to get raises; the company was profitable enough. Instead, they got permission to hire a full-time accountant. Mel, the manager, interviewed several applicants and settled on Wyatt.

"Did the Japanese owners suggest you hire Wyatt?" Monk asked.

"No. They just said hire someone."

"Did Mel check his references?"

"I assume so. It's standard procedure."

"If Wyatt were a criminal," Monk said, "what kind of criminal would he be? Other than a killer, I mean."

"What kind? Is this like a game? Like what kind of animal would he be?"

"No, it's serious. Use your imagination. If last week someone told you Wyatt had committed a crime, what conclusion would you jump to? Would he be a thief? A professional hit man? Maybe an anarchist who built bombs?"

"An anarchist? Wyatt?" She almost smiled. "If I had to guess, I'd say embezzler. Only because he was our accountant. I really don't know anything."

"I'll bet you know his birthday," I suggested.

"March twenty-fifth. I bring cupcakes in for everyone's birthday. Brought." And she drew in her breath, like a sniffle. This confirmed my theory about her office persona, but I was sorry I'd asked.

"Wyatt kept to himself," she added. "Politically, he was probably conservative. That's a guess. There was no girlfriend or boyfriend we knew about. At our Christmas party, he came alone. No one cared enough to be curious about him."

"Well, something happened," Monk said. "For some reason, he wanted you dead."

"You mean he wasn't crazy?"

"We have a theory," Monk said. I loved how he said *we*. It wasn't just Natalie's silly theory. "Wyatt may have had a secret life. Your friends were killed because they stumbled across some information about this life."

"You think I know this information?"

"You may not realize it," I said. "Maybe he accidentally left something on a desk. Or said something. Maybe someone called the office. Or you saw someone drop him off at work."

"And that's why he needed to kill three people?" Sarabeth bit her lip. "Four. Am I still in danger?"

"You're not," I assured her. "You have an armed police officer right in front of your door. Twenty-four/seven."

"That's right," said Monk. "We think he has a

full clip in his sidearm, but we're not sure. He says it's a full clip, but he wouldn't show it to us."

"Adrian," I hissed.

"It probably is a full clip. That's my guess."

"I don't know anything." Sarabeth's hands shook and her eyes began to fill.

"Natalie, wipe her tears," Monk ordered. "Never mind. I'll do it." And he took a travel packet of Kleenex from his breast pocket, shook out the top tissue, and started dabbing at the corners of her eyes.

I had never seen Monk do anything like this. Once, while interrogating a quarterback during the halftime of a division play-off game, he'd used a sanitary wipe to try to remove the black smudges under the player's eyes. But this was different. Monk was actually feeling someone else's pain.

"You're a nice man," Sarabeth whispered.

"I'm not," Monk whispered back. "But I'll try harder."

A buzz from inside my PBS tote alerted me. For some reason, I didn't want to interrupt this moment. Plus, I think cell phones aren't allowed in the ICU. I took it outside, past the armed guard to the corridor.

"Hi, sweetie." It was my daughter, Julie.

Julie Teeger was in her senior year at UC Berkeley. With maintaining her class schedule and trying to line up an internship after graduation, she felt guilty about not spending more time together. And with all the work of opening an agency and dealing with my partner and four dead bodies (three office workers and a Guatemalan drug runner), I was feeling even guiltier.

"Hey, Mom. Are you free for dinner? A Teeger night in?"

"Absolutely." I would make myself free. Our get-togethers are often quasi-spontaneous. One of us calls the other out of the blue. I try to do a little shopping and get home before she drives over the bridge. Sometimes, due to a murder or Monk, I don't make it to the store. Then we scrounge the refrigerator and pantry and come up with something. Those can turn out to be the best meals. And a lot of fun, because it feels like a challenge in a TV cooking show. That reminded me. I should tell her about Randy and Monk and the murder at Summit Chef. She'd get a kick out of that.

"How's the new business?" she asked. "I'm still waiting for an Evite to your grand opening."

"That's been delayed," I said. "We're too busy to open."

"Glad you're busy. Are you and Adrian working the mass murder downtown? It's all over the news." She also called him Adrian, and has for much longer than I have.

"Triple homicide," I corrected her. "Yes, we are. But I should save it. We don't want to run out of things to talk about."

"We never run out," she corrected me. It was true. The two of us could talk and talk for hours, like girlfriends.

After hanging up, I walked back to the officer at the door to Sarabeth's room. He was halfway through an apple and held it in his mouth while he wiped his hands and got up to unlock the door.

It was during those few seconds that I glanced through the protective glass panel, a feature only designed into doors of the ICU rooms. I was at just the right angle to see the bed. Monk was standing there, his back to me, straightening the sheets and tucking in the bedspread. I could see Sarabeth, waiting patiently for him to finish, staring off into space. There was something about the look on her face. Something . . .

I know that in retrospect, when you look back at an event and play it over in your mind, you often think you sensed something wrong when you really didn't. I think we all have the ability to reinvent memories to suit what we later find out to be the truth. Then we smile wisely and say we'd had this premonition.

But I swear to you, even then, I knew something was wrong.

# 10

## MR. MONK AND THE INTERN

It started out as one of our better Teeger nights.

I was late arriving home. Daniela had called at the last minute and talked me into an AA meeting. I felt I had to go, and not just because she was a client on a case that we were doing absolutely squat about. I liked Daniela, and I found the meetings soothing and inspiring. Plus, I'd been consistently unable to convince her that I wasn't an alcoholic.

The misunderstanding happened months ago when Monk and I accidentally attended an AA meeting while he was trying to score some individually wrapped oatmeal cookies. Ever since, the more I tried to deny my alcoholism, the more convinced Daniela became that I was in denial.

Julie's car was in the driveway when I pulled up. Miraculously, there was a spot at the curb, so I grabbed it. From the moment I opened the door, I felt like I was in an Indian restaurant. The house was full of the unmistakable scent of curry. Red and yellow scarves were draped over the reading lamps to give the living room some soft Eastern ambiance. Julie must have dredged up an old Ravi Shankar CD from some bottom drawer somewhere, because the monotonous strains of sitar music were wafting through the house. (True story: I once had a Ravi Shankar CD playing for two hours before I realized there was a flaw in the disc and the same song was playing over and over. It was almost impossible to tell.)

"Are you doing an internship in India?" I called out. "Is this your way of breaking the news?"

Julie's laugh was coming from the kitchen. "I was just in the mood," she said. "And the online recipe looked easy. I didn't realize how much chopping was involved. I think I have enough onions for an army. I hope it wasn't a typo."

I joined her, washed my hands, grabbed a knife, and followed instructions, chopping carrots and mint and measuring out fifteen different spices.

I don't cook every night, especially not time-consuming dishes. But I welcomed the chance to do something simple and manual while we caught up on each other's lives. Julie offered me a glass of my own Chardonnay, but I turned it down, perhaps as a tribute to Daniela and the meeting I'd just attended.

An hour and a half later, when we were sitting down to our shrimp curry, we had gone through boyfriend stories—hers, not mine, which don't exist—the sagas from Summit, and a brief outline of the current cases. Julie has been hearing Monk cases since she was eleven, so what might have seemed like crazy mysteries to the average poli-sci student sounded perfectly normal to her.

"So what's happening with the body in the vacant lot?" she asked. "The guy is obviously hiding something. Have you looked through his house or talked to his neighbors?"

I suppose a normal mother doesn't discuss murder over the dinner table. I wouldn't know. "Don't make me feel guilty," I said. "We've been so busy with the triple homicide, I haven't even thought of the next step in the Pickler case. Maybe tomorrow we'll have time to refocus."

"It's your first case in the new office. You'll have to frame your first dollar and put it on your wall. That's what businesses do for luck."

"I'll do that," I said.

Then I switched subjects and turned into a mother. Julie was graduating this spring and planning for law school. But she hadn't been able to get into her top-two choices, Stanford and Harvard. This had been a big disappointment, evenings of long, tearful phone calls. But she was bouncing back and wanted to take a year off to do an internship in a law office. Somewhere local, I hoped.

"You know, my client Daniela is a senior partner. Working for her would look good on your résumé."

"She won't mind hiring the daughter of an alcoholic?"

"Recovering alcoholic," I said, and we toasted

with the Chardonnay I'd poured for dinner. "Daniela's firm practices all types of law. Corporate. Criminal. Civil. Class action."

"Actually, I was hoping to do an internship closer to home."

"Closer than the business district?" It sounded like a joke.

"Emotionally closer. I was thinking an unpaid internship at the firm of Monk and Teeger."

"Where?" I actually said that before realizing what she meant. "Are you serious? No. Spending a year with Monk and me is not going to help get you into law school."

"That's just it. I'm not sure I want to be a lawyer."

"Julie." I took a deep breath. "Just because you didn't get into Harvard or Stanford . . . They're the two most competitive schools in the country. I know it was rough. But if you spend a year at a great firm and get a little more realistic in your choice of schools . . ."

"Mom, I've thought this through. I want to be a police detective. Or a private investigator like you."

"No, no, no." I don't know why it took me by surprise. Julie was practically raised with detectives and had been on a first-name basis with more than one killer. She'd been in the background of dozens of cases and in the foreground of several more. But I'd never once thought that any of this had been appealing to her.

"What? You don't want me to be like you?" I think she was annoyed by my three emphatic no's.

"Julie, you're young. There's so much more you can do with your life."

"More than what? More than you? I thought you loved your work. I thought you were proud of your life."

"I am proud. But I got here . . ." How could I explain? "This is not what I intended. Yes, I love it. I love Adrian and the work. But if I was starting from scratch . . . Sweetie, you can be anything in the world. You're graduating from Berkeley. You don't want to waste that."

"It's an education. I'll have it no matter what. And the police academy prefers college graduates."

"Police academy? Why do you want to sell yourself short? You're too smart."

"Monk was a police officer," she countered. "So were you."

This was in fact true. I had served for a brief stint in the Summit police department. But that was beside the point. I wasn't a sweet, educated twenty-one-year-old related to me by birth. Kids don't understand.

"Or I could be like you," Julie said. "Get my license and open my own detective agency."

"That was a fluke," I said. "I just happened to get eleven years of training with one of the most brilliant minds in the world. Warped but brilliant. What do you think the chances are of you finding a brilliant partner?"

"Maybe I'm the brilliant partner, huh? You tell me that I'm selling myself short? But it's you who's selling me short. Maybe I'm the next Monk."

The girl had a point. She was smart and insightful and tenacious. But I think most mothers would be on my side. I'd just gone from visualizing my little girl writing torts in a safe, wood-paneled office to shooting bad guys or hanging from a cliff. . . . True. I'd done both myself and a lot more. But it was still a mental adjustment.

"Why don't we start after graduation and see how it goes?" she said. "You can use my help. You're falling behind on the Mafia case, right?" She pointed to the file folder out on the coffee table.

"I'm not having you get involved with that. When Sal Lucarelli asks how my beautiful daughter is doing, he's not being nice. It's a threat."

"I can do simple stuff. Looking into Henry Pickler's background like we talked about."

"You remembered his name?"

"What if I can do a little investigating and connect him to the Mexican cartel? Wouldn't that be helpful?"

"I need to show you season four of *Breaking Bad*."

"I'll be an intern. I won't put myself in danger. Even though you put yourself in danger all the time."

I took another deep breath. When was Ravi Shankar finally going to get to a new song? "Okay, sweetie," I said. "Let me think about it." Meaning no.

"Why do you always say no?"

It was somewhere around here that Captain Stottlemeyer came to my rescue, arriving on the front porch and ringing the bell. He hadn't called ahead, but I welcomed him with open arms.

"I can come back," he said, looking through the window and waving at Julie.

"Don't you dare leave. Your timing is perfect."

"Oh," he said, a little startled. "That's too bad."

"Just mother and daughter stuff. What's up? And don't say you were in the neighborhood."

"Thanks for the warning." He smoothed both sides of his mustache, a classic stalling technique. "By the way, good catch with the name. It helps to know we're dealing with a fake identity. Keeps us from going down too many dead ends."

"Is that why you dropped by?"

"No. I guess I'm here because of Devlin. The chief and the commissioner are itching to set up a review board and she's feeling the pressure."

I nodded. "Adrian and I are doing all we can. What have you gotten from the FBI? They have great resources. Maybe we can set up a meeting."

"The FBI isn't involved. This doesn't involve federal law or go over state lines. And with just three deaths, it's not a mass murder."

"They're very strict with their rules, aren't they?"

"I've never seen her like this," said the captain, lowering his voice. "You know her. Confidence is her key asset. She can be wrong and rude and a pain in the butt. But her self-confidence is what always makes it work. Now she's second-guessing herself. She's got a team of twenty tracking this guy down and she's a mess. I've never seen her so indecisive and disorganized."

"She offered to personally pay us for helping."

"Whoa." This was obviously news to him. "You see? If this doesn't turn her way, I'm afraid she might put in for a transfer or even quit the force. She mentioned it once, casually. But nothing is really casual with her."

"Quit the force? She can't. Amy is a born cop."

"She let a killer escape a locked-down building dressed as an EMT. That's what everyone thinks. Even if he got out some other way, she was the one in charge."

That did seem to be bad. "Well, as Adrian says, 'The truth is the truth.' All we can try to do is find it."

"That's all I'm asking," said Stottlemeyer.

By the time the captain drove away and I went back inside, Julie and I had both calmed down.

Neither of us mentioned the internship. We kept to small talk as we cleaned the kitchen and filled the dishwasher and sat down with some cookies and milk. We let ourselves be grossed out by a half hour of *Tosh.0*, a show that I never watch on my own but keep on my DVR just for her.

Julie had to get ready for an early class, so she didn't stay overnight in the shrine that used to be her bedroom. I stood on the porch and watched her drive off around the corner. Then I went straight to bed. It had been a long day.

Sometime during the night, I received a voice mail from the captain asking us to come to the station for an early meeting with the president of East Decorative Imports who had just flown in from Tokyo to deal with the massacre.

I got the message the next morning and immediately found myself in a rush. First was the call to Monk, telling him he had to alter his morning routine in order to be ready for me to pick him up. "Cut out your second shower and your second exfoliation," I advised. Then I hung up and dealt with my own, much shorter routine.

When it came time to race out the door, I grabbed my PBS tote and my car keys and the triple-murder file from the coffee table. It struck me at the time that the Pickler file wasn't there. It had been sitting right beside the other file, or so I thought.

At the time I thought I'd just misplaced it.

# II

# MR. MONK REARRANGES
# THE FACTS

Mr. Takumi Ito was a tall man by anyone's standards, well over six feet, dressed in a dark European-cut suit that just seemed to accentuate his height. He sat straight and composed in the captain's office but looked tired and a little befuddled. I think I'd be befuddled, too, coming to a foreign country and dealing with this senseless violence.

"The man has escaped," he said, addressing the captain. "That's what they say on the TV. You have no idea where he is?"

"We have our best people working on it." Stottlemeyer's eyes wandered out his office window to the command center at the far end of the bull pen near the elevator. Lieutenant Devlin and a sergeant borrowed from another major crimes unit were organizing cards on a corkboard. "It would be a lot easier. . . . Why aren't there any cameras in your building? A warehouse like that with valuables? You'd think there'd be cameras."

"We're a small company, Captain. At one point we discussed having them installed, but they never seemed to get around to it."

"It must be difficult, running a company from thousands of miles away."

"That's why you hire good people and trust them." A second later he was struck by the irony. "At least you try. The poor families. I must go visit them. And Sarabeth. I'm so grateful she survived."

"I am, too," said Monk, "even though I just met her. Do you know what kind of flowers she likes? I was thinking of flowers."

"I don't know," said Ito. His English was flawless, with maybe just the hint of an Australian accent. "But thank you for reminding me about flowers. I'll have my driver pick up some. It will be a long and sad day, I'm afraid."

"Did you know them well?" asked the captain. "The victims, I mean."

"I knew them all," said Ito. "Mel Lubarsky worked for the company in Tokyo, before we expanded. His wife was very happy when we decided to open operations in the States. I believe her people live in San Francisco. Katrina Avery and her husband both worked for East Decorative. He is employed in the loading dock. Ex-husband, I should say. They're divorced now. Caleb Smith was single. I believe he lived with another man. But I met him only once, on a visit eighteen months ago."

"What about Wyatt Noone?" asked the captain. That was the question all of San Francisco wanted answered. What about Wyatt Noone?

"I've spoken with him on the phone but we never met."

"What was he like on the phone?" asked Monk. "Pleasant? A good vocabulary? Any particular kind of accent?"

Ito mulled this over. "As I recall, he didn't indulge in much talk. Perhaps a South American accent?"

"South American?" I asked. "Like Hispanic?"

"No, I'm sorry. From the American South. A Southern accent. But I'm not certain about accents."

"So he never gave you a chance to know him," said Stottlemeyer.

"Not at all. I had in fact planned a trip here next week to meet Mr. Noone in person. Unfortunately, this situation forced me to come early."

"Why?" Monk asked. "I mean, why were you planning to come at all?" He pursed his lips, paused, and said the next sentence casually, as if asking about the weather. "How much do you suspect he stole?"

"Excuse me?" said Ito.

"The reason why you decided to visit for the first time in over a year. The reason why you wanted to meet the accountant. We've been considering all kinds of motives, from madness to spying to terrorism. But you say it was embezzlement. How much?"

It wasn't the biggest leap of logic, given Wyatt

Noone's false identity, the office massacre, and what Sarabeth had suggested. But to Takumi Ito it must have seemed like mind reading. "That's not something I feel comfortable talking about," he replied.

"I understand," said the captain who was also just coming up to speed. "But we would really appreciate your cooperation. Whatever information you can give us we'll do our best to keep confidential."

"Or we can just subpoena your company records and draw our own conclusions," I said. I wasn't sure if this was even possible, but it didn't stop me from saying it.

Ito straightened his cuffs, one by one. "We're not sure exactly how much. A little under two hundred million."

Our mouths all fell open. "Dollars?" I asked.

"Yen," he clarified. "Sorry to alarm you. About two million U.S. We are selling more antiquities this year, many from Malaysia and Indonesia. All legally exported. Mr. Noone's accounting was not very sophisticated. But since our American profits were growing nicely, no one thought to look into it. It was just by luck that someone in the Tokyo office noticed a discrepancy."

"And you're sure it was Wyatt?" I asked. "Not one of the others?"

"His signature was on all the paperwork. That's why I needed to talk to him."

"He must have known you would find out," said Stottlemeyer. "Sooner or later."

Ito agreed. "In a company our size, two million does not go unnoticed. I wanted to handle this quietly. I pretended my upcoming visit would be routine, just checking in, as you say. Do you think the murders had something to do with it?"

"It's a strong possibility," said the captain.

A combination grunt and moan formed in the back of the throat of the elegantly dressed man. "Then I was perhaps the catalyst for this. If no one had found out . . . If I hadn't told them I was coming, they might be alive."

"You had no way of knowing," said the captain. His voice was kind and reassuring, a tone that he'd used on me many times in the past. "We have reason to believe that Noone always intended to run. He planned his disappearance carefully. It was just a question of when."

"Although . . ." Monk had his hand raised, like the annoyingly smart kid in school. "It doesn't quite make sense, does it? If this was his plan, to steal as much as he could, then disappear, why would he need to kill anyone at all? Why not just disappear?"

It was a good question. Embezzlement certainly seemed like the right direction. But none of our scenarios, not even this one, seemed to cover all the bases. Now even the annoying smart kid was starting to look annoyed.

Mr. Ito stayed for another fifteen minutes, answering every question as best he could. But he knew even less than we did. For example, he still thought Wyatt S. Noone was the killer's name and that the police had a decent chance of finding him.

All three of us escorted Mr. Takumi Ito to the elevator. He opened up a sharkskin holder and handed each of us a business card, performing the action double-handed and formally, with a little bow, like part of a tea ceremony. I responded by reaching into my PBS tote and scrounging around for a Monk and Teeger card. I made sure to straighten out the bent corner before handing it to him, also with a little bow. It felt kind of comical, and I was glad I could make his mouth turn up slightly at the edges.

Devlin was nearby. She could barely wait for the elevator door to shut before pouncing. "Monk." She mimed grabbing him by the jacket sleeve and pulling. She didn't touch him, but it was still enough of a threat to make him sidestep with her to the corkboard. She pointed to it. "What do you think?"

The corkboard was the largest one in the building, but it was already plastered with details: photos of the victims; a list of all the known facts of Noone's existence, a map of the city with pins that marked possible sightings called into the police hotline number. The airport, train, bus, and BART systems were also represented, but with next to no information under those headings.

"Noone didn't have a car, at least not under that name. Sarabeth Willow says he always walked or took public transportation. We circulated a photo of him to ticket stations and to the security lines at the airport. It's not a very good one." Devlin pointed to the two photos at the top center of the corkboard.

The one on the left had been taken at a company Christmas party and showed a medium-sized man with a lumpy bald head, standing between two of his victims, Sarabeth and Katrina. He was wearing a reindeer sweater and a closed-lipped smile, perhaps a little drunk. The one on the right was a blow-up of the same photo. This was a little fuzzier and featured only Noone. It didn't look like it would be much help to anyone, no matter how diligent the TSA agents were. "We sent this out to all the media, not that it will do much good. He was very camera shy. The only reason this one probably happened was because he was tipsy and off his guard."

"What you're doing is a mess," said Monk. "A total mess."

"Monk, please. We're doing our best." Devlin looked exhausted and as close to tears as I'd ever seen her.

"I'll fix it. Don't worry." Monk rubbed his hands together. "First thing. We need to straighten all the photos and center them. Then we'll divide the whole board into sixteen grids, the same amount of information in each grid."

"You are not changing the board," ordered Stottlemeyer, grabbing him by the sleeve. "This is the lieutenant's operation."

"But how can she think straight?" Monk demanded. "Messy board, messy mind."

"No. He can change the board," said Devlin. It was a sign of just how exhausted and desperate she was.

"About time you got with the program," Monk said. He performed a satisfied, half smile and reached out to start his rearrangement. "Photos at the top, that was good, if sloppy. But the map should go right underneath and on the right side. . . ." Then his eyes fell on the photo of Sarabeth Willow, the last in the line of victims, and he stopped. "What does this mean?" He pointed.

Sarabeth's sweet, smiling face was framed by a question mark on each of the side margins, the only photo in the group with any notation.

"She's the sole survivor," said Devlin. "It's standard procedure. We only have her story for exactly what happened inside."

"Only her story?" I was confused. "The sharp-shooters saw Noone with his shotgun. You have the 911 calls from Sarabeth and Katrina. What else could have happened?"

"We don't know," said Devlin.

"A question mark?" Monk tilted his head. "Are you saying Sarabeth's a suspect?"

"Not an active suspect, no," said Devlin. "But any time you have only one survivor, you need to keep open the possibility. . . ."

"Possibility of what?" asked Monk. "That she and Noone were in cahoots? That they planned this massacre together? Killed three people? Sarabeth's friends? And then she stood there and let him shoot her twice in order to divert suspicion?"

Devlin shrugged and nodded. "When there's a lot of motive involved—money and/or desperation—people have been known to take bullets. You've seen it yourself. Maybe he didn't mean to shoot her so close to an artery. But she survived. That's the critical thing. And it makes her a suspect."

"C'mon, Monk," said Stottlemeyer. "That's the way we think on every case. You keep your scenarios open."

"Not this time. We're closing that scenario down. It's a waste of manpower and mental energy. Not to mention an insult to a wonderful, heroic woman who risked her own life . . . in order to hide out and escape a killer."

"Monk?" asked the captain. Everyone was looking at my partner, the three of us, and the sergeant borrowed from major crimes. "What's going on?"

"Nothing," I said. "Monk thinks it's a bad theory."

"A horrendous theory," Monk agreed.

"Hey." Stottlemeyer stared Monk in the eyes. "Are you getting a little sweet on Miss Willow?" He would have smiled if it hadn't been so serious. "This isn't like you, buddy."

"What happened to Ellen in New Jersey?" asked Devlin. "Weren't you just out there to see her?"

"Ellen rejected me because her brother is a murderer, which is not my fault. I'm on the rebound with Sarabeth. I'm not even sure she likes me. But it's a good thing."

"It's a crush," I tried to reassure everyone.

"Well, it's not a good thing," said the captain. "For a whole host of reasons. Mainly because she's involved in this case. I'm not saying she's an accomplice. I truly didn't think of her until this minute. But this case is important. You need to keep a clear head."

"Sarabeth was a victim," said Monk. "You may as well say Mel Lubarsky was involved. He was in the office, too."

"Yes, Monk. But he's dead."

"He could still be involved. He even looks like Wyatt Noone. See?" And with that, Monk tore off Wyatt's photo with one hand and Mel's with the other. The pushpins clattered to the floor, but he didn't seem to notice. He was that upset.

Monk held them up side by side, the blurry shot

of Wyatt at last year's Christmas party and a smiling shot of Mel cropped from a vacation shot in front of the Eiffel Tower with his wife. Monk had a point. The two men did look a bit alike. The same general build and height. Wyatt might have been slightly younger but it was hard to tell with his shaved head and Mel's head of brown, wavy hair, just receding a bit with age.

"You're actually right," said Stottlemeyer. "There is some resemblance."

"I should have noticed that," Devlin scolded herself. She reached for a file on the nearby desk. "Mel doesn't have any brothers. But we can check his other male relations. Cousins. Nephews."

"You should," said Monk. "I'm not saying there's anything to it. But Mel's the guy who hired Wyatt in the first place—without references or a verifiable work history. If you're going to start blaming one of the victims, I'd suggest starting with him, not a woman like Sarabeth."

"But she's alive and Mel is dead," said Stottlemeyer again.

"Ha," said Monk, and made his version of a raspberry sound, with no spit and very little sound. "It wouldn't be the first time a killer betrayed his partner. It kind of goes with the territory."

"We'll check Mel out," Devlin promised. "We'll check everything."

"Did you really arrest Ellen Morse's brother?"

asked Stottlemeyer. "Yes, of course you did. Why am I even asking?"

I had my PBS tote under my arm and felt my phone vibrate. I always keep it on vibrate in the police station. To me it's like being in a theater or a church.

I saw who it was and took a deep breath before answering. "Daniela, hi. We're actually with Captain Stottlemeyer of homicide right now, discussing your case."

"Good. The captain might be able to help us out. I'm with your intern. She's been arrested."

To my credit, I did not say, what the hell do you mean, my intern? Although I almost did. Instead, I said in my calmest voice, "Ah, yes. Julie. I'm sure it was just a misunderstanding. May I please speak with her?"

I stepped aside, leaving Monk and Devlin to fight over the symmetry of the corkboard. "Mom?" came a soft, hesitant voice. "I'm so sorry."

"Julie, where are you?"

"I'm in Henry Pickler's house, like we discussed."

"We discussed no such thing, young lady. You stay right there. I'm coming."

"The police want to take me to the station and book me. I'm kind of guilty."

"Don't say that." Life was tough enough. My daughter was not about to add a criminal arrest to her résumé. "We'll get you out of this."

# 12

## MR. MONK AND HIS DREAM HOUSE

Daniela had been right. Captain Stottlemeyer was able to help. As soon as I pulled him away from the corkboard and explained the situation, he made a call to the sheriff's office in Millbrae, which is just south of South San Francisco—which is not a part of San Francisco at all but a totally separate town, despite its name.

It was surprisingly easy to get Monk away from the board. All I had to say was Julie was in trouble and he forgot all about symmetry. Monk is like an uncle to her. He and Julie had even worked on a case or two, with Julie filling in for me as his assistant. Devlin also asked if there was anything she could do. Everyone at the station loved Julie. Except for me. Right now, I wasn't too fond of her.

Most of Millbrae is dominated by the San Francisco airport and the kind of developments that often get built around airports. But there's a section farther south, not far from the tony environs of Hillsborough, where the lots are larger and you might be able to squint and fool yourself into thinking there's some nature around that's not part of a backyard or a state park.

The Pickler residence was in just such an area. It was a large split-level ranch, straight out of the seventies, complete with a sunken living room, shag carpeting, and harvest gold appliances. I know the place sounds overwhelmingly depressing, but it wasn't. When you walked in, you found yourself entering a spotless, perfectly maintained tribute to that era. It was like a museum to a gentler, more innocent era of terrible taste. And you instantly knew two things. One, this had been Henry's childhood home. It had to be. And two, a lot of money and attention had been spent to keep it looking this way.

Daniela Grace met us at the door. Julie Teeger waited nervously by the modular sofa under the bay window. I recognized the wallpaper color from my own childhood, a soft Moon Landing blue. The captain's call had succeeded in getting rid of the police presence, so it was just Daniela, Monk, and the two Teegers.

"Mom, I am so sorry."

"Don't say anything. We'll talk about this later," I advised. It was my own version of the Miranda warning. Anything you say now can and will be used against you, sweetie.

"Hey, Adrian." Julie and Monk hadn't seen each other in a month or more. They greeted each other with their usual air hug. "How's it going?"

"Can't complain," said Monk.

"You can't? Really?"

"That's a figure of speech. Don't hold me to it."

Daniela seemed a lot more forgiving than I would be, given the circumstances. "I remember when my son was an intern at my law firm years back," she reminisced. "He once tried to help by rewriting an entire tort in street English without telling anyone. We had six lawyers show up at the meeting and no one could make heads or tails of it." Daniela smiled. "He wanted to help. That's how it is with the children of alcoholics. They have this need to take care of their parents."

Great, I thought. On top of being an alcoholic, I'm a bad mother.

"I didn't do much illegal," Julie insisted. "I found an unlocked side window, so there was no breaking, just entering. And I wasn't taking anything. I just wanted to look around, the way Adrian does."

"The house has motion sensors and a silent alarm," explained the lawyer. "Since Henry's in jail, I'm listed as the alarm company contact. The police called me as they were on their way. Luckily, I live in Hillsborough. I arrived shortly after they did."

"So there won't be any charges?" I asked. That was a relief.

"No charges," said Daniela. "Between my presence here and the call from your captain . . ."

Her smile was mischievous. "Julie had your permission to be here; you had my permission; and I had Mr. Pickler's."

"Good," I said, ignoring the lie about Julie having my permission. "So, long story short, we're free to look around."

Monk was already a step ahead of us. This time he didn't have his hands up. He was walking slowly through the rooms as if under a trance. "Beautiful," he said again and again. "This man has excellent taste."

I knew exactly where Monk was coming from. He hated change. His earliest memories centered on the sixties and seventies, which fit in perfectly with Henry Pickler's décor. Monk wouldn't call it nostalgia, but I would. The problem with living in the past, of course, is maintenance. But the Pickler house had been eerily and spotlessly maintained.

"We're acting under attorney-client privilege," Daniela warned us. "The upside is that we have his permission to go through the house. The downside is that nothing we find pertaining to the death of Mr. Rivera can be turned over to the police. Nothing at all relating to motive or means or opportunity."

"That's ridiculous," said Julie. "What are we even doing here?"

"Acting in the interests of our client," said Daniela. "That's what happens when you work for a lawyer."

"Not to worry," said Monk. "Henry Pickler couldn't be involved with that drug runner. Just look at this place."

Monk restarted in the living room, hands raised this time. He made a slow, clockwise circle through the split-level, interrupting his inspecting every now and then for an appreciative little grunt or nod. "It goes much faster when everything's perfect," he murmured.

"I know," I said. "But when everything's perfect, you don't get clues."

"It's a trade-off," he acknowledged. Then he stepped into the kitchen and came to a halt, his eyes almost bugging out. To me it looked like a normal kitchen—if you took into account Pickler's affinity for harvest gold and yellow Formica and linoleum floor tiles. But to Monk, it was like he'd been slapped in the face. "This must be where it happened."

"The murder?" Julie asked. "Cool."

"Not murder. But whatever made him go outside and do whatever he did. It happened here."

"How do you know?" asked Daniela.

"Because it's a disaster. Look." And he circled the room clockwise. "Smudge on the microwave handle; one whole-wheat crumb under the toaster; plate in the sink, sponge not properly wrung out; dinette stool number two out of alignment. The Henry Pickler I know would never leave it like this unless there'd been an emergency."

"You can tell that the crumb is whole wheat?" Daniela asked. That was such a newbie question. Of course he could.

"What type of emergency?" I asked Monk, and began to list the possibilities. "Phone call? Someone at the door? An alarm going off? Hearing something outside?"

Monk crossed to the window above the sink. The floral chintz curtains were open to a view of the backyard.

The backyard was nothing but a rectangular lawn running the length of the ranch-style house and going back perhaps fifty feet. There was no patio or garden to interrupt the perfection, just a flat, weed-free lawn with every blade of grass in place, cut to exactly the same height. At the end was a white picket fence and beyond it a large, unruly field, also a piece of Pickler property, purchased decades earlier when prices were cheap and Henry's parents were concerned about protecting their privacy.

"This was at night," Monk thought out loud, "when a decent person like Henry would have his curtains closed—unless he happened to hear some commotion outside. Then he would open them." Monk pointed toward the vacant lot. "Out there. That's the crime scene, isn't it?"

Two minutes later, we were outside, walking along the edge of the brush of the large lot. The crime scene tape had been taken down but parts of it still dangled from a few trees. Monk led the way and we followed in his footsteps.

As we walked, Julie took it upon herself to recite facts from the report she'd stolen from my coffee table. "Esteban Rivera was shot with a nine millimeter, probably with a silencer on the barrel. The body wasn't moved, except for a few yards by Henry Pickler. The San Mateo County coroner estimates the time of death at less than half an hour before the patrol car passed by and caught Mr. Pickler. The gun and silencer were never found."

"The police combed this field thoroughly," Daniela told us. "They haven't dug it up because there were no signs of recent digging. And because Henry's shovel showed no signs of use."

"I'll bet it was a perfectly clean shovel," said Monk. "Polished and shiny."

"It was," said Daniela. "Is that a clue?"

"No. Just a sure bet."

"I have a theory," said Julie.

Julie was allowed to have theories, of course. But it was always intimidating to voice one around Monk, especially for an intern who hadn't been hired yet. I was kind of proud of her. "Go ahead, sweetie."

"Thanks, Mom." Julie stood up straight and spoke clearly. "What if Pickler was looking out his window and saw the murder go down in his field? After the killer leaves, taking the gun,

Pickler goes out with a shovel to bury the body." Her posture began to deflate almost as soon as the last words were out of her. "That doesn't make sense, does it?"

"Why would he bury someone else's victim?" asked Daniela. "On his own property? Why not just call the police?"

Julie was still thinking. "Maybe the killer already buried the body and Pickler just dug it up?"

"With a clean shovel? And a clean corpse? Not to mention a field with no holes in it?" Monk shrugged his shoulders. "Even your mother comes up with better theories. No offense."

"None taken," Julie said.

"None taken," I said. We said it pretty much in unison and it made us smile, the first smile we'd shared since I got here.

Monk had not moved from the field's edge. There were probably bristles in there and dead leaves and insects and soil, better known to my partner as dirt. He turned slowly in a tight little circle, three hundred sixty degrees. "That's an apple tree," he said, indicating a gnarled, unpruned tree not far from the picket fence.

"I believe it is," said I. "Do you want me to pick you an apple?"

"Just commenting on nature," he said, then made another tight three sixty, this time looking farther into the distance.

Surrounding the overgrown lot were a dozen or so houses, all with a comfortable amount of privacy and on decent-sized lots. In the middle of his second three sixty, Monk stopped and focused on one house in particular. It was a modern white construction, modern in the old-fashioned sense with square angles and big square windows. From the eighties, I would have guessed. It was set on a mound slightly higher than the others and, despite the white stucco wall, had an unobstructed view from the second-story windows.

"That one," said Monk, and began to lead the way up the street. The rest of us followed.

"What's he doing?" Daniela asked. She was huffing along at the back of the pack, with Julie keeping her company.

Julie explained. "Adrian noticed the position of the house and the lights around it and the security cameras. He thinks they might have seen something."

"The police already spoke to the neighbors," said Daniela.

"Well, we're not the police," said Julie. I did not like the way she said *we*.

A woman answered the door after two evenly timed rings of the bell. Monk took a reflexive step back, bowled over by the stench of her perfume. Or maybe it was from the shine of her lipstick and makeup and silver lamé tank top. She might have been in her twenties, although her fashion choices gave her the look of an underage cougar.

"Are you the lady of the house?" Monk asked. He wrinkled his nose to fight the smell.

"That depends what you're selling," she said, smiling and brushing back her long blond hair. Then she took in all four of us. "What's this about?"

"We're investigating what happened over there," said Monk, pointing back toward the field. "Were you here on the night of the drug dealer's murder?"

"Why, yes," she said dramatically. "Yes, I was." Her eyes turned misty. "Horrible. Although I didn't hear a thing or even know about the poor man until the police showed up. I was watching a rerun of *Sons of Anarchy* with the sound turned up, so that might explain it."

Her name was Cyndi Locklear, with a reversed *i* and *y* as she put it when she spelled it out. She wasn't shy about standing in her doorway and telling us every detail of her life. She never even asked why three women and a man with a wrinkling nose were asking her questions.

Cyndi was originally from Las Vegas—yes, actually a native, born and raised there in a Mormon family, although she herself stopped going to church ages ago. A Jack Mormon her parents called her, even though she had no idea who Jack was. Oh, and did she mention?

Her boyfriend rented this house for her. Carlos was this crazy-busy businessman and didn't spend as much time with her as he should. She was really getting fed up. I mean, why did he make her move to this boring suburban wasteland if he was just going to be gone all the time? You know?

I felt sorry for Cyndi, all dressed up all the time with no place to go. Her talkativeness was probably a result of loneliness, I guessed. But she didn't make it easy to get a word in.

"Your sexual paramour is concerned about security," Monk said, pointing to a white camera positioned at the right side of the house above a window.

"My what?"

"Boyfriend," I clarified.

"Then why didn't he say boyfriend?"

"Because there's s-e-x involved, not just boy friendship." Monk squirmed.

"Sure, there's sex involved. But it's very friendly sex." She watched as Monk squirmed twice more. "Hey, look. He squiggles every time I say sex. Sex, sex, sex, sex . . . Isn't that cute?"

"Adorable." I had to get her back on topic before Monk worked himself into a seizure.

"Sexy, sexy, sexy sex."

"Cyndi!" I raised my voice and pointed. "That's a security camera."

"Really?" She looked over, as if seeing it for

130

the first time. "That must be left over from the owners. I think. I wouldn't know."

"Didn't the police ask you about the cameras?" asked Daniela.

"I'm not even sure they work. I hope they don't, now that I think about the stuff Carlos and me do out by the pool, you know? Sexy sex. Are any of them even pointed in the right direction? The field is way over there."

"We won't know until we look," said Daniela. "Perhaps we could talk to Carlos."

Monk was the first to hear the overpowered engine. He cocked his head and tensed slightly. How he knew the car was heading toward this driveway, I don't know. But he was right. Ten seconds later, a red Lamborghini pulled in. Cyndi squealed with delight and clapped her hands. "Carlos. Carlos."

The man stepping out of the Lamborghini was middle-aged and relatively short—thick around the middle but not fat, just powerful. He stared directly at Cyndi and pretended not to see us, even though the four of us were almost blocking the door and hard to miss. "Inside," he growled as he powered through both us and the doorway.

"Sorry," said Cyndi with a giggle and another toss of the hair. "My man's home. Gotta go." And she shut the door in our faces.

A second later, Monk had turned on his heel and was striding down the street. This time Daniela tried to keep up. "So that's it?" she said, talking into his back, her heels clattering. "You're just leaving? Don't you want to stay and talk to this Carlos character? He's right there."

"I don't," said Monk.

"Why not?" she demanded. "Because the man is tough and threatening? You're a private detective. That comes with the territory."

"I found out what I need to know." Monk increased his pace and we all struggled to catch up. It was like race walking.

"What? What did you find out?" asked our lawyer. "That there were security cameras that might have picked up something that night? A passing car? Someone walking by? Those details could help us. Are you not even going to try to get access?"

"We're not going to get anything out of those cameras."

"How do you know that?" Daniela stopped in the middle of the street and stood her ground. "Mr. Monk, talk to me."

We must have been far enough away from the white modern house for Monk's comfort. He turned to face Daniela but didn't go back. They were like two gunslingers facing down each other in the middle of a street.

"The police can get a court order," said Daniela, firing first. "For the cameras."

"Even if those cameras were working and

facing the right direction, we'll still get nothing out of them."

"But that's why you dragged us over there, to check the cameras. And now you're just giving up?"

"That man was Carlos Menendez," Monk said. "I'm surprised you didn't know his face."

"I did," said Julie. "His picture was in the case file." She smiled at Monk, as if she'd aced an extra-credit question on a test.

"Very good," said Monk. "So, maybe you can explain to Ms. Grace and the other Ms. Teeger why Carlos Menendez is important."

Julie stood by Monk the Gunslinger as she faced down Daniela and me. "Carlos Menendez runs the Menendez drug cartel. He was Esteban Rivera's employer at the time Mr. Rivera was shot in that field, right next to his girlfriend's house."

"Very good," said Monk. "Now, if everyone is finished with their questions, can we please get the heck out of here?"

# 13

## MR. MONK'S BEDSIDE MANNER

"Breaking and entering? Julie, what were you thinking?"

"Not breaking," she argued again. "Besides, you and Adrian do the same thing."

"But we've never been arrested for it." Never? Okay, I'd have to think about that. Monk and I have been arrested so many times, even for murder, but I don't think ever for breaking and entering. It was my own fault for telling Julie so much about our exploits and making it sound exciting.

"You still did it. You just didn't get caught."

"The difference, young lady, is that we're a team of professionals who know what we're doing. You're a twenty-one-year-old who could have ended up with a criminal record. How do you think that would look on a law school application?"

"I'm not going to law school, remember?"

"All right. Let's say a police academy application. Or an application for a PI license. Not to mention the danger you were putting yourself in."

"It was the empty house of a man who was in jail."

"It could have been more than that; you didn't know. And meanwhile, not a soul knew you were there. Not a partner or the captain or anyone."

"Okay, I get it," said Julie in a tone that said maybe she finally did. "I shouldn't have done it."

After we'd closed up Henry Pickler's tribute to the seventies, making sure this time that no side windows were unlocked, Monk had wanted to go back to his apartment. But it was a workday and I insisted on dropping him off at the office. "Just in case we get any street traffic." It was a remote prospect but one that made him shudder all the same.

Out in the parking lot of our strip-mall home, Julie and I sat in the old Subaru, the scene of so many mother-daughter confrontations over the years. A light rain was pelting the windshield. "Did you miss any classes this morning?" I asked, trying not to make it sound like an accusation.

"I missed a lecture. No big deal. Jennifer recorded it for me." Her mouth curved up in the slightest of smiles. " 'Ethics in the Workplace.' "

"Well, you just had a mom-lecture on ethics in the workplace, so it probably amounted to the same thing."

"I think the mom-lecture made more of an impact."

"Good to hear."

Julie got back in her own car. She promised to

call tonight, then drove off, heading back to Berkeley while I headed back into work.

Monk was at his desk, in the middle of a call and not looking happy. "I'll tell you exactly what kind of detective agency we are, ma'am. We're the kind that couldn't care less why your fiancé emptied out your 401(k) and disappeared. My guess is the man had his reasons."

My reflex was to rush up and grab the phone and apologize to whoever was on the other end. But I was too late. Monk had already hung up.

"Is this what you've reduced us to, Natalie? Taking cases from desperate, stupid women with easy-to-forge signatures who give their younger boyfriends all their banking information?"

"You didn't take the case, Adrian. You took the phone call."

"It still took time and annoyed me." Monk reached for the can of Lysol in his top drawer and sprayed down the handset, ignoring the fact that he was the only one who ever used that phone. "How was your conversation with Julie?"

I sighed. "I have a feeling it's not over."

Monk nodded. "Julie was smart out there today. She could be an asset." I never should have let it slip that Julie was lobbying for an unpaid internship with Monk and Teeger. If only I'd left out the word *unpaid* . . .

I tried to change the subject. "So tell me. What happened to your theory that Fat Tony killed

Rivera? Last time I looked, you were ninety percent sure."

"I still am," said Monk. "Just because Rivera was shot outside the girlfriend's house doesn't change that. The Lucarellis were sending a message. 'We can strike you anywhere, even outside your sexual paramour's place of residence.' Such an attack makes it personal, not just business. Menendez has a wife and family in Mexico. It could be construed as a threat against them, too."

"But it still leaves us with the big question," I pointed out. "What is Henry Pickler's part in all this? Why won't he say anything?"

"Don't have a clue," Monk said, "which is what I need. I can't work without clues, Natalie. Why don't you get me a clue?"

The business phone rang again and Monk fixed me with one of those looks. "It's been like this since we got back. Almost twice an hour." He let it ring. But not for long.

Here's a secret about Monk you might not know. Part of his obsessive-compulsive nature compels him to complete things. A doorbell cannot go unanswered, even if his answer is "Go away." If you knock "shave and a haircut," he will always knock back "two bits." And if a phone rings and if I refuse to pick it up, which I was doing right now . . .

"This is why we need an unpaid intern," Monk

said. His phone hand was already starting to shake. "Where's Julie?"

"We are not having this discussion, Adrian. And I'm not your assistant. If you want that phone answered—"

"Hello?" he said into the freshly cleaned handset after the sixth ring. I was never going to get him to say, "Monk and Teeger. Consulting Detectives. How may I help you?" I wasn't even going to try.

When you've known someone long enough, you get to recognize how they talk on the phone. Not just the words but the tone. Is the caller a stranger? A friend? An acquaintance? Someone you have to be nice to? Someone who has to be nice to you? There's also the voice you adopt when you're talking to family. In this case, Monk was almost mute, voicing a few comfortable grunts but showing no real impatience. Every twenty seconds or so he would murmur something like "good" or "fine."

"Hi, Ambrose," I called toward the phone.

"Natalie wants to talk to you," Monk said quickly, and held out the handset.

Ambrose is Monk's older brother. If you think of Monk as Sherlock Holmes, with a trusty sidekick, an irascible police captain, and criminals that outfox everyone in the world but him, then Ambrose would be Mycroft Holmes.

For those who don't know, Mycroft was Sherlock's older brother. He was acknowledged by everyone to be smarter than Sherlock and could have been an even greater detective, but the man didn't have Sherlock's energy and was so antisocial that he rarely left the confines of his private men's club.

Ambrose Monk might indeed be smarter than Adrian. But he's also more damaged. He has lived in their childhood home his entire life. For nearly all of his adult life, Ambrose, a true agoraphobe, never left the house. And he was a bit of a pack rat. Every piece of mail that arrived at the door, he had hoarded in the hope that the father who had deserted them might come back and want to sit down and read a hundred Lands' End catalogues in chronological order.

Ambrose's saving angel turned out to be Yuki Nakamura, a Japanese American biker chick with multiple tattoos. I realize how odd that sounds, but what can I say? It's true. Yuki arrived with her own set of problems, including a very dark past.

She came into the Monk family house as Ambrose's assistant, helping him with his free-lance business of writing instruction manuals. If you've owned anything from a toaster to a tractor and bothered to read the manual—in English, Japanese, German, Braille, or a dozen other languages—then you're familiar with Ambrose and Yuki's body of work.

I grabbed the phone as soon as Monk held it out.

"Ambrose! Where are you? How are you? When are you coming home?"

All right, I did say Ambrose never left the house. My mistake. I left out the part where he and Yuki got married. For their honeymoon, she convinced him to tour the entire United States in a mobile home. He would never have to leave the safety of the RV, never have to deal with the outside world. He would be able to see it all through a spotlessly clean Winnebago windshield.

"It's been almost a year," I said. "Tell me everything. How's the weather wherever you are?"

"Identical to San Francisco weather," reported the stilted, slightly formal voice. I never thought I'd actually miss that voice but I did. "That's primarily because we're in San Francisco. We've been home for a week, but it took Yuki a few days to get me out of the RV and into the house. As you may know, I'm not fond of change."

"I know. I know. Welcome home."

"Excuse me?" Monk raised a hand. "You shouldn't tie up the business line with personal calls."

I ignored him and kept Ambrose on the phone long enough to wrangle a dinner invitation for that evening. Monk included, of course.

The best thing about eating at Ambrose's is that I never have to explain Monk's food restrictions because Ambrose shares them all and a few more. No hint of fruit in the entrée, all the meats well done, no food types touching one another on the plate. Soup is okay, but no stew. Stews are anarchy. The list goes on.

"We're in fact going to partake in Japanese food tonight, Natalie. So please warn my brother."

"Japanese? How daring."

"What about the Japanese?" Monk asked. I didn't respond.

"Yuki encourages me to try new things," said Ambrose. "She assures me the food will be cooked. And spices will be optional, in little containers on a separate table in the next room. No wasabi unless requested in advance."

"Sounds like fine dining. We can't wait."

After the call, I informed my partner of our dinner plans. He was not fond of Yuki, not in the least, starting with her tattoos and ending with her once having killed a man. But she had done a lot for Ambrose in the past few years, and Adrian recognized the kind of caring and understanding that goes into loving someone of the Monk species.

We shared a late lunch of Spam sandwiches and Fiji Water. I informed him that tomorrow I was bringing lunch and that it wouldn't be Spam. Then we headed over to San Francisco General. Monk felt it important to have yet another interview with Sarabeth Willow.

When we walked into Sarabeth's private room half an hour later, he was disappointed to find the two visitor chairs already occupied. "We can come back," Monk said before even bothering to say hello. "No need to rush. Is five minutes okay? We'll wait out in the hall until you're gone in five minutes."

"Adrian, Natalie, come in please. So good to see you." Sarabeth was looking much better, her cheeks blooming with some color and maybe just a little makeup. She was no longer connected to tubes, just a heart monitor, which is standard procedure for an ICU. "I'd like you to meet my friends." They were both seated on the same side of the bed, displaying sad, half smiles. "This is Helena Lubarsky, Mel's wife. And Todd Avery. Todd used to be married to Katrina."

At some point very soon we were going to have to take half a day to visit the victims' families. Now here they were in front of us. I considered it an opportunity. Monk considered it their brazen attempt to poach quality time with his rebound girlfriend.

"Nice to meet you both. We're so sorry for your loss." In our line of work, I wind up saying that a lot.

"Thank you," said Helena. She was in her early forties, slim and stylish in a rather showy way. Helena was dressed in darker colors, blue and gray, but not black. "Are you the detectives? Sarabeth's been telling us about you."

"We are," I said. "We're from the firm of Monk and Teeger. I'm Teeger. He's Monk."

"Adrian is famous." Sarabeth threw my partner a sly wink. "As well as very handsome. They say he can solve anything."

"Then why hasn't he found Wyatt?" asked Todd. He immediately apologized. "Sorry to be so blunt. But in this day and age, you'd think anyone could be found."

"We'll find him," I said. "Maybe you can help."

"We'll do anything," said Helena. "That maniac killed my husband and ruined my life."

"Katrina was a wonderful woman," said Todd, "even if we couldn't make the marriage work. She didn't deserve this." Todd was also in his forties with even, handsome features, a sandy crew cut, and just enough heft to keep him from being a middle-aged heartthrob. "If there's anything I can do to help, Mr. Monk, just ask."

Monk asked. "What can you tell us about Wyatt Noone?"

"I'm afraid I told you all I know," said Sarabeth with a helpless sigh.

"I wasn't asking you," Monk said, then turned to the visitors. "What did Wyatt tell you about himself? Do you have any pictures of him?"

Todd and Helena traded an embarrassed glance. "We were just talking about that," said Helena. "I don't think either of us actually met Wyatt."

Mr. Noone had been adept at keeping a low profile, so Monk and I had been prepared to be disappointed. Just not this disappointed. "Never met him?" I asked. "He worked with your husband for a year. You never ran into him at a party or when you visited the office?"

"I work a dayshift myself," said Helena. "The one time I dropped by to see Mel, Wyatt was in his office with the door closed. I didn't think much about it."

"How about you?" I asked Todd. "You worked in the same building. He was the company accountant. How could you never meet?"

"I don't know," said Todd, looking even more embarrassed. "The third floor is its own little world, totally separate from the warehouse and on a different schedule. Once or twice I may have seen him in passing—in the elevator or in the parking lot. I'm not sure."

"You didn't have any contact with him?" asked Monk. "This man was your financial manager."

"E-mails and phone calls," Todd said. "That's how most business gets done."

"Did he have an accent on the phone?" Monk asked. "What kind?"

"An accent?" Todd had to think for a second. "Hell, yes," he said, treating it like a victory. "A Southern accent. Very pronounced. Does that mean anything?"

"The Southern accent was fake," Monk explained. "That's the go-to accent for fakeness, for some reason. I suppose it's easy to do, at least a bad one. And it changes the tone of your voice."

"It's funny you didn't mention a Southern accent," I said to Sarabeth, "when you were describing Wyatt to us earlier."

"Didn't I?" She looked confused. "Well, I suppose it's because you didn't ask me."

"It's because we didn't ask her," said Monk. "My fault." Then he turned his attention to Todd. "It's hard to believe you never met him. How about the office Christmas party? We have a picture of him. Weren't you at the party?"

"Wyatt was gone by the time I came upstairs," said Todd.

"It's true," Sarabeth confirmed. "Wyatt left early. Said he had a headache."

Wow, I thought. Whoever this Wyatt was, he was good. I turned to Helena. "What do you know about him? Your husband must have had stories. Everyone brings home gossip from the office."

"Sure," said Helena. "Mel talked about him all the time. Where to begin?"

But the stories they told, Sarabeth included, seemed perfectly ordinary. The cheap gift Wyatt gave for the Secret Santa exchange. Wyatt's taste for classic country music, especially Dolly Parton. A bottle of cranberry-prune juice he kept in the company refrigerator because he thought it would help with his new diet. He drank it religiously and wound up spending hours in the bathroom, even though no one noticed him ever losing an ounce.

145

"He scrawled his name on the bottles," said Sarabeth with a chuckle, "as if anyone would try to steal this concoction. Can you imagine the taste?"

"Wyatt was quite the character," agreed Helena. "From what I've heard."

"I wonder why your husband hired him in the first place," Monk said.

"I wish he hadn't. Believe me."

"Did Wyatt and your husband know each other from before?"

She thought about his question for a second. "Mel never mentioned him. No. He just showed up for the interview, I guess."

"And you're sure you never met him?"

"Outside of a few pictures, I've never even seen him."

"And Todd." Monk looked him in the eyes. "As far as you know, your ex-wife and Wyatt were never romantically involved?"

Todd tensed, as if the idea of Katrina even looking at another man was impossible. "No way. Katrina hated him. I don't know how many times she told me Wyatt never should have come, that he was more trouble than he was worth."

"More trouble than he was worth," said Monk. "That's an interesting way of putting it."

He continued to ask questions, first to Helena, then to Todd. I knew better than to interrupt. There had been a subtle change in his tone, as if the investigation was growing more focused in his mind.

When we finally said our good-byes, Todd and Helena were still there, unmoved from their chairs. Monk and I headed toward the nurses' station and the stairwell at the end of the elevator bank. He prefers using the stairs, and I only insist on the elevator when it's more than six flights or I'm wearing heels. The ICU was on the third floor, so the stairs it was.

"People can't take a hint," Monk muttered, still thinking about Sarabeth's visitors. "Now I'm going to have to come back."

"Why were you asking questions like that?" I had to ask. "I know you, Adrian. You were treating Todd and Helena like suspects. How can they be suspects?"

"Well, it was suspicious of them staying so long and monopolizing the chairs."

"No, it wasn't. Come on. Is there something I'm not getting?"

Monk cricked his neck and rolled his shoulders. "Devlin may have been right. I know how strange that sounds. But even a broken clock is right twice a day."

"I'm sure Devlin will feel honored being compared to a broken clock."

"I didn't say that she is right, just that she may be. Wyatt Noone may have had outside help."

# 14

# MR. MONK AND MR. MONK

I instantly changed our trajectory, guiding Monk away from the stairwell and toward the little sitting area that served as the ICU's lounge. I took a few sanitary wipes and cleaned off one plastic chair for him and another for myself. I didn't care for myself, but by now it was a habit.

The nurses' station was a good distance away and we were the only ones there, but still I lowered my voice. "What do you mean, outside help?"

"I mean what the words normally mean. Noone managed to stay off everyone's radar. Even people working in the same building. He got hired without any verifiable references, which seems impossible for an accountant. There's nothing of any consequence in his employee file, meaning either no one demanded references or they've been removed. The man was either brilliantly lucky or luckily brilliant. Or he had an accomplice."

"And you're thinking it's Todd or Helena."

"Well, besides the fact that neither of them can take a hint . . ." Monk faced me in his chair and leaned in. "We could be dealing with a double motive: two million dollars in embezzlement plus the getting rid of a spouse. Spouse killing is a very popular motive in this screwed-up world. For instance, Helena could have talked her husband into hiring Noone in the first place. Or Todd could have facilitated Noone's escape from the warehouse. We still don't know how Noone got out of there."

I took his reasoning a step further. "Or Todd and Helena could have been working together. Two accomplices. I mean, people who don't take a hint are probably capable of anything."

"I can't tell if you're mocking me or agreeing with me."

"I'm not sure myself. It could go either way."

"I wonder how much longer those two are going to be here."

I found Monk's theory about an accomplice fascinating—not because I really believed Todd or Helena were part of Noone's conspiracy, but because he was purposely ignoring the one real possibility—Sarabeth, the sole survivor, a woman who had worked every day with Wyatt Noone for a year. But I knew better than to bring up that subject right now.

We were back on our feet, heading for the stairs, when the elevator doors opened and Takumi Ito stepped out. The businessman seemed to have aged a year since we'd seen him this morning. His slim-cut suit fell wrinkled and limp over his shoulders and an unnatural stoop made him look a good three inches shorter. "Mr. Monk. Ms. Teeger." He bowed ever so slightly. "You are here to see Miss Willow?"

"We'll be back tomorrow," said Monk. "If you want any time with her, you're going to have to get in line. It's a zoo in there."

"She has visitors," I translated. "Helena Lubarsky and Todd Avery."

"Ah," said Ito. "I visited Mrs. Lubarsky after leaving the police station. Then I paid a call on Caleb Smith's roommate. They were not romantically involved it seems, just sharing the rent. Very nice man. After this I was going to visit Mr. Avery. I'm glad he's here."

"It will save you a trip," I agreed. I felt so sorry for him, having to deal with eight hours of jet lag, plus a two-million-dollar loss, plus spending all day shuttling between the police and the relatives of the victims. "Is there anything we can do to help?" I asked.

"Thank you, no. You're very kind." But then he thought. "Would either of you know of a good Japanese restaurant? After a day like today, I could use the comfort of home."

"There's a neighborhood called Japantown," I offered. "It's not very far. I don't have any favorite restaurants there myself. . . ."

"Would you care to join me for dinner, Ms. Teeger? Mr. Monk?"

"We'd love to, but I'm afraid we have plans." I

was sorry to have to say it. The man looked so traumatized.

"You should have dinner with us," Monk said. "My brother's wife is cooking Japanese, partly because she is Japanese. I'm sure they'd love another guest. It will be no bother at all."

Huh? This was very un-Monk behavior. I actually looked behind him just to see if anyone was sticking a gun in his back. No one was, so I played along. "Yes, that would be lovely. Yuki is such a good cook." I had no firsthand proof, but I said it anyway.

"No, that would be imposing," Ito said. I could sense that he wanted to say yes.

"Not a problem," Monk said. "Please join us." I had to look again. Still no gun.

"Well . . ." Ito smiled. "To tell the truth, I was not looking forward to an empty table. I would be honored to join you, if that's okay."

"If you want wasabi, you have to order it in advance," said Monk.

"Whatever you have I'm sure will be wonderful."

I took out another of our business cards and wrote on the back the time and the address. I also asked him please not to bring anything. The pleasure of his company would be enough. After he disappeared down the hall to Sarabeth's room, I got on the phone to Yuki. It was fine with her, just as I'd thought. And she would break the news gently to Ambrose.

Only after it was all settled did I turn to Monk. I'm always saying how Monk cocks his head to one side when he's puzzled. Now it was my turn. "What was that about?"

"What? You mean asking him to join us? For one thing, he's Japanese, so he might actually like the food. Plus he might mention this to Sarabeth, and I want her to think I'm a nice person."

"You won't do it for me, but you'll do it for a woman you just met?"

Monk sighed dramatically and headed for the stairs. "Well, excuse me for trying to be empathetic."

"No, no," I said, chasing behind. "I'll take it where I can get it. Good for Sarabeth."

Dinner that night was quite pleasant. I might even say lovely. And despite instructions to the contrary, Takumi Ito brought a gift for his hostess, an expensive bottle of saki that needed to be chilled.

We hadn't seen Ambrose and Yuki for almost a year. For most of that time, we didn't hear a word, just the occasional call saying they were still alive and in love. Sometimes a mysterious package would arrive in the mail, something they'd bought on their travels and sent home so it wouldn't crowd up the RV. Monk kept them all in the storage unit in his building's basement. One of

152

the first things he did on arriving at the house was to set up a time for Yuki to come over and retrieve them.

"We can make a game out of it," he told her. "Empty the storage unit and wash it down with bleach. Ambrose and I used to play games like that as kids."

"Teenage high jinks." Ambrose sighed. "Those were the days. Ooh, remember bassoon Wednesdays?" He turned to the rest of us, beaming with the memory. "Every Wednesday we used to sit around the living room, listening to Mother play the bassoon."

"We don't want to bore people," Monk said. "I'm sure every family has its bassoon stories."

"In our family it was tympani Tuesday," I said, trying to repress a grin. "We all had our own set of tympanis. You could hear us for miles."

"Well, I'm sure you rich folk could afford tympanis," huffed Ambrose. "Some of us had to make do with bassoons. By the way, did you get the chain saw we sent?"

"We did," I said.

"Chain saw." Takumi Ito burst into laughter. "Now I know you're all joking."

"Actually, the bassoon and the chain saw are true," I informed him.

Monk nodded. "Luckily we knew the chain saw had come from Ambrose and not from some horror-film kook sending me a message. What do you want with a chain saw? Isn't it illegal to send them through the mail?"

"That's a story worth telling," said Ambrose.

Yuki smiled and reached up to clasp her husband's hand. "We were in Oregon," she explained, "driving by the edge of a national forest. That night we happened to park the RV right by an antilogging protest. Well, one thing led to another and my hero Ambrose wound up saving a thousand-year-old sequoia from being slaughtered."

"You mean he actually got out of the RV?" Monk asked.

"Only for a minute," Yuki said. "It was after the chase with the logging truck."

"You were being chased by a logging truck?" I asked.

"No, no. Yuki exaggerates," said Ambrose. "We were chasing the logging truck. But even that's not technically true. We were chasing the ambulance that was chasing the logging truck. Accuracy is very important when you're telling a story."

"But you're missing the point, sweetie," said Yuki. "They were asking about you getting out of the RV."

"You're right. That was the most exciting part. You should have seen the pine needles. They stuck to everything. My left shoe and my right shoe. Even my trouser cuffs, if you can believe it.

At first I didn't notice the needles, maybe because of all the sirens and the explosion. But once I got back into the RV . . . Boy, oh boy. For the next two days, I was picking out needles—"

"Forget the needles," I demanded. "What about the chain saw?"

"Oh." Yuki patted Ambrose's hand and they shared a secret little grin. "Let's just say, that is one chain saw that's not going to be cutting down any more sequoias, thanks to the U.S. Postal Service."

"I hope you didn't mail me evidence in a criminal case," Monk said. He regarded his older brother, the rebel, with wary eyes.

"No, no," Yuki assured us. "Just a civil case."

There were maybe a dozen stories like this. And even though we only heard a few details of each, I was amazed that Ambrose could have such adventures all within a few arm's lengths of the safety of his movable home.

Takumi Ito didn't say much. He seemed happy just listening as the Monk family caught up. It must have been a nice break for him, I thought, not having to talk about the senseless tragedy his company had been through, although I'm sure it was never far from his mind.

The meal itself was as promised. The salmon was perfectly cooked and lightly seasoned. The white rice was in separate bowls. And the broccoli rabe was stir-fried, with the chaos of sesame seeds kept on the side for the more adventurous eaters. Yuki had to be one of the best Japanese biker-chick chefs in the world, although I'm sure the list wasn't very long.

When it came time for second helpings, I joined Mr. Ito out in the living room where the soy sauce and other exotic spices had been set up on a sideboard. The white porcelain saki bottle was also on the sideboard cradled in a soup bowl full of ice. He poured for both of us, filling up the little handleless cups.

"Thank you again, Ms. Teeger. This evening is just what I needed." There was exhaustion in his voice, but not the tension I'd heard earlier in the day.

"I'm glad," I said. "I was a little worried. It's not everyone who can get enjoyment out of the Monk brothers."

"They are absolutely splendid. In the United States, I think you make reality TV stars out of your eccentrics. In Japan, we call them national treasures."

"It probably amounts to the same thing. And please don't suggest a reality show about Adrian. I can't imagine where that would lead. No place good."

It was nice to hear him laugh and it gave me a warm feeling to be at least partly responsible. "Tomorrow will be easier," I promised, and toasted with my cup of chilled saki.

Ito toasted back but didn't drink. "I was the one who made them hire an accountant," he confessed. "They would have been happier doing the work themselves and getting a raise. But our company rules prohibit them getting paid more than their Japanese counterparts. I thought I was doing them a favor. Instead, three of them are dead and I've placed my whole company in jeopardy."

"It's not your fault. You had no idea who they would hire." I toasted again, deliberately, like a mom trying to force her kid to take his medicine, and this time he sipped.

I brought the bottle of saki back to the table with an extra cup for Yuki. The three of us settled in while Adrian and Ambrose began arguing over the proper way to catalogue a collection of maps. Adrian said alphabetically. Ambrose said it had to be by continent, north to south, west to east. Yuki suggested burning the maps and using Google Earth instead. We all agreed to vote on it, and the result was three to one to one. Adrian and Ambrose both lodged formal protests.

At exactly ten, Ambrose and Yuki said good night and ushered us out the door. It seems that Ambrose had read somewhere that a dinner party should last somewhere between three and four hours, making the ideal length exactly three and a half. Since we had all arrived punctually at six thirty, he had no choice.

"A wonderful evening," Ambrose called out from the safety of the doorway, arm in arm with his smiling wife. "I wish you could have stayed longer. I really do. But I don't make the rules."

I was home well before eleven and checked my phone for the first time since I left. There was a message from Julie and I called back without bothering to check it.

"I just wanted to apologize," she began. "Again. I shouldn't have broken in."

"That's all right, sweetie. I understand."

Call me cynical. But when my daughter calls to apologize—again—it usually means there's something else in play. I accepted the apology and went on to tell her about my evening with the Monks.

Julie knew Ambrose and Yuki well. She sounded a little disappointed that she hadn't been there for the fun. "Maybe when I'm your intern, I can snag those invitations, too." Okay, so that's what this was about. "What's happening on the Pickler case?" she asked, trying to sound nonchalant.

"Nothing since your break-in yesterday."

"You mean you're not working on it? Pickler's got to have some connection with the Lucarellis or the Menendez family. If he's willing to sit in jail for a murder he didn't commit—"

"You are not our intern," I interrupted. "You're a college senior who needs to concentrate on her last few months of school."

"I know that. But after graduation. Does Adrian know I volunteered?"

"This is not Adrian's choice. It's mine. As a mother and a partner, I get two votes to his one."

"What about my vote?"

"You're the plaintiff in this case. You don't get a vote."

# 15

# MR. MONK TAKES A DAY OFF

I can't tell you how nice it was sleeping in on Saturday. I didn't even look at the clock, just reveled in the luxury of not having to be in the office. In my half-awake stupor, I realized how spoiled I'd been all these years. As hard as Monk and I worked on cases, it was never a strict schedule, having to show up exactly on time day after day, year after year, doing the same thing. And I'm not even talking about the people who wind up getting shot by their crazed coworkers.

I was jolted fully awake at 8:35 by the phone on my nightstand. It was Lieutenant Devlin. "Oh, I'm sorry," she said, responding to my grogginess. "I forgot it was the weekend."

"That's okay. You're working the weekend."

"I have to. Every day we don't catch him makes it less likely we will. Do you guys have anything new?"

I sat up and adjusted my pillows. "Adrian thinks Wyatt may have had help."

Devlin growled. "That's what I kept telling him. Any lone survivor needs to be investigated. Sarabeth . . ."

"It's not so simple. He has this blind spot for Sarabeth."

"Well, I don't," said the lieutenant. "I'll check a little deeper, see if any neighbors or friends ever saw her with Noone. I can also let her accidentally find out I'm looking. That kind of pressure can be good. Let the bad guys know you're interested and they'll make mistakes."

"I'm not saying she's a bad guy. I'm just saying Adrian won't go there."

"I'm familiar with his blind spots," Devlin said. "Like the time he falsely accused Ellen Morse of murder because she owned a store that sold fossilized poop."

"Yeah," I agreed. "Looking back, I'm kind of amazed that relationship lasted as long as it did."

Devlin got off the phone to rally her troops. I finally rallied the strength to get out of bed and put on my bathrobe. I pushed the button on the coffeemaker, fork-split my English muffin, and put it in to toast, then performed my daily hide-and-seek with the *San Francisco Examiner* (in the azaleas to the left of the porch). And all this time, despite it being my day off, I was thinking about work.

Before I even unfolded the paper, I was on the phone. By then it was after nine and, according to the rules of etiquette I'd been raised with, the phone was fair game. "Daniela, hi. It's Natalie. Hope I didn't wake you."

"Wake me? Dear, I'm heading off to the County Office Building in Redwood City. What can I do for you?"

"On a Saturday?"

"That's the same thing the assistant DA said. Why does everyone think justice takes time off?"

So much for my guilt-free weekend. "If you can take a second, I'd like to talk about the case."

"Mr. Monk had a breakthrough?" Daniela asked, her voice rising. "That's great news. Henry's been rotting away for days."

"Uh, no," I had to admit. "No breakthrough."

"Oh." Her voice lowered. "I was hoping you'd have some brilliant insight for me by now. I mean, that's why I hired you people. Not that you promised a miracle in your brochure. But you did lead me to believe . . ."

"We often do deliver miracles," I said. "But each case is different. Daniela, I was wondering if I could have access to the Pickler house again? If you remember, we cut short our examination of the premises."

"When we went over to talk to the drug boss's floozy. Of course. I'll have a messenger drop by with a key and the access codes. I'll do it right now."

It seems everyone was working on Saturday, messengers included. "That would be great. We have Pickler's permission, right?"

"Access to the home during incarceration is

included in my firm's boilerplate contract with clients, although he may not realize it was included."

"Are you okay with me going in?"

"I'm okay." There was something about the way she emphasized the "I'm."

"How about Henry? Is he okay with it?"

She laughed, a melodious cackle. "Henry has annoyed the hell out of me. This would be so much easier if he told me something. Anything. So, go ahead. I'd love to find out what he's hiding." Daniela Grace, it seemed, was someone you didn't want to annoy. "Of course, whatever you find is included under client-attorney privilege. The police can't be informed."

"Got it. No police."

"No matter what you find."

"Got it." This was all part of our brave new world. Only time would tell if it was a world we could live in and still hold on to our souls. "Why are you meeting the assistant DA?"

"I'm trying to get the charges dropped. Henry's GSR test came back negative." That was cop talk for gunshot residue. "Combined with the police failure to find the weapon, it might be enough to get him released. Barring a Monk and Teeger miracle, it's the best we can hope for."

"Don't rule out the miracle," I said in a confident tone I didn't feel. "Good luck with your meeting."

Waiting for Daniela's messenger gave me half an hour of Saturday leisure. I didn't call Monk to join me today. He had a session with his psychiatrist, Dr. Bell, postponed from yesterday when Julie's quasi-arrest interrupted our schedule. Monk was down to one session a week now, except for emergencies, like his wedding anniversary or a tough case or a particularly traumatic breakfast. On average, I suppose it was more like one and three-quarter times a week.

This house search was something I felt I could do. Julie and Daniela had both made me feel guilty about our lack of progress. And I was a licensed PI, after all. I didn't need Monk with me every step of the way.

I parked on the street, one house down from the Pickler residence. This was an old habit I didn't feel like breaking, even though my visit was technically legit. I used the keys and the alarm codes, then walked into the pristine time machine—the entry hall with its shag carpeting, the sunken living room with its circular fireplace, the dining room with its clear plastic chairs, and the harvest gold kitchen.

Monk had already examined these rooms, so I started by going down half a flight to the lower section of the split-level where I found the master bedroom. It was divided precisely into two halves, each with a blond wood dresser with flat drawer fronts and no handles. Very seventies

Scandinavian. There was a mirror above each dresser and a little seating area and walk-in closet for each half of the couple. In the middle was a king bed, the one communal part of the room, perfectly made and tucked in like a soldier's cot.

The next thing I noticed about the bed was the pillow arrangement. Two sets of two pillows, as if Pickler's wife had just walked out this morning. I have to tell you, I was touched by the sight. The woman had been gone eight months and still he preserved her side of the bed, as if she might return any second.

As for the rest of the room, I didn't frame the view but I tried to be just as thorough—not that it did much good. The wife's walk-in closet was empty and perfectly clean. Henry's closet seemed like an ordinary man's closet, if the man had OCD and kept everything on identical wooden hangers spaced evenly across the bars. The drawers were just as neat and organized. And, to my disappointment, there was nothing stashed in the bottom of the sock drawer. Come on, people. Isn't that what a sock drawer is for?

I even checked under the bed, something I never do at home, since my vacuum wand doesn't reach all the way and I don't want to be reminded of the multiplying dust bunnies. Of course there were no dust bunnies under Henry Pickler's bed, just a plastic bin filled with a white winter comforter.

The only item of any interest was a framed

wedding photo sitting on the blond wood table by Henry's bedside. It showed the couple in the first moments of their five-year marriage, facing the camera, arm in arm. Henry smiled sheepishly while Becky looked happy and at ease. She was a shortish woman, almost as slight and trim as her husband, with sharp features that promised not to age very gracefully. This was the only photograph in the room and once again I was touched by the man's devotion to his wayward wife.

Beyond the bedroom was Henry's office. I intended to be just as focused here as I'd been in the bedroom but, to be honest, I was out of my element. Henry was a freelance Web site designer, and I knew next to nothing about this. The office was predictably organized and neat. A huge Apple monitor sat on an even huger curved desktop. There was no clutter. But all four walls were covered with corkboards, ten of them, all neatly organized with printouts of projects, photos, and swatches of fabric and color chips, plus details of the Web sites he was working on. One of them was decorated with beaches and sunsets and a central image of the Taj Mahal. It seemed to be the inspiration for some travel site.

I wasn't at all surprised by the corkboards. People with OCD tend to be very visual. Monk had had a corkboard on his bedroom wall for almost a dozen years, adding to it, taking away from it, as he slowly figured out the most important case of his life, his wife's murder. The physicality of the clues and photos and clippings and reports helped him internalize the facts. It's a gift and a curse, as my partner likes to say. Everything in your line of sight has to be symmetrical and even. The upside to that is you're attuned to the smallest things being out of place. In Henry's case, staring at his corkboards . . . I had no idea what might be out of place.

From the boards, I turned to the file cabinet, a two-level vertical type where you pull out the drawers and are facing the long side of the files with the tabs lined up in front of you. They were in alphabetical order, of course, mostly old projects and taxes and one surprisingly boring file labeled *Personal*, which didn't seem to contain anything noteworthy. I don't know what I'd been expecting to find—perhaps something filed under *D* for drug dealers. (I actually looked under *D*.) That was the moment I realized what a mistake it had been to come here without Monk. I'm sure he could have found something.

As I pushed myself up from the lower drawer, my right shoulder nudged the edge of the desk, which jiggled and nudged the mouse sitting to the left of the keyboard. A few seconds later and the humongous monitor came to life. It startled me. But then I recalled how Henry had been arrested out in the field, without having a chance to come back in and turn off his system.

I found myself staring at the frozen screen image of a Facebook page. Staring back at me was the smiling face of Becky Pickler.

It was framed in a picture on her Facebook Timeline. Once again I was touched, but also a little creeped out. I guess the lesson here was that when you leave your husband, you should also remember to unfriend him. Unless you want him following you every time you have breakfast with a friend or repost a cat video—or think about going out with a man.

The picture on the screen was from several months ago, far down on Becky's Wall. Easter Sunday to be precise. It was a solo shot of her on a rugged coastline, casually posing beside a towering pine. Behind her was a blue-gray evening sky, somewhere around dusk. A sliver of the moon floated low in the background sky, like a Cheshire cat grin. The reason I knew it was Easter was deductive logic; her post date combined with her comment: "Easter weekend with a new friend. I don't want to jinx it by saying too much. He's Australian, working here on a visa. When I get to know him better, I'll send one of him." Below the post were half a dozen comments from old friends, telling her not to be such a tease and asking when was she coming back to visit.

I took the mouse and tried scrolling up the page to something more recent. But the screen was frozen, which was just as well. I should try to avoid doing anything to alert our Web site expert that I'd been on his system.

I scanned the room again, secure that I was leaving the office just as I found it. Then I went through the door into a double-bay garage and glanced around the wall for a light switch. Just moments into my search, an overhead light went on. My immediate reaction was that Pickler had installed a motion detector. How very thoughtful. And then I saw that the light was part of the garage door system—and that the garage door was slowly going up. The sound of an engine purred outside in the drive.

My instinct was to run and hide. That's always my first instinct. But the problem with an OCD home is that everything is so neat and symmetrical that there's often no place to go. I wasted precious seconds, frozen, as the door continued to rise. Then I ducked back inside the house.

You would think I'd have headed straight for the front door. I probably should have. Except I was curious just who this could be. Pickler was in jail. And Daniela wouldn't have possession of her client's garage door opener. In fact, no one would have had the opener, except maybe Becky Pickler. Was that it? Had Becky heard about her husband's arrest? Was she finally coming home? This would be my chance to meet her.

I was two rooms away in the master bedroom,

when the door between the garage and the office opened and a voice called out. "Hello? Who's here? I know someone's here." That's another problem with an OCD homeowner. They always know when there's someone's there. The voice was Henry Pickler's.

Several possibilities raced through my tiny brain. Scurry out the front? (But what if he sees me drive off?) Hide under the bed? (Then how do I get out?) But something Lieutenant Devlin said this morning came to mind. "Let the bad guys know you're interested and they'll make mistakes." And although I had no proof that Pickler was a bad guy or had done anything worse than keeping a secret . . .

"Mr. Pickler. In here."

When Henry walked into the bedroom, he found me by his walk-in closet. I had already taken two shirts out and laid them on the bed. "Who are you?" he demanded before realizing. "Oh, you're the detective working for me."

"That's right, sir," I said with a smile. "Natalie Teeger. Daniela asked me to come by and pick up some personal items for you. She didn't know how long you'd be incarcerated."

"Daniela just got me released." His thin face squirmed into a frown. "Why would she send you for things if she just got me released?"

"Well, she didn't know you'd be released. The last time we talked, she was showing the assistant

DA the results of the GSR test. Congratulations. It looks like she was successful, huh?"

"The murder charge was dropped," he said, not sounding that happy about it. "Apparently, even in this fascist state, they can't hold you for refusing to explain your actions in your own backyard. They still have some other trumped-up charges. But Daniela will deal with those."

"So that's good," I said. "What a surprise. So I suppose you won't be needing a change of clothes."

"Did Daniela give you the keys and the codes or did you just break in?"

"Mr. Pickler." I tried to look offended. "She gave me everything, including her permission as your attorney."

"And that's why you're here, to pick up some extra clothes for me? Nothing else?"

"Some underwear and toiletries. I noticed in your bathroom; you and my partner, Adrian, use the same exfoliant. He swears by it."

"Even though we can't wear our own clothes in jail, you were going to bring me clothes?"

"I was hoping they'd make an exception. But it's all a moot point now, isn't it?"

"And that's the only reason you invaded my home?"

"Yes." I looked him straight in the eyes. "What else would I be doing here?"

"Snooping around?"

"What?" I faked just enough outrage to keep him guessing. "You are my client. I'm bound by law not to do anything to endanger your legal welfare. If you choose not to confide in us, that's your choice. I'm sure, as a law-abiding citizen, you have nothing to hide."

"Another fascist argument, Ms. Teeger. If a person has nothing to hide, then he doesn't need privacy. Is that what you're saying?"

"No, I'm just saying I believe in my client. Why should you have to explain every movement you make on your own property?"

Henry looked like he didn't believe me. Totally understandable. "What were you doing before I got here? Not just picking out clothes." He glanced around the bedroom, then back toward the home office. He must have seen something in my eyes, because he went right into the next room, heading straight for his file cabinet.

"I did not invade your files," I said, just for the record. "Why would I do that?"

I followed him into the office and my eyes flicked past a row of corkboards to the monitor on his desk. The screen had gone into sleep mode again and I breathed a sigh of relief. Again, Pickler must have seen something in my eyes. I'm really going to have to work on my poker face.

Instantly he forgot about the files. "You were on my computer," he said.

"No," I lied.

"Yes, you were. Look." He crossed to the monitor. "I'm left-handed, so I leave the mouse on the left side. Now it's on the right."

I hadn't even noticed. What a stupid mistake. "Not me." I tried to think fast. "The cops must have done that. They searched your home after the arrest. Right?"

"Maybe." My explanation seemed to make a begrudging kind of sense. But when Pickler moved the mouse back to the left, the screen once more came to life. And once more, Becky Pickler stood along the rugged coast, smiling under the sliver moon of an Easter Sunday.

"That's my wife," he said, studying the moonlit face. "But of course you know that. You seem to know everything."

"The screen is just the way you left it. I mean . . ." I was stammering like an idiot. "Just the way the police left it, I assume. If they were in there looking, which I think they were." Shut up, Natalie.

"Why are you interested in my wife, Ms. Teeger?"

"I'm not."

"Have you been talking to Becky?" He sounded defensive. "What did she say?"

"Nothing. Is your wife involved in this?" The words had just come out of my mouth.

"What do you mean, involved?"

"Are you protecting her?" I guessed. "Is she

involved with the mob or the Mexican cartel? Is that why she had to leave town?"

"My Becky?" He tried not to laugh, but the air bubbled in his nose until he erupted in a guffaw. "That's rich. Becky cleaned houses. You can ask Daniela if my wife was some kind of mobster. I haven't seen Becky in eight months. I have no idea where she is."

"You have some idea. That photo's on her Timeline. You and she are Facebook friends. You check up on her. You still love her, Henry."

This guess was enough to take the air out of his sails. He nodded slowly. His shoulders slumped. "I look in on her every now and then, not to comment, just to look. She still lists her residence as Millbrae. So no, I don't know where she is. Somewhere in Washington State."

"Do you think she'd come back if she knew you were in trouble? You should get in touch."

"Is that the way you think I want my wife back? Out of some sense of pity or obligation?" His voice cracked. "You really think that will help the marriage?"

"I'm sorry," I said. And I meant it. "You're right."

"I've been released. The murder charge was dropped. There may be other charges, whatever the fascists can think up, like moving a body on your own property. But the worst is over. Thanks to Daniela."

"You're right." The man was obviously in love

and in pain, and I was ashamed of myself. It's strange how quickly these things change. Henry Pickler wasn't telling me anything more than he had before, which was nothing. But it no longer seemed so important.

Our job was officially done. And so what if he was keeping something from us? Everyone has a secret or two. Okay, his secret happened to involve a dead gang member in a field. But so what? He wasn't paying my salary so that I could snoop through his house.

As for Esteban Rivera, the San Mateo County Sheriff's Office would have to look for another killer, if they wanted to look that hard. Monk could point them in the direction of Fat Tony, but it was doubtful they'd come up with much. Mob killings aren't the most rewarding investigations, especially when you don't have a dedicated homicide squad.

Henry and I had come to a truce. We engaged in awkward chitchat as he walked me to the front door. He'd missed a few days of nice weather, I informed him. And yes, that was my car parked down the street. No, jail hadn't been that bad, he said.

"If I had to do it over, I probably wouldn't say anything to Becky about her flossing. She's a grown woman who can make her own decisions." He smiled sadly, showing off his well-flossed teeth. "In her posts, her gums still look nice. Who knows? I may have been too harsh."

# 16

# MR. MONK MAKES A HOUSE CALL

I came out of Henry's house feeling strangely let down. I had wanted to hate him. I'd wanted him to be involved in some complex scheme worse than murder, a scheme that had forced him to go out with a shovel and try to bury a stranger. But by the end of our time together, I was entertaining the thought that he'd just been offended by someone being killed in his vacant lot and felt the need to go out and clean up the mess.

Returning to the old Subaru, I checked my phone and found a message from Dr. Bell. I didn't bother to listen but called him back right away. It was a lesson I learned years ago. Calls from Monk's psychiatrist always needed immediate attention.

"Natalie. Sorry to bother you on a Saturday. But Adrian canceled."

"I'm sorry," I said. "That doesn't sound like him."

"No reason for you to be sorry. I came into the office especially for our session and got a message saying that he was helping a lady friend do security on her house. He made a point of saying that this lady friend was not Ellen but someone nicer. Are you the friend, Natalie? I'd like to speak to Adrian if he's there."

"No, I'm not the friend."

Dr. Bell seemed taken aback. "He never mentioned a new friend. Do you know what he means? Does it make any sense?"

"Those are two different questions. Yes, I know what he means. And no, it doesn't make sense."

"Does Adrian have a new girlfriend? I can't tell you what goes on in our sessions, of course. . . ."

Dr. Neven Bell might have restrictions about what he could and couldn't discuss, but I didn't. "Ellen completely broke things off less than two weeks ago. Adrian pretends it's no big deal. But you know that it is. And the fact that he's falling for the first single woman that he's come in contact with since being back from New Jersey . . ."

"The first? That's not good."

"Wait," I said. "It gets worse. The woman is the only surviving victim of an attack. Adrian has been visiting her in the hospital and feels very protective."

"Well, feeling protective can be a coping mechanism. It isn't necessarily bad."

"It is when the woman might have a connection to a triple murder and Adrian refuses to even consider her possible involvement."

"Is that a real possibility?" he asked. "I don't think Adrian would jeopardize an investigation."

"Not on purpose, no."

"The main thing I'm worried about . . ." Dr. Bell paused. "Unfortunately, I can't tell you what Adrian has or has not told me."

I could guess. "He hasn't told you anything about this woman. That worries you because he normally doesn't keep secrets." I didn't wait for him to say yes, no, or maybe. "In fact, Adrian tells you every minute detail of his existence. I know because afterward he often tells me what he told you, and it covers everything from his breakfast this morning to his anger issues with his mother to a breakfast eighteen years ago. I wouldn't be surprised if you wound up having to go to a psychiatrist yourself just to deal with it."

"I do go to a psychiatrist," he admitted. "A lot of therapists do. And yes, I am concerned that he hasn't brought up this woman."

"Her name is Sarabeth Willow, by the way, the survivor of the Stockton Street shooting. She may have absolutely no connection with the killer, but Monk's infatuation is not a good thing, not from a police point of view."

"And not from a psychological point of view— although I cannot discuss—"

"I get it."

"Good. Can you have Adrian get in touch with me as soon as possible? I was going to go visit my grandkids this afternoon. But I'll keep the rest of the day open in case Adrian wants to have a session. I think it's important for him to discuss this."

I promised Dr. Bell I'd do my best to get him there. My next call was to the hospital to verify Sarabeth's release. My call after that was to Lieutenant Devlin to get Sarabeth's home address. Devlin had not been happy that their one eye-witness to the massacre had been let go. But the hospital agreed to Sarabeth's request to continue her recovery in familiar surroundings, and the department's only choice was to follow her home and set up a twenty-four-hour rotation of officers to protect her.

Just from spending a little time with Sarabeth, I would have guessed she lived in a painted lady, one of the cozy, colorfully painted Victorian row houses that decorate the city, especially in the lower Haight. It seemed to be her style. And I was right.

Her address was on Haight Street itself, just a few blocks from Buena Vista Park. It was a one-bedroom, ground-floor rental, and she'd probably been there forever. Most of these lovely little historic houses had been taken back by single families and renovated to within an inch of their lives, but a few were still tiny apartment buildings with reasonable rents.

An SFPD cruiser was parked illegally in front of a hydrant and would probably be there for a while. I parked at a newly vacated spot across the street and performed a perfect job of parallel parking, a driving requirement in this town. As I walked by, I waved at the officer behind the wheel who must have recognized me. He waved back and didn't try to stop me from ringing the lowest of the four doorbells.

"Who is it?" said a cheery female voice. Before I could reply, the door opened and Sarabeth Willow was ushering me inside. "Natalie, so good of you to visit. I tell you, I've never felt so safe in my life." She was in a bright floral housedress, or what we used to call a housedress, with half sleeves and a modest scoop neck. She was taller than I remembered. Or maybe it was just that her apartment was so small.

"No, no, no," shouted Monk from somewhere in the back of the minuscule apartment. "What did I tell you about security?"

"It's Natalie," said Sarabeth, still managing to be cheery as she led me through the living room and into the bedroom. She took small but steady steps.

"First you look through the peephole, then you ask 'who is it?' Look at the face. Listen to the tone of the voice. If it's not someone you know well . . ."

Sarabeth remained amused. "It's your partner, Natalie."

"Looks mean nothing. Natalie has a very common face. That's why you need to hear her speak. If you have any doubts about her identity, call me."

"You don't have a cell phone," I pointed out.

"Well, Sarabeth has your number. She can call you and you can relay the message." Monk was standing by the bed. He had just finished making it and now, a second later, was unmaking it, folding down a corner of the quilted comforter. "Now, get back in, missy. You shouldn't be out of bed."

"Adrian." I rolled my eyes. "You made her get out of bed to answer the door?"

"I had to test our security procedures, which did not go well." He clapped his hands twice quickly, like a grade school teacher. "Sarabeth, get back in bed. Natalie, go back outside. We'll try again."

"We are not going to try again," I said firmly. "We're going to let Sarabeth get some rest. Is there anything we can get you from the kitchen?"

"A Fiji Water would be nice. We did a little shopping before getting here."

"Not you. Sarabeth."

"That's so sweet, Natalie. Yes, a little iced tea. There should be a bottle of sweet tea in the icebox."

"It's right beside the Fiji Water," said Monk. "That's my way of asking you to bring me some Fiji Water."

Sarabeth smiled. "I think she knows that. Please get something for yourself, Natalie, dear."

The apartment was old-fashioned, but not in the same way as the Pickler house. Under normal circumstances, Monk would have found it claustrophobic and depressing. But none of this, not the chairs with the tattered doilies or the mismatched pillows, seemed to be annoying him at all. Maybe after the first blush of rebound wore off, he would start seeing things with his usual, critical eye.

As promised, the iced tea was in front, next to the Fiji Water. I looked around the rest of the refrigerator, hoping to find some fruit juice for myself. A purplish pink bottle of something was in the back, partially hidden by a bottle of ketchup and an oversized jar of mayonnaise. I reached in for the juice and checked the label. Then I put it back exactly where I'd found it.

I stood there nearly a full minute, trying to process this. What in the world would Sarabeth be doing with a half-empty bottle of Earthway brand cranberry-prune juice? It was just yesterday when everyone in the hospital room, including Sarabeth, was making fun of Wyatt and his obsession with the benefits of cranberry-prune. I reached past the mayo again and checked the date stamped on the neck of the juice bottle. These organic brands don't have the longest shelf lives and this one was still a week away from its expiration.

There could be an easy explanation, I thought.

Sarabeth could have decided to try the juice on her own, for example. She could be a convert to the juice lifestyle, although the woman did also own an oversized jar of mayonnaise. But in order to hear this easy explanation, I would have to let her know what I'd just seen—and what I now suspected. I didn't want to do that.

"Thanks, Natalie. Just what I needed."

I handed Sarabeth the iced tea, with four ice cubes and a bendy straw, then gave one of the Fiji bottles to Monk, keeping the second one for myself. "Did you ever see Wyatt outside of work?" I tried to make the question sound casual.

"She already answered that," Monk said. "No, she never did."

"That's right," Sarabeth confirmed. "We went bowling once, as a group activity with the people from the warehouse. But Wyatt called in sick that day."

"And he's never been to anyone's home, as far as you know? He's never been here, for example?"

"No," she said. "I never even thought of inviting him. Why do you ask?"

"I was just hoping we could get a reliable set of his prints. Everything the police recovered from the office is either an elimination print from one of the other employees, or is smudged."

"Sorry. I don't think Wyatt ever saw anyone in a social setting." My answer had seemed to satisfy her, a lot more than her answer satisfied me.

"You should be safe for now," Monk advised. He was busy drinking his Fiji Water and checking a list. "Just don't go outside or into your backyard. I'll come back later and replace the lock on the back fence. You'll have the only key."

"You think old Mr. Simonton across the fence is going to break in and attack me?"

"You never know," said Monk. "Maybe someone will kill him in order to get access to your yard. I've seen that happen."

"I didn't think of that," she said, then reached out over the comforter and touched his hand. "You make me feel so safe."

Monk removed his hand but didn't wipe it. "Do you want to go over the procedures? It shouldn't take more than an hour. We'll start with Natalie coming to the door again. This time change your voice, Natalie."

"Not now, dear," said Sarabeth. "I think I need a little rest." She seemed about to close her eyes. "How long do you think the police will be here, guarding me?"

"Until we catch him," Monk said. "And if we don't catch him, then forever."

"I don't think forever is a good option. Do you honestly think I'm in danger? I would love the freedom to get around on my own. Without a police escort."

"Get around?" Monk scoffed. "You can barely walk."

"I'm getting stronger every day," she said, following it with a dramatic yawn. "But I'm afraid I do need my rest."

"Good idea. Come on, Adrian." I mimed pulling him by the arm but he didn't respond. I had to actually pull his arm, which is a fairly drastic measure for a man who hates being touched.

Out in the living room, the two of us paused by the front door. "Dr. Bell told you I was here," he said accusingly. "What ever happened to doctor-patient confidentiality?"

"I don't think it applies to a voice mail cancellation of a session."

"Well, it should."

"The doctor is very concerned about your rebound relationship with Sarabeth."

"You told him?" Monk looked horrified. "You blabbed about my private life, Natalie? To my doctor? What ever happened to partner-partner confidentiality?"

"It doesn't exist. And the fact that you haven't mentioned this woman to your psychiatrist is not a good sign."

"The only reason I didn't mention her was because I know what he's going to say and we'd wind up wasting an entire session talking about it."

"That's what you're supposed to do. And that's exactly what you're going to do now. We're going straight over to Dr. Bell's. He canceled a visit to his grandkids this afternoon just to see you. He's that worried."

"No can do. I need to stop by the hardware store and buy a new lock for Sarabeth's back fence."

"Adrian!" And this time I didn't even mime grabbing his arm. I just grabbed and started pulling him out the door.

"Do you think she'll be okay?"

"Sarabeth? She'll be fine."

"I like it when people need me. And she likes me, I can tell. Do you think she's attractive? I think she has a special kind of beauty."

"It's hard to tell with the housedress," I said. But I wasn't thinking about the housedress. I was thinking about the bottle of cranberry-prune juice. How was I going to phrase this? "Do you think Sarabeth knows something she's not telling us?"

"Do you mean that she may not really like me? That she has a boyfriend?"

"Yes." That was one way of putting it. "Do you see any evidence of her having a boyfriend? Something around her house?"

"Are you referring to the bottle of juice in her refrigerator? She explained that. She'd been trying out Wyatt's juice diet, but it didn't go well with her system."

"But she didn't throw out the bottle; she kept it in her fridge. And it's a fairly new bottle. And at the hospital, she indicated that she didn't know what it tasted like."

"No, Natalie. Her exact words were, 'Can you imagine the taste?' Apparently she could imagine the taste, because she has a half-empty bottle in her refrigerator."

"So you're not even going to allow the possibility."

"It's not a possibility. Sarabeth is not that kind of girl."

# 17

# MR. MONK AND HIS DAY OFF

From the car, I called ahead to Dr. Bell, who, true to his word, had postponed his family Saturday in order to wait for us. I dropped Monk off at the homey little office complex on Otis Street and made sure he got safely inside. Then I went home to try to enjoy what was left of my day.

Settling on the front porch with a glass of white wine seemed like the perfect way to decompress and mull over what had happened at Sarabeth's apartment. But the wine was barely out of the bottle when I thought of a better way to relax. I poured it back in, every drop, screwed the top back on, and returned it to the fridge. Then I made a call.

"Are you in the mood to go to a meeting?" I asked.

"Of course," said Daniela without a moment's hesitation. "Let me check a schedule."

She found a meeting starting in an hour, in the basement of a church just a few blocks off the Bayshore Freeway. We'd been there once before. The people tended to be nice and the location was about halfway between our neighborhoods.

I bet I know what you're thinking, because I'd probably think the same thing. Isn't there something dishonest about a nonalcoholic going to AA meetings? Isn't there something cowardly and sad about not sitting down with Daniela and explaining the weird circumstance that led me to go to my very first meeting and say, "Hi. My name is Natalie and I'm an alcoholic," even though I wasn't.

First of all, I did try to explain. More than once. All it did was solidify in her mind that I was in denial and needed a sponsor like her to help. Second of all, outside of my first visit, I never again claimed to be an alcoholic. Now I go to open meetings, ones where you don't have to share. I just sit and listen, which is perfectly allowable. Third of all, I actually get a lot out of this process. Hearing the stories of people's struggles with addiction is inspiring and helps put my own life in a healthier perspective.

It was a small group on this late Saturday afternoon, perhaps a dozen active participants and a few shy or curious observers like me. The church was in the heart of a working-class neighborhood, with a brick basement, a small podium, and folding chairs scattered in a semi-circle.

A man named Patrick (no last names) was speaking about last night, his Friday night temptation as he called it. He'd been sober for a month and had refused to go out with the boys on purpose. But his grown son had just moved back in and, despite being specifically warned against it, the boy left a forty-ounce bottle of Country Club Malt Liquor in the house. There it was in the back of the refrigerator, hidden behind the leftovers, just staring out at him when Patrick opened the door for a late-night snack. And speaking about things hidden in the back . . . My mind started wandering.

Today Monk had seen what I'd seen in Sarabeth's refrigerator, and he came to the same conclusion. But then his power of denial kicked in. I've never seen it affect his judgment before, not like this. He still saw everything and could make the connections no one else could. But to ignore one of the few real leads we had . . . Maybe this was a sign of just how much he'd been hurt by Ellen's departure.

When I looked up from my reverie, Patrick had moved away from the podium and my reaction was to join the usual round of supportive applause. Only this time, no one was with me. I'd got off four or five little claps before Daniela threw a hand over my wrists. "What are you doing?" she hissed. "He started drinking again and you're clapping?"

"Sorry," I said, then said it a little louder. "Sorry. Sorry, Patrick."

At the end of the hour, Daniela and I hung

around with the others, mainly so I could apologize again to Patrick and voice my support for his brand-new ten hours of sobriety. "Day by day," I told him, then watched the poor man walk out of the basement room and up the stairs.

"Don't beat yourself up," said Daniela, and handed me the coffee that she'd poured from a leather-bound thermos into one of the foam cups. She always brought her own coffee, just for her and occasionally for me. At a few meetings, she even brought her own folding chair. Much more comfortable. She'd stopped when Jerry, a Teamster—sober six years—accused her of being too snooty. But the good coffee she wouldn't give up.

"You've been distracted tonight," said Daniela as we took our first sips. "I know why."

"You do?" I didn't know how that was possible.

"You feel bad for not taking part. Next time, I want you to stand up and share your story."

"I'm not sure I'm ready." No, I was not at all ready to stand up and lie about being an alcoholic.

"Yes, you are, Natalie. It's about commitment. You need to realize the truth, however unpleasant, and commit to a solution. I can't do it for you. Mr. Monk can't. Even he has his limitations. If you believe in sobriety—if you believe in any-thing—you have to become proactive."

"I need to be proactive," I agreed. "Yes. You've given me a lot to think about."

We stayed for another few minutes, sharing a few of the gluten-free cookies Daniela always carried in her Gucci handbag. Then we wandered up the stairs to the parking lot.

"Thanks for joining me on such short notice," I said as we arrived at the empty space between my Subaru and her Mercedes. "And for hiring us. I'm sorry we couldn't be more help."

"Oh, it's not over," said Daniela. "The sheriff's office dropped the murder charge. But Henry's just out on bail. The pending charges are failure to report a crime and obstruction of justice. That's the big one. They consider him a material witness. As long as he refuses to talk, they can prosecute, even if they don't have a suspect. If they arrest someone and go to trial, Henry could face contempt of court."

"What does Henry say about this?"

"He's disappointed. He expected it to go away."

"Well, at least he's home. Did you ever contact his wife, Becky? Does she know?"

"I e-mailed her several times after the arrest. She finally got back to me. I'm afraid she's not in a conciliatory mood."

"All because of her flossing?" I genuinely felt sorry for the guy. "I think he still loves her."

"Well, maybe they'll patch things up if I keep him out of jail. How does this sound? Henry testifies that he saw the murder from his window, although he can't possibly ID anyone. When he went outside to check, he found the body and tried dragging it to the street—in order to take it to the nearest hospital."

"That doesn't account for his shovel."

"I know, dear. But without the truth, it's the best I can do."

"What if the police get their hands on Fat Tony?" I asked. "Caught and convicted. Then the obstruction of justice goes away."

"Easier said than done."

"Not for Monk and Teeger."

"Is that something you and Mr. Monk are willing to go for?" Her gaze narrowed, burrowing into my eyes. "Henry will pay, of course. But I'm just as happy losing this one. I know that's a horrible thing for a defense attorney to say. But I'd rather have my client serve a little time for being stubborn. It beats pitting you against Lucarelli's people and risking my friend getting hurt or killed."

"I appreciate it," I said. It was nice to know she considered me a friend. "But we're investigators. It's what we do. And the next time you have a tough case, I don't want you hiring someone else because you think I might get myself hurt."

"You have a point," she admitted. "I probably would think that way."

"Then it's settled. We'll get on it right away. And don't worry. We've faced down bigger crooks than Fat Tony."

We finished our coffees, every last drop, and I took both foam cups. "Incredibly good coffee," I said. "Very dark and smooth. Was that kopi luwak, by any chance?"

"Very impressive," said Daniela, looking very impressed. "The finest coffee in the world. I used to buy it locally, but the shop went out of business. I'm down to my last few pounds."

"Poop."

"Excuse me?"

"You bought it at Poop on Union Street. I used to be friends with Ellen Morse, the owner."

"Yes. Poop. So I don't need to tell you how the coffee's made. Tell me, how is sweet Ellen? Have you kept in touch with her?"

"Her brother was just arrested for murder."

"Oh my." Daniela took a second, just a second. "Well, if you talk to her soon, give her my e-mail or my number. I'd love to stock up on some more kopi luwak."

Before getting into my car, I phoned ahead to Mickey's, my favorite comfort food establishment, and ordered their famous beef and pork meat loaf with sides of mashed potatoes, gravy, and green beans. No rolls, of course, because I'm watching my weight. Twenty minutes later, I retrieved a foil-lined bag from their pickup window and was on my way back to the house.

Halfway there, I decided to take a little detour to

Haight Street. A police cruiser was still in front of Sarabeth's apartment. I rolled down my window and motioned for the officer behind the wheel to do the same. "Hey, Natalie."

"Hi, Joe." It was Joe Nazio, a patrolman I knew, since he often took over the desk duties at the precinct house. "Is Adrian in the apartment?"

"Yep. He's been there for a while. Are you going in?"

"No. I just wanted to keep tabs on him."

"Is Monk involved with this woman?" asked Joe. "I'm curious because he brought two suitcases with him."

I was surprised but not shocked. "What size?"

"Kind of medium."

"He may be involved," I admitted. "But she's injured and he's Monk, so I'm not sure how deep the involvement goes."

"Is that kosher, spending the night?"

"I don't think there's a law against it."

"Well, if he's protecting her, maybe I'll take a break and get some food."

"You can't do that."

"Yeah, I know. What do you got in your car? Smells great."

I wound up parking right behind the cruiser, getting in beside Joe and sharing my oversized portion of meat loaf and side dishes. Joe shared a bottle of warm lemonade from his backseat and wondered aloud why there weren't any rolls. I told him about my diet and he dutifully told me that I didn't need one.

The two of us kept an eye on the street and talked about the joy of raising girls. Joe is the father of a six-year-old and thinks it's the easiest, most gratifying thing in the world. I didn't want to spoil his fun with any of my war stories. He'd find out soon enough. Despite the wad of paper napkins, we made quite a mess of the whole front seat.

"This was fun," I said, swallowing the last of the green beans and wiping a streak of grease off the middle console. "Adrian never lets me eat in the car."

"Even when he's not in the car with you?"

"Even when I'm alone, driving to see my folks in Monterey for the weekend. He always knows."

By the time I finally pulled into my own little driveway, I had a plan. I settled into the living room couch with my first glass of wine and speed dialed Amy Devlin. She picked up on the second ring.

"Here's our plan," I said. I didn't need to introduce myself, because she knew my voice.

"What do you mean, here's our plan? I'm the lead investigator and you're telling me what the plan is?"

"Yep," I confirmed. "You hired us for our expertise and here it is. We focus on Sarabeth Willow."

"Sarabeth?" She sounded confused. "I thought Monk eliminated her."

"Monk isn't thinking straight. You're getting your expertise from the other half of Monk and Teeger."

"I'm not sure I'm comfortable with that," Devlin said, separating each word.

"I'll explain it all later and you'll agree with me. Officer Joe Nazio says that Adrian arrived at her apartment this evening with two medium-sized suitcases. That means he's sleeping overnight on her couch, but not doing his morning routine there. That requires at least four suitcases."

"I'm not sure where you're going with this."

"Since it's daylight saving time, Monk will be back at his place by seven a.m."

"What if it wasn't daylight saving time?"

"Then it would be six. Monk's internal clock doesn't change with the seasons. Don't worry, Amy. I have this all planned out."

# 18

## MR. MONK AND HIS SUNDAY PLANS

It was exactly seven forty-five when Captain Stottlemeyer rang the bell, climbed the single flight of stairs, and knocked on the door.

"Leland, nice to see you. Good timing." Monk ushered him inside. "I just finished my morning haircut." The captain's timing, of course, had not been accidental. I had Monk's morning schedule memorized. "What can I do for you?"

Stottlemeyer made himself at home while Monk used a minivacuum, the kind designed for computer keyboards, to suck up the last little pieces of hair from his temples. "It's an election year, Monk. You know what that means." The captain and I had rehearsed this. "It means the police commissioner wants to crack down on the Lucarelli family."

"How does that involve you?" Monk said, shouting over his self-inflicted din. "You're homicide. Is there some unsolved mob homicide I don't know about?"

"Not in the city. But there is one in Millbrae."

Monk shut off his vacuum. "I already investigated that. For what it's worth, the culprit is Fat

198

Tony Lucarelli, which is what I told the sheriff's office. But there's no proof."

"Then we get proof. The commissioner won't care how the case is broken. He just wants a Lucarelli going to jail before the good citizens vote."

"What about the triple murder?" asked Monk.

"We have manpower for both. There's only so much we can do with a suspect who disappears without a trace."

"What about Sarabeth? I promised I would spend the day with her. Jogging her memory about Wyatt. Protecting her. Stuff like that."

"She already has protection," said the captain. "Besides, it's Sunday. I think she can do with a day of rest."

Monk crossed his arms. "You mean a day of rest from me? Is that what this is about?"

"No, Monk, I need your help. And it's not the worst idea to give her a little space to recover. She just got home." Stottlemeyer pointed to the cordless phone on the kitchen wall. "Tell her you'll see her Monday. Then you'll come with me. We'll figure out how to get Fat Tony. It'll be like the old days, just the two of us."

"Okay, I'll try," said Monk. "But I can tell you right now, she'll be disappointed." He took the phone and dialed the number from memory. Sometimes I think he has the whole phone directory committed to memory.

I got all of this later in the day from Stottlemeyer. According to him, there was disappointment involved. But it was all on Monk's part, since Sarabeth didn't sound crushed at all by the prospect of a Monk-free day. When Monk promised that he would drop by after work tomorrow, she said, "Okay," and seemed perfectly fine.

Sarabeth also didn't sound disappointed when Lieutenant Devlin called and informed her that the twenty-four-hour guard was being removed from in front of her painted lady. According to what Devlin told her, Wyatt Noone had been sighted in Vancouver, B.C., and no longer posed an immediate threat.

I was with Devlin when she made that call. The two of us were half a block down on Haight Street, with a clear view of Sarabeth's door, when Officer Nazio's daytime replacement pulled away from the curb. "Now all we have to do is wait," said Devlin.

I don't know anyone who is fond of stakeouts. But we were fairly sure that if anything was going to happen, it would be today, the one day that Sarabeth could count on everyone leaving her alone.

We were based in Devlin's car, a red Grand Am, one of the last Grand Ams ever made. It stood out more than I would have liked. But Sarabeth had seen my old Subaru. Today I parked it farther down the block, facing the opposite direction, just to give us flexibility.

As with most stakeouts, it started with a certain excitement and devolved into boredom and irritation with everything the other person does. As noon approached and no one had come into or left the ground-floor apartment, I got out to stretch my legs—and walk around the block to Page Street to buy something I didn't need from the 7-Eleven so that I could use their filthy restroom.

It's little unexpected moments like this that make you believe in God or destiny or fate. If I hadn't gone around the block at just the right moment and bought the pack of Twizzlers and hadn't waited in line to relieve myself, then I never would have emerged on Page Street in time to see Sarabeth Willow exiting from someone else's ground-floor apartment. An elderly man waved her on her way, and I was close enough to hear her thank him before she turned west and started walking. Her pace was measured and slow, but better than I would have expected for a woman recovering from a bullet wound to the stomach. Dangling from her left shoulder was a small green backpack.

I dialed four on my speed dial—one was for Monk because he insisted on being either one or ten, which didn't exist, two was for Julie, three was for Stottlemeyer, four was for Devlin—and waited an endless few seconds. "Suspect heading west on Page on foot. Turning right onto Scott now."

"Follow procedure," said Devlin. Over the phone I could hear the Grand Am roaring to life.

The procedure was simple. I tailed our target on foot, updating the lieutenant as she maneuvered the maze of one-way streets. As I had hoped, Sarabeth was crossing Oak Street, heading for the westbound Muni stop on Fell, which gave us a minute or two to regroup half a block away.

"How did she get on Page?" Devlin and I were only ten yards away from each other but still on our phones.

"I didn't count on a back exit," I explained. "But at least we got her." The number one rule of a stakeout is to cover all exits. In this case, there had been only one. I hadn't even thought of the back gate, since it dead-ended into the yard of a neighbor, old Mr. Simonton, as I recalled from Sarabeth's conversation yesterday.

This development told me three things: one, Sarabeth was on good terms with Mr. Simonton; two, she was smart enough to make up a plausible story for needing to use his front door instead of her own; and three, she was being cautious. She wanted to get out and didn't completely trust that we had removed her bodyguard. I also felt I was on my way to proving a fourth, that I'd been right and Monk's new girlfriend was guilty of something.

Somewhere a cell phone rang. The distance and the street noise combined to make it barely audible. Sarabeth pulled it out of her backpack. I wasn't close enough to hear, but I could see her face radiating a smile as soon as she answered.

As the Seventy-one, the Haight-Noriega, pulled up, Sarabeth said good-bye, got on the bus, and swiped her pass. I got off my own phone and back into the Grand Am. Devlin kept us in the bus lane, thirty yards back, with no vehicle in between. Reaching around to the back, I dusted away a week's worth of fast-food wrappers, and grabbed the binoculars. From what I could see, Sarabeth was sitting by herself, on the right side, by the window, about six rows from the rear, completely unaware of our presence.

She stayed seated as the Seventy-one angled its way left through the edge of Golden Gate Park and emerged onto Lincoln Way, the road that marks the park's southern boundary. At the Ninth Avenue stop, I barely noticed the bald man, middle-aged, carrying himself carefully as he got on the bus. He was at the front of a group of three and planted both feet on each step before going up to the next. Devlin's inner alarm may have gone off sooner, but mine didn't activate until the seemingly frail man sat down next to Sarabeth—on a half-empty bus with plenty of seats.

"Can that be him?" I asked, focusing the binoculars. Could it be that easy? In the midst of a city-wide manhunt, could our guy actually be getting on a public bus and settling in beside one of his victims?

At each stop the bus made, I refocused the binoculars. The green backpack was now on his lap, not hers, and they seemed to be talking.

We stayed in this procession through the left turn onto Twenty-third Avenue, still in the bus lane. It was shortly after the Lawton Street stop, when the blue and white lights began flashing in our rearview mirror and whoop-whoop of a siren ruined everything.

"We're in the bus lane," I moaned. I had thought of this before, but really! Since when do the San Francisco police enforce the bus lane?

"Damn," said Devlin. She pulled over as quickly as she could. "Natalie, follow on foot. Don't let them get away."

"What about the cops?"

"There's only one. I'll take care of him and catch up."

"Where's the camera?" I shouted.

"Go, go, go," she shouted back, which I took to mean, *It's under food wrappers or in the trunk or maybe I forgot it. Go!*

Devlin got out of the car at the same moment I did, her hands raised. "Get back in the vehicle," an amplified voice blared. "Both of you. Now."

I didn't obey, but grabbed my phone and started running, trying to keep my eyes on the bus and wondering where the next stop might be. The next to the last thing I heard was Devlin speaking in a loud but calm voice. "We're officers in pursuit. I'm going to reach into my jacket and pull my ID."

"Don't do it," said the bullhorn. "Ma'am, I'm warning you. Get back in your vehicle." Uh-oh. I knew for a fact that Devlin hates being called ma'am.

There was very little foot traffic on Twenty-third, but that didn't stop me from running in a zigzag, as if the officer had forgotten about Devlin and was training a bazooka on my back. I saw the bus do one more half stop, no one getting off or on, then make a right turn onto Noriega. At least I thought it was Noriega. I was still more than a block behind.

By the time I made my own right turn on Noriega, it was too late. My heart sank as I saw the Seventy-one blending in with three other buses in the bus lane, all taking in and letting off passengers—plus three cars and a taxi also in the bus lane, driving undisturbed, just to rub salt in the wound. Damn it. It wasn't fair.

I walk-ran another five blocks before admitting to myself it was useless. Then I doubled over at the waist and tried to catch my breath. I don't care what they tell you. One Pilates class a week can in no way prepare you for this.

I didn't want to go back to Devlin with nothing

to show, but what could I do? Had we really come this close, only to be foiled by a traffic cop protecting the sanctity of the bus lanes? As I turned the corner back onto Twenty-third, I wondered who I would see lying spread-eagle over the hood of the cruiser—Devlin or the traffic cop. It could go either way.

It turned out no one was on the hood. Two more patrol cars had joined the scene, and Amy was in the center of the action, toggling back and forth between a phone in one hand and a police communicator in the other. I wasn't sure which of the uniformed officers had pulled us over, but I was sure he was feeling terrible.

I remained on the sidelines until my breathing had returned to normal. "Don't apologize," Devlin said as she saw me walking her way. She pocketed her phone. "It is what it is."

"Can you send someone to stop the bus?"

"Already done. They stopped it at the end of the line on Ortega. Neither Sarabeth nor the bald guy was on it. The driver is being questioned."

"I should have started sooner. Run faster."

"Teeger, stop it. You're the one who figured she would go. Without you, we wouldn't have had the stakeout."

"So what do we do?" I asked.

"I'll tell you what we don't do. We don't let Sarabeth know we're onto her. When she comes home, we set up a real stakeout. Maybe we'll get a second chance. We'll also get a warrant for phone taps, cell and landline. Meanwhile, I'll call Judge Markowitz and get a record of Sarabeth's recent calls. When she left the house today, I assume she was talking to him."

"How about following the money?" I suggested. "If they were both involved in the embezzlement, the money has to be somewhere. Two million dollars."

"Good idea, Teeger. We may not have enough probable cause to examine her bank accounts, but we can certainly check her recent deposits and withdrawals. She'll have some serious explaining to do when we find her."

A chill went right through me. "If we find her. What if we just blew our last chance?"

"Then we have two of them gone. I just hope she's not as good at disappearing."

# 19

## MR. MONK AND THE EMPTY CONVERTIBLE

Saturday night, after I'd spoken to Captain Stottlemeyer, he went out to the twenty-four-hour car wash on Harrison and had his boat of a Buick detailed. It seemed like a lot of trouble to me. But to the captain, it beat the prospect of an early-morning lecture on vehicular germs and then wasting half an hour while Monk did his cleaning magic on the front passenger seat.

By eight thirty a.m., Monk and the captain were on the road to Millbrae. By a few minutes after nine, they had arrived by the side of the vacant lot, shaking hands with a highway patrol officer and a deputy sheriff from the county. Monk had brought his own wipes for the handshakes. He's not helpless.

"I was raised in Millbrae," said the deputy sheriff, looking around the suburban landscape. His name was Clayton Jones. "Half a mile from here. Worked for the Millbrae PD until the city in its wisdom eliminated it last year." Stottlemeyer would describe him as a mid-thirties career cop with a sandy crew cut, who resented losing whatever seniority he'd had within the force. "It's all about saving money, isn't it? Public safety be damned."

"You realize that Pickler didn't shoot Mr. Rivera," said Monk.

"I know the DA released him," said Jones.

"Which means Mr. Rivera's murder is still unsolved." By the way, this is kind of an old-fashioned tradition, to refer to a murder victim as *Mr.* or *Mrs.* or *Ms.* Even for a drug dealer. It just seems respectful.

"That's what the evidence says. Of course, if this town still had a police force . . ."

"Got it," Stottlemeyer interrupted. He was not fond of Clayton Jones' attitude. "Did you know the Picklers? Was there anything about them that would help us understand? Drug use or behavioral problems?"

"I actually went to school with Henry. Quiet kid. Real straight arrow, but with a lot of pent-up emotions, if you ask me. That's why a town needs a police department, to keep track of the weirdos."

"What about the parents?" asked the captain. "Are they still alive?"

Clayton Jones shrugged. "I don't recall their funerals. Maybe they're living in a home some-where. The Picklers kept to themselves, if you know what I mean."

"Was Henry always so clean and neat and organized?" asked Monk.

"I guess. Is that important?"

"Very important. Oh, you mean important to the case? No."

"The whole family was weird," Jones continued. "Look at their house. They had money but they never changed anything. Not in forty years. They even bought the lot behind them, just so the view wouldn't change. In today's market they could sell it for a ton."

"How did they make their money?" asked Stottlemeyer.

"It was always family dough. Trust funds. But no one really knew them. I was surprised when Henry found a wife. Of course, she didn't stay very long, did she?"

Monk bristled. "There's nothing weird about having a woman leave you in the lurch. Happens all the time."

"But there is something weird about dragging a corpse in the middle of the night." This was the fourth man in the group speaking up. Highway patrolman Tim Hooper had been one of the officers to come across Henry and arrest him. Like Jones, he had graciously agreed to give up his Sunday morning. He kept looking at his watch, anxious to get back to Redwood City in time for church with his family.

Hooper didn't have much to add to the mix. He and his partner had caught Henry by accident. Literally by accident. They had been doing speed control on the 280 and were trying to cut across on surface roads to the 101 where a two-car accident had been reported. Somehow Hooper took a wrong turn, what he thought would be a shortcut past a construction delay. It was his partner, keeping his eyes peeled for a street sign, who first noticed the movement in the shrubs of the vacant lot.

"Was Pickler dragging the body into the lot or out of it?" asked Monk.

Hooper scratched his head. "Hard to say. He saw us almost as soon as we saw him and tried to duck into the bushes. As for the lot, it was trampled both ways, in and out. We gave him plenty of chance to explain himself. But he just froze. Petrified. We were petrified, too. The body was still warm, with a big hole in the back of the head."

"And no gun?" the captain asked. "He couldn't have thrown it away or hidden it?"

"We were all over that lot," the patrolman attested. "Short of digging for oil, there's nowhere he could have got rid of it."

"Maybe, maybe not," said Jones. "But if this town had a police department . . ."

"What the hell does that have to do with it?" demanded Stottlemeyer. He was tired of hearing Jones blame everything on cutbacks. Everyone had to deal with cutbacks.

Deputy Jones calmed down a notch and tried to explain—cops knowing the local beat, community trust, outreach to the neighbors. "In the old days, we could have solved this without some outside homicide cops."

"Don't flatter yourself," growled the captain.

During this whole last part, Monk stopped paying attention. His eyes wandered across the lot to the rear of the Pickler family home. "Why isn't the car in the garage?" he asked.

Stottlemeyer paused. He has this sixth sense about when to really listen to Monk. "What do you mean, buddy?"

"We can't really see the driveway from here. But I can see the edge of a chrome bumper. The glint caught my eye."

"Who has chrome bumpers these days?" asked Jones.

"Shut up," advised the captain. "Go on, Monk."

"Strikes me as odd. Pickler wouldn't park in the driveway. And I don't think he would let guests do it. He wouldn't like to be blocked in like that."

"Let's check it out," said Stottlemeyer.

A minute later they had blocked the entire street in front of the house with two civilian cars and one cruiser from the sheriff's office. The first thing Monk noticed was the open door to the double-bay garage. The first thing the captain noticed was the convertible—sleek, low, and black, with the top down.

"A real classic," said the captain admiringly. "A 1973 Jaguar XKE. When I was a kid, I was in love with these more than with girls. From what I hear of the Picklers, I'll bet it's all original. One owner."

"It's his," Monk confirmed. "But with the top down like this and the forecast of rain and the garage door open . . . Oh, and the keys in the ignition."

Monk knelt on the manicured gravel that was no longer manicured. "This is his usual path in and out." Then he pointed to the depression leading to and from the tires. "Almost perfectly lined up every time. But look at this other stuff." There were tire marks in front of the other bay, different marks, and little mounds of gravel pushed in every direction. "One car. Large. From the footprints, I'd say a sedan rather than a coupe."

"Cut to the chase, Monk."

"Sorry, Captain. You can ring Pickler's doorbell to make sure. But I'm saying abducted."

Deputy Sheriff Jones' eyes went wide. "Abducted? No."

Monk shrugged. "You can say kidnapped if you prefer. Snatched. Carried off. Taken against his will. Carted away."

Stottlemeyer was already halfway through the open garage, making his way to the connecting door leading into the house. "Stay there," he shouted back to everyone.

"You're going to trigger the alarm," said Monk. "I'm just warning you."

Stottlemeyer made the trip back in less than twenty minutes.

When he pulled up in front of Albert's Barbershop, two black-and-whites were already in front, with a third positioned across the back alley. The yellow and red lights were flashing on all three. No sirens. The captain was trying to give the Lucarellis fair warning but not to spook them. He wanted Sal to have time to figure out his options and calm down his troops. The old gangster was reasonable that way.

No one stopped the captain and Monk as they walked into the shop. Albert himself had even swept away the trimmings in anticipation, leaving a neat little trail to the door in the back. Stottlemeyer knocked out of respect and was about to turn the knob when it turned from inside.

The captain stood in the doorway, facing a slight, pale man he'd never seen before. Although he had a pretty good idea. "Henry Pickler?"

Pickler nodded, and stepped aside to let them enter. For a neat and obsessive man, he was not looking his best. His shirt collar was crooked, both his shoes were scuffed, and his black Windbreaker had a tear in the left pocket. He didn't say a word, but the captain assumed Pickler was glad to see them.

"Adrian, Adrian. I should have known." Sal Lucarelli was in his usual spot by the rolltop desk—rolled down, of course. He was smiling, which is not always good. "Please don't tell me you tracked down our friend Henry without visiting his house and doing your thing. Because that would really upset me."

"I visited his house," Monk admitted. "I could tell he left against his will. That information presented me with two possibilities—you or Carlos Menendez. I ruled out Mr. Menendez since he already knows who killed his employee, and it wasn't Henry." Monk turned to Pickler. "By the way, we put the top up on your car and left it in the garage. We didn't have time to stay and use those dust wipes of yours on the interior."

"Actually, Monk wanted to stay," said the captain with half a smile.

"Thank you," said Pickler. "So you didn't wipe down the interior? I always wipe down the interior."

"Sorry," said Monk.

"We thought it might be more important to come and save your life," the captain suggested.

"What are you talking about?" Sal chuckled. "Our buddy Henry doesn't need saving. Henry knows I don't get out much anymore, what with my gout. He agreed to come of his own free will, didn't you?"

Pickler eyed the tear in his Windbreaker. "Yes."

"And he'll be leaving of his own free will."

"So why did you come to visit?" the captain

asked, then raised a hand. "I want an answer from Henry, not you."

"Tell him, Henry," said Sal. "Go ahead."

"I came to talk about what happened that night." Henry was measuring his words. "Mr. Lucarelli wanted to know—"

Sal cut him off. "I was curious about his involvement with this Rivera guy. Henry was gracious enough to enlighten me. And believe me, it was quite an enlightenment. I was impressed."

Stottlemeyer threw Henry one of his patented stares. "So you tell a mobster, but you won't tell your lawyer or the police?"

"I can be very persuasive," said Sal.

Stottlemeyer took Pickler by the shoulders. He couldn't help noticing a painful little wince. "Did he hurt you? You can tell us, that's okay. Nothing's going to happen. This whole building is surrounded."

"They didn't hurt me," said Pickler.

"You can take Henry away and question him," said Sal. "Be my guest. It's not going to be in his best interest to talk."

"Did they threaten you?" asked the captain.

"Did they threaten your wife?" asked Monk.

Sal and his goons seemed to find the whole thing amusing, especially Fat Tony who was actually laughing. "How I wish I could share the details," said Sal. "But Henry made me promise. And I don't want to cross Henry."

At this point everyone in the room laughed—except Stottlemeyer, Monk, and Pickler, who was looking scared to death.

"I don't appreciate being on the outside of your inside joke," said Stottlemeyer.

"That actually happens to me all the time," said Monk. "It's annoying, yes, but you get used to it."

"We are not getting used to it, Monk." Then the captain strode across the room to the air hockey table and stuck his finger an inch from Fat Tony's bony chest. "We know you shot him, Tony. I don't know how you got Pickler involved in your dirty work. But we're getting to the bottom of this. And you're going to jail."

Tony tossed the nub of his carrot onto the hockey table. It was small and light enough so that the air pressure made it vibrate. "This ain't your case, Captain. Not unless you're the sheriff. Are you a sheriff now?" Then he went into his John Wayne impression. "This town ain't big enough for the two of us, Pilgrim." This also got a laugh, which didn't make the captain any happier.

"Esteban Rivera was last seen being forced into a vehicle ten blocks from here. Your vehicle. That's kidnapping on my turf. And it gives me all the authority I need."

"My vehicle? Really? Because, from what I hear, the vehicle couldn't be identified." Tony watched the carrot bob. "Which is a shame, since

I'm sure it would prove I had nothing to do with any such crime."

At this point, according to what the captain told me in his blow-by-blow, there wasn't much left to say, although I'm sure he delivered a few more growls and pithy attempts to save face. When they walked out a minute later—Monk first, followed by Pickler, followed by the captain—no one tried to stop them.

"We'll give you protection," the captain said as soon as they hit the fresh air and the patrol cars.

"Protection?" Pickler laughed in one of those irritating, unfunny ways. "You can't possibly give me protection."

"We can," said the captain. "Tell us what you saw from your kitchen window and all of this can go away."

"You don't know what the hell you're talking about."

# 20

## MR. MONK AND THE PAWNSHOP

Monk and I didn't have a routine set in stone. My assumption was that I would pick him up five days a week and drive to our little strip mall with the reserved parking space out front and the sign EMPLOYEES ONLY.

I was running a few minutes late that Monday morning. But I knew better than to pull up in front of his apartment and honk. I'd tried that once and had to physically restrain him from calling the Department of Public Health for violation of Article 29. That's the noise control ordinance that, among other things, prohibits the honking of car horns except in the case of imminent danger. I had to promise that I would voluntarily turn myself in, but I never did.

I called his house phone from my illegal spot on the street. No response. The front bell and the second-floor bell also provided no response. So I retrieved my Subaru before it could be towed and drove the five minutes to Monk and Teeger. Maybe he's already there, I thought, ready to embrace our new life. Miracles are always possible.

He was there, all right.

To be specific, he was at the storefront on the other side of the strip mall, 24-Hour Holiday Pawn. Monk and the proprietor and two officers from an SFPD squad car were gathered just inside the dusty establishment, all of them talking and trying to be heard.

"Natalie, thank goodness. Come on, come on." Monk joined me as soon as I got out and mime-dragged me into the shop. "Please explain to Mr. Wittingham that I need to inspect the premises. There may be a lot more where this came from." Monk pointed to a gorgeous sterling silver punch bowl taking up the entire countertop by the cash register. Being a detective, I had already clocked the gaping empty space in the front window display.

"What exactly happened?" I asked.

"Since you didn't call to confirm our schedule, I was forced to walk into work this morning. . . ."

"You have a phone, too, Adrian. You could have called me."

"Be that as it may, you didn't call and I walked to work—and you weren't here. I was forced to look in the window of the pawnshop."

"How many times do I have to tell you not to go into pawnshops?"

"I didn't go in. I just looked through the window. It's your fault because you weren't here."

"I wasn't here because I went to pick you up."

Monk and pawnshops don't go well together. It's not just the dust and the chaos and the fact that everything is tattered and used. Everything also has a story. Monk can look at a set of bowling pins and know that the former owner clubbed his business partner to death with one of them. He can glance at a set of poker chips and know they were used by con men in a blackmail scam. He can also look at a sterling silver punch bowl and know . . . Hmm. "Okay, Adrian, what's wrong with this punch bowl?"

"You mean beside the fact . . ."

"Yes, beside the fact that it's a punch bowl and dozens of unsanitary people make a point of drinking from the same container. What's wrong with it?"

It looked pretty normal to me—huge, polished, and traditional, with engraved flourishes, the kind of thing rich people get for their anniversaries or when their sailboat wins the annual regatta. Monk pointed to a blank space in the middle of all the flourishes, an oval perhaps eight by six inches. "That," he said. "That spot is blank."

"Yes, Adrian. That's where the engraving goes."

"And why isn't there an engraving?"

"Umm. Maybe they didn't want it engraved."

"Natalie, open your eyes. It's a presentation piece. The only reason to spend thousands of dollars on a bowl with a big space for an engraving is to put in an engraving. Yet this one is blank. And don't say they had the engraving removed. I checked with a magnifying glass. It was never there."

"Okay, I'll bite," said I. "Why is there no engraving?"

Monk lowered his voice, even though everyone was still close enough to hear. "The lack of engraving isn't conclusive. That's why I called the police. Mr. Wittingham allowed me to use his phone."

"He actually had the nerve to call the police on my phone." Wittingham was understandably upset.

"Thank you, sir," said Monk, then turned back to me. "Since it was in the window, I assumed the bowl was a new acquisition. I asked a sergeant about burglaries at the high-end jewelry shops. There was a break-in two weeks ago at the Tiffany's on Union Square. One of the items was a punch bowl, not yet sold or engraved."

"He's right," said one of the officers with a sheepish grin. "It's the same bowl."

You see how he does it? A simple observation—something that doesn't quite fit—then a phone call to confirm it. Yeah? Well, neither do I.

"I had no idea it was stolen," said Wittingham. "I need to keep my dealer's license, so I'm always legit. I'll give you a copy of the seller's form and the receipt, no problem."

"A hundred to one the ID is fake," said the same officer. The other picked up the bowl, ready to confiscate it and eventually return it to Tiffany & Co.

"I'm sorry, Mr. Wittingham," I said. It's an occupational hazard in the pawn business to be the buyer of stolen property. In most cases, it works out. The broker gets a good price and resells it at a premium without anyone being the wiser. But in most cases, you don't have M&T setting up an office fifty yards away.

"You're sorry?" Wittingham said. "What about me? I'm out eight hundred bucks."

"Eight hundred?" I had to laugh. "And that wasn't a clue to you that the bowl was stolen?"

"What can I say? The guy was a bad bargainer."

"Was this the only thing he brought in?" I asked. "No other silver pieces, like the punch bowl cups?"

"Nothing." The pawnbroker was a small, round man with round-framed glasses and a vintage 1980s rock T-shirt that was spattered with a couple of vintage food stains. He looked at me seriously, as if for the first time. "Who are you, lady? Are you this guy's keeper?"

"I am," I said. "I mean, I'm not. I mean, Adrian and I are co-owners of the detective agency, where the sandwich shop used to be. It's nice to finally meet you. I've been meaning to drop by. I hope we can all be good neighbors. Natalie Teeger." I held out my hand and wasn't surprised when he didn't shake it.

"Your co-owner is trying to get me arrested."

"Not arrested," said Monk. "I'm just saying you should let me inspect the rest of your premises. Who knows what else we'll find?"

"Not without a search warrant."

"Search warrant?" I glanced around at the hundreds of items on the shelves in glass-topped displays. "This is a retail establishment, open twenty-four hours. You can't stop him from walking around and looking."

"Sure I can," said Wittingham. "I can ban anyone. In fact, I'm banning the two of you from ever entering my store again. For life. I'll put up your pictures on the wall. Welcome to the neighborhood."

"He's right about banning you," said the officer who did the talking. "We can take it from here. Thanks again, Monk. This is the easiest case we've had all year."

Seven neighbors to go, I thought as Monk and I walked back across the parking lot to open up for the day. Less than a week and he had already made enemies with one of the eight other shops in our little mall. I wondered which would be next, the Laundromat or the UPS store.

I unlocked the M&T storefront, turned on the lights and off the alarm. Monk made chamomile tea and we settled into our matching desks, sipping tea and doing what countless other office workers do every Monday morning—discussing what we did on Sunday.

Monk went first, starting with Stottlemeyer's unexpected visit and taking me straight through to Henry's rescue and their confrontation with Sal at the barbershop. I had already been debriefed by the captain, so there weren't any surprises, except for how much Monk had enjoyed spending the day with his old partner.

"Leland could have handled it on his own, but I think he really wanted to work a case together, like old times." Monk was practically beaming and I felt a little guilty about having used the captain as a distraction. "And how about you, Natalie? What did you do?"

"Nothing much. I hung out with Amy Devlin a little." I knew as soon as I said it how ridiculous it sounded.

"You hung out with Devlin? On purpose? Were you working on the No One case?"

"No, no," I lied. "We just hung out. We took her car. We walked around."

Monk looked like he wanted to pursue this quirky behavior of mine. But then the phone rang, the office phone, and he forgot all about me. His face lit up. "I gave her this number," he said, and picked it up after the second ring. "Sarabeth, hi. This is Adrian Monk."

Okay. I suppose I need to do some explaining.

After the disastrous tailing attempt on the Seventy-one bus, Devlin and I weren't sure we would ever see Sarabeth again. Within an hour, the department set up an official, round-the-clock stakeout on the Haight Street apartment, just in case. And the gamble paid off.

Around six that evening, a detective sergeant in an unmarked vehicle noticed Sarabeth Willow walking east on Haight, returning home as if nothing had happened. This time she didn't disturb Mr. Simonton on Page Street but came in through her own front door. Noticeably absent was the small green backpack.

When Devlin found out, she was ecstatic. Not only did this mean that Sarabeth wasn't on the run—our worst-case scenario—it meant she probably wasn't aware of having been tailed. Her exit onto Page Street had been merely a precaution, one that she didn't feel like repeating on her return. Devlin's only disappointment was the missing backpack.

"Why don't I come over now?" Monk said, a little too eagerly. "I made Spam sandwiches for Natalie and me, but I'm sure she won't mind. Do you like Spam? It's the perfect food. Great! I'll see you soon."

"I thought we were going to spend the day working the No One case," I said right after he'd hung up.

"I am working it. At some point, Sarabeth is going to remember something crucial about our mystery man. It could be when I'm sitting by her bed helping her recover, or when she gets up to make me a snack. And when it happens, I'll be there to fit the pieces together."

I think he actually believed this. And it could happen, given his track record, so who was I to argue?

I found a legal spot to park on Page Street, directly opposite Mr. Simonton's house. I escorted Monk around the block and was with him when he rang the bell. Sarabeth answered the door in her floral housedress, genuinely pleased to see my partner and artificially pleased to see me. "Natalie, how nice of you to drop Adrian off." Drop him off? I could take a hint.

I remained on the doorstep to the garden-level apartment. I waited until the door had closed behind Adrian and Sarabeth and they'd moved away from the front window. Then I walked across the street and down the block to the red Grand Am. The front passenger door was already open for me, and I got in as quickly as possible.

Devlin was in street clothes, a Forty-Niners sweatshirt, black jeans, and Nike runners, her spiky hair scrunched up under a baseball cap. She had made room for me. But between the usual garbage and disorder and the supplies for a lengthy stakeout, it was a pretty tight and smelly fit. "Are you having second thoughts?" she asked.

"No," I said with some conviction. "Are you?"

"I don't know," she admitted. "I mean the whole point of getting Monk and Teeger committed to this case was Monk. No offense. But he's the mad genius. It seems stupid to keep him in the dark about Sarabeth. What if he can help?"

"You don't know him like I do," I said. "All we have on Sarabeth is that she sneaked out the back and met a man bearing a resemblance to Wyatt Noone."

"Plus she's the only person alive who knows him. Come on, I've seen Monk focus on bad guys with less proof."

"Not when he's got a blind spot."

"Are you saying he can't be objective?"

"Okay," I said, and settled into my faux leather bucket seat. "Let's say for a minute Adrian wasn't on the rebound from Ellen. Let's say he's not willing to fall for the next woman to smile his way. Let's say he's not afraid that he'll be spending the rest of his life as a lonely outcast."

"Is that how he feels? Wow, I have to start being nicer to him."

"I'll remind you. But even taking all of that out of the equation, Adrian Monk is a terrible liar. Can you imagine him being in there right now, at Sarabeth's bedside, and not letting it slip that we saw her and Noone together?"

Devlin sighed. "I've done undercover work with Monk. He's pretty terrible."

"Remember the time he went undercover as a clown at a kid's birthday party? He blew his cover and wound up being kidnapped."

"I remember."

"The only break we've caught is this Sarabeth connection. But if she gets wind of it, if she suspects her phone is tapped and she's under surveillance, all that goes away. We lose whatever advantage we had."

Devlin nodded in reluctant agreement. "It still makes me nervous."

"Why? Because it makes you dependent on a mere mortal like me and not on the Einstein of crime?"

"I think you mean Einstein of crime detection."

"Crime detection doesn't sound as good. Amy, look, I'm nervous, too. But after all these years, I know Adrian's strengths and weaknesses. When it comes time to bring him in, we'll do it. But not now."

Devlin didn't answer.

"Was it Adrian who arranged for Sarabeth to feel free enough to sneak away and get on that bus? No, that was me."

"That was you," she had to agree. "You want a bottle of water?"

"No, thanks, I'm good."

We spent the next two hours sitting side by side, saying next to nothing, staring at the door and front windows of the ground-floor apartment of the painted lady on Haight Street.

# 21

## MR. MONK AND THE SCENE OF THE CRIME

"I need to speak to Adrian."

I'm not sure if I was doing this out of boredom or because I wanted to move things forward. As long as Monk was in there, I knew our suspect wasn't going anywhere or making any calls.

Once again Sarabeth had answered the door in her colorful housedress. From the faint odor on her breath, I could guess they had finished the sandwiches. "Natalie, come on in. You just missed lunch. I have to tell you, Spam is a wonderful thing. I had no idea."

Monk was in the little eat-in kitchen, wiping the plastic tabletop clean. "Can we have a moment?" I asked Sarabeth.

"You can say anything in front of her," Monk said a tad defensively. "Sarabeth and I don't have any secrets."

"Okay." *Actually, you do have secrets,* I wanted to say. *At least Sarabeth does.* "Adrian, I need you with me in the field. We have two big cases. And we have an obligation to Lieutenant Devlin. She's not saying anything, but I know the commissioner has set up a review board." I looked over to Sarabeth. "I'm sorry to drag him away."

"But she needs protection," Monk said. He had finished his second wipe of the kitchen table and was starting his third. "The police, in their wisdom, removed the squad car."

"That's because they no longer consider her in danger."

"Adrian, it's been a delight having you here," Sarabeth said, all sweetness. "But Natalie's right. I've got good locks now, thanks to you, and I'll follow all your protocols, I promise."

"We can review them once more," Monk said. "What do you do if you hear a noise in the chimney? I know that's a trick question since you don't have a chimney. But if you did have a chimney . . ."

"Sweetie." Sarabeth took him by the shoulders and he didn't flinch. "Three of my good friends are dead. We need you out there finding Wyatt. I'll be perfectly safe. I'll stay right here."

"Do you promise to stay here?"

"I promise."

Monk wasn't about to listen to me, but he listened to her. When we stepped out of the house, the Grand Am had been moved around the corner and out of sight—although I've never dismissed the possibility of his having X-ray vision.

"I hope you're happy," Monk whined as we walked.

"Happy's a relative thing. Where do you want to go? I say East Decorative Imports. If we figure out how Noone left the building, that'll go a long way to clearing Amy's name." Monk didn't bother to answer, which told me he approved. "Good. I already called Mr. Ito. He's meeting us there."

"Did you investigate the survivors of the victims?" We were driving on Broadway and now heading east, miraculously hitting all the green lights. "Mel Lubarsky's widow and Katrina Avery's ex-husband?"

"Yes," I answered somewhat truthfully. Devlin's people had done checks on them both. "Neither one seems to have a connection to our mystery man."

"I still think Noone had inside help."

"So do I."

At the main entrance on Stockton, I rang the office/showroom buzzer. We took the stairs to the third floor and emerged onto a spare, elegant space decorated with statues and soothing rock fountains and drops of blood soaked into the wood-paneled floor. Remnants of yellow crime scene tape hung from a pair of Tibetan prayer wheels on either side of the reception desk.

Monk took a moment to stand in the middle and absorb it all. He didn't raise his hands to frame the scene but turned in a slow, deliberate circle. He was just about to move on when something outside the front windows caught his eye.

They were two large, side-by-side windows, typical of a warehouse, each consisting of nine panels of glass and looking out onto an old, five-story office building on the other side of Stockton. The sun was just beginning to inch its way past the corner and into the street below.

"What?" I asked. I knew he had seen something. "What's wrong?"

Monk wagged his head at an angle, as if shaking loose a drop of water from his left ear. "Nothing."

"It's not nothing. I know your looks. That's not your 'aha' look or your 'interesting' look or your 'something's not symmetrical' look. That's your 'something doesn't make sense' look. What is it? What doesn't make sense?"

"You can see the same thing I'm seeing."

"Adrian, that's not fair."

"It's nothing," he insisted, and forced himself to move on, focusing his gaze onto the floor. We followed the trail of stained wood back to the largest office where Mel, the first victim, had been gunned down.

"Mr. Monk. Ms. Teeger. Please come in."

Takumi Ito sat at a handsome teakwood desk, his tall, lean frame slumped back. Ledgers lay open on either side of the computer screen. "Forgive me for not getting up. I'm not sure I have the strength." He certainly didn't look or sound well.

"What's the matter?"

"It's worse than I thought," said Ito. "The losses may be three or four million now."

"Three or four . . . How can that be?" I asked. "A company this size? How could no one notice?"

"It's absurdly simple," he said, and held up one of the ledgers. "East Decorative sells original pieces worth tens of thousands U.S. to serious collectors. We also sell copies worth maybe a few hundred apiece to decorators and businesses. Mr. Noone was fulfilling orders for original pieces and substituting copies. Then he listed the sales as copies and pocketed the difference."

"And this was easy to do?" I asked. It sounded easy.

"It was child's play. That's the expression, correct?"

"Child's play," I confirmed.

"Our copies are very skillful, down to the rust and the verdigris. They go through customs with labels confirming them as copies, but it's not hard to remove the labels. I spent all weekend comparing receipts and invoices. We're going to have to make good on everything. As you can imagine, our whole business depends on a reliable reputation."

"Could one person have done this?" asked Monk.

Ito was puzzled. "Of course, one person did it.

Are you saying there was someone in addition to Mr. Noone? Who?"

"You answer my question first. Could it be just one person?"

"Yes. As I said, child's play. Being the accountant, he had access to the invoices. And the warehouse is right below us. Now please answer my question, Mr. Monk. Was there someone else?"

Monk chose his words carefully. As with everything, work life and personal, he likes to be precise. "I don't know. There are aspects that make it look like a partnership—how Noone got hired in the first place; his ability to keep a low profile; and how he managed to escape the building. But, as you say, the actual embezzlement could have been done by one. And when you're planning to kill three people, partners are always dangerous." Monk shrugged. "There's something I'm not quite seeing."

Not quite seeing? I liked the sound of that. It meant he was keeping an open mind, maybe even open enough to think about Sarabeth.

"Mr. Ito?"

Todd Avery stood in the office doorway, dressed for work—work gloves, back-support belt, a clipboard in his hands. "Hello," he said, looking a bit surprised to see us. "Monk and Teeger, right? Good to see you. Mr. Ito?" He returned his focus to his boss. "I had a few questions about the deliveries."

"You're back at work?" I asked Todd. "So soon?"

"Todd is our foreman," said the company president. "He was gracious enough to come in. Our business can't stop or it may never restart. We have some local deliveries that were due last week. Todd, I'll meet you at the loading dock in a few minutes."

"Thanks," said Todd, but he didn't move from the doorway. "How's the investigation? I'm sorry for interrupting but the police aren't saying much. Are you going to catch this bastard? That's all I want to know."

"We're getting close," I said, partly to calm him down and partly to gauge his reaction.

"That's good," he said. "I never thought I was into revenge. But you want things to make sense. A man kills your ex-wife, the woman you once planned to spend your life with. Then he disappears. There has to be more to it than that."

"I agree," said Monk. He has a special place in his heart for the husbands of murdered wives. "That's what we do, try to make sense of things."

Ito nodded and I nodded. We all seemed to want to make sense of this. "Todd, I'll meet you on the loading dock."

We waited until the foreman left, listening for the door to the stairwell to close behind him. "Is there anything more I can do for you?" Ito asked. "I wish I knew more myself."

"We'd just like to look around," I said. "The first time we were here, the place was in lockdown. We didn't get to take our time."

Ito waved his hand across the space. "Please feel free. Nothing is off-bounds. If you have any questions, I'll be on the ground level with Todd."

For the next ten minutes, after Ito left, Monk wandered the offices and the showroom displays. I tried to stay out of his way. But I noticed that he kept gravitating to the reception area. Katrina's office, then reception. Mel's office, then reception. Caleb Smith's office . . . And on each return, he seemed to be pulled toward the large front windows facing the receptionist's desk.

I waited until his next gravitational pull. "What?" I asked again. "What are you looking at?"

"I told you before, nothing."

"You know I'm going to bug you until you tell me."

"It's just a little discrepancy, nothing big."

"Then why won't you tell me?"

"You're a detective, Ms. Detective. Figure it out."

"Okay, I will," I said, but without much conviction. I hate these little challenges of his.

Monk stepped away from the window just as I stepped up. Stockton Street looked exactly the same as it had on a dozen other occasions. The windows of the office building opposite us were tinted for privacy or energy efficiency or both. Street traffic was relatively heavy. The tops of a dozen or so heads paraded below me. Another dozen were crossing at the corner and one was jaywalking. If only I knew what I was looking for . . . A third of the way down the block, a Dumpster was positioned not far from a fire hydrant. Did it have something to do with the Dumpster? I wondered. Could Wyatt Noone have escaped into the Dumpster? Not with half of the San Francisco police force looking on.

I stayed at the window, not wanting to give up. And that was when I saw the red Grand Am pulling in behind the Dumpster.

"It's not a clue," Monk said from across the room. "Just a discrepancy. I'm sure there's an explanation." He must have been saying something like that, but I wasn't paying attention. I was too focused on Lieutenant Devlin sitting behind the wheel of the Grand Am.

*What is she doing?* I asked myself. She's supposed to be on stakeout. She wouldn't have left except in an emergency. Even in an emergency . . . The only reason why a hardnose like Devlin would drive away from a stakeout . . . I glanced directly below to the street in time to see a glint of light as the front door to East Decorative Imports swung shut.

"What are you doing? Natalie?"

What I was doing was gingerly opening the door to the stairwell, just enough to stick out my head and listen. "Shh."

"Is Mr. Ito coming back up?" Monk whispered. "Why are we whispering?"

I noticed that the elevator didn't engage. But there was definitely someone on the stairs. One pair of soft feet. Then the sound of another stairwell door closing.

"Adrian, let's check out the second floor. You're done on this floor."

"No, I'm not."

"Yes, you are." There must have been something urgent in my voice, because when I turned to mime-drag him into the stairwell and down the stairs, he was right behind me. When we reached the landing, I stopped and quietly laid down the law. "You don't need a hazmat suit, Adrian. We don't have the time. You can hold your breath if you want, but I wouldn't recommend it." Then I slowly opened the door to the warehouse.

I couldn't tell you if anything had been moved or changed, but the upper warehouse level looked just as shadowy and creepy as before. Just inside, Monk made a move to switch on the lights, but I stopped his hand. That was enough to tell him that we were in stealth mode. He cocked his head to one side, silently asking, "What next?" Then he must have heard something, something I couldn't hear, because his finger went up and he pointed it directly ahead through a lineup of weapon-wielding Shivas from India with eight arms apiece. Did we want to go toward the sound or away from it? I nodded yes.

I knew exactly what to expect. But I had no idea why she was here or what she was doing or how Monk would react, which made things fairly tense. As far as I could tell, we were retracing the path she had taken from the stairwell to her hiding place during the confusion of the mass murder. My mistake, triple homicide.

"Adrian."

She must have just heard us, because we found her in the middle of a walkway, backed up by a quartet of four seated Buddhas made of tin, all identical, about four feet high and looking too fat to ever get their legs into a lotus position. Sarabeth just stood there, a little out of breath.

"Sarabeth," Monk said, confused. "What are you doing? You promised me you wouldn't leave the apartment."

"I know. But I was feeling better. And I knew Mr. Ito would need help keeping the place going."

"But you promised." Monk turned to me, accusingly. "You knew she was here, didn't you?"

"I saw her through the window," I said, which was almost true.

"Why didn't you tell me," said Monk, "instead

of dragging me down here like she was some kind of thief?"

"Don't blame Natalie," said Sarabeth.

*Hold on,* I thought. Wait a minute. He wasn't blaming me. All of a sudden, she was shifting the focus.

"When Natalie took you away, I started to get stir-crazy. It's not her fault. It's mine. I should have kept my word."

"You should have," Monk grumbled. I could tell he wasn't completely convinced.

With a snap and a fluorescent buzz, the overhead lights went on. "Hello? Who's there?" Down the row of Shivas, I could see the slim silhouette of Takumi Ito, followed by the bulkier mass of Todd Avery.

"Mr. Ito? Todd? It's me, Sarabeth."

"Sarabeth," said Todd, and almost broke into a run. "What are you doing out of bed? Mr. Monk, you shouldn't have let her get out of bed."

"Don't blame Adrian," said Sarabeth. "It was all my fault."

"You should be at home," said Ito, joining in the reprimand.

Sarabeth reiterated her desire to come back to work. Ito refused and entrusted us to get her home immediately. "Todd and I will take care of business just fine," he said.

"But you don't know the system."

"I'm learning the system very quickly," Ito told

her. "For example . . ." And he pointed to the four Buddhas. "These are the ones we've been looking for, Todd. They should be on the loading dock."

"Are they copies?" I asked.

"Cheap copies," said Ito. "They don't even pretend to be good. We need to get these wrapped in blankets and out the door. Am I right, Sarabeth?"

"If that's what the computer says." Sarabeth threw them a tired smile. "It looks like I'm not even needed."

"On the contrary. You're needed too much. Maybe next week, if you're feeling up to it. By then I hope to have hired a few people. You'll have a new boss to boss around." Everyone chuckled except for Monk and me.

Todd stayed to deal with the statues, getting on his two-way radio to talk to someone in the loading dock. Ito made us promise again to take Sarabeth directly home and escorted us as far as the stairwell before he headed one floor up and the rest of us headed one floor down.

"We don't have to go, Adrian," Sarabeth said, looking sweetly contrite. "You came here to investigate and now they're making you take me home."

"That's okay," he said. "I can come back later."

"If you want, we can stay. Mr. Ito doesn't have to know."

"No," said Monk. "It's more important for you to keep your word."

When we got to Haight Street, Sarabeth asked Monk if he wanted to come in, but he said no and she didn't press the point. He remained silently strapped into the front passenger seat as we watched her unlock the door to the ground-floor apartment and step inside.

I checked the rearview mirror just before pulling out—and caught a glimpse of the red Grand Am pulling into a space near the far corner.

# 22

# MR. MONK AND
# THE OTHER MAN

Just a few months ago, Monk almost drowned. I know that doesn't sound serious. At least not for us. Monk and I are always almost drowning or getting shot or poisoned or pushed out of hot air balloons. It comes with the territory.

But this last time was bad. He'd been in the water for more than fifteen minutes and had to be put into a medically induced coma while the swelling in his brain went down. After he was revived, the doctors were concerned about the chance of permanent brain damage. Everyone breathed a sigh of relief when, just a few days later, Monk solved another very thorny case.

But I knew better. I was at Monk's side the whole time, and his recovery had been touch and go. As for the thorny case, I actually had to do some of the solving myself when he couldn't quite remember a suspect's name or a vital clue. Even now, months later, he would have little lapses, especially at the end of a long day. Sometimes I would catch him just staring into space, which is normal for a lot of people, but not so much for Monk.

When we got back to Monk's apartment that afternoon, he was a little like that. Quiet and moody and distracted. When he finally did speak, I was relieved to find out he was just mad, nothing more.

"I know what you and Devlin were up to." He was sitting in the middle of his sofa, his hands on his knees. "A bit of advice. On your next stakeout, don't use a red car or park illegally. It draws attention."

"I'm sorry, Adrian. I really am. But you totally dismissed Sarabeth as a suspect and I wasn't willing to do that. Do you want to know where we followed her?"

I sat in the chair across from the sofa and told him the whole story—how Devlin and I had sent him off to work with Captain Stottlemeyer while we sat in the Grand Am to see where Sarabeth might go. I'd felt bad about deceiving him and just a little better about finally being honest.

"We're supposed to be partners," said Monk. "We're supposed to make decisions together. Or are we only partners when you want to be partners?"

He certainly had a point and wasn't wrong about it. On the other hand . . . "I know, Adrian, and I'm sorry. But you do have these blind spots. You were opposed to investigating Sarabeth. Now look. She's our best lead."

"I do not have blind spots. I've arrested loved

ones. I arrested more than one of your boyfriends, remember? And Linda Fusco. The captain
was all set to propose when I put her in jail for
murder. And let's not forget the girl Randy
Disher was dating a few years back, the one who
got him believing in fortune cookies. Oh. And
Ellen Morse's brother in Summit? That was just
this month."

"I'm surprised you have any friends left."

"What's that supposed to mean?"

"It means you're more than willing to arrest
other people's loved ones. But would you be as
willing to go after Sarabeth?"

"If there's a reason to."

"There's a ton of reasons," I said. "She sneaked
out the back. She met a man on a bus who could
be our bad guy. She promised you she'd stay
home and then sneaked into the warehouse, just
a few yards from where the SWAT team found
her. I don't know what any of that means, but it
means something."

"It's a little incriminating," he had to admit.

"I just wish we could have caught the guy on
the bus."

"Okay. Let me think about it." Monk was still in
the middle of the sofa, hands still on his knees.
"Can you get me a bottle of Fiji Water?"

"Anything you want."

"People think better when they're hydrated. Not
a cold bottle from the fridge. A room-temperature

one from the cabinet above the stove. You'll need to get the stepladder from the laundry room. And make sure you wipe the bottle with a clean towel and get a clean glass. No ice."

It took me less than three minutes to follow his instructions, but that gave him all the time he needed. When I came back into the living room, he was standing up and on the phone. "I won't take no for an answer," he said. His voice was soft and intense. "I'm coming over tomorrow morning and I'm staying until we catch this guy. Around the clock. I don't want you going off again, not unless I'm there with you."

I felt like throwing the bottle right at his head —and the glass, too. No ice.

"Yes, they removed your protection, but you're still in danger. As long as it takes, I'm there. See you bright and early." He hung up and looked my way. "That was Sarabeth. Did you wipe the bottle?"

"Adrian." I was livid. "What the hell was that?"

"The phone call?" He looked confused. "I thought this is what you wanted."

"You thought I wanted you to spend all your waking hours protecting Sarabeth?"

"I thought you wanted another chance to catch Mr. No One."

"And how will babysitting Sarabeth help us do that?"

Monk has this patient tone of voice that sounds

anything but patient. "I wasn't telling her I would be over in the morning. Well, I was telling her that. What I was saying, in my own way, was that she has until morning to go wherever she needs to go and do whatever she needs to do."

"Oh." I had to smile. "You're right."

"I assume Devlin won't let her slip away this time."

"I hope not." I was just about to call Devlin and give her a heads-up when she called me. "Is Sarabeth on the move?" I asked.

"How did you know? Yes, out the front. Going west. My gut says she's heading for the bus again." Her voice was almost drowned out by the roar of the Grand Am.

"We're coming," I said. "Call for backup. We can't let her disappear."

When Monk absolutely has to move quickly, he does. As soon as we got in the Subaru, I handed him my phone. Devlin was keeping us in the loop with a constant stream of texts, and he read them aloud. *"Waiting for Seventy-one." "Crossing park." "On Lincoln."*

"I can't believe we're getting a second chance," I said. I was almost giddy and had to warn myself not to speed. The last thing we needed was another diligent traffic cop.

*"Off bus. Ninth Ave."*

"That's where the bald guy got on last time. He must live nearby."

"You want me to text her that?" asked Monk.

"She knows," I said. "Besides, you don't know how to text."

"I'm neither a scientist nor a fifteen-year-old, if that's what you mean."

When we caught up with Devlin, she was out of her car, on Judah between Ninth and Tenth, half a block after the street divides into two one-way sections. She was standing on the westbound section. I parked right behind her in a space reserved for the nursing staff. The words on the sign didn't even register until we got out of the Subaru.

"Nursing staff?" I asked.

"She went in there." Devlin pointed to the two-story building, a plain prefab, seventies-style brown stucco with a wheelchair ramp going up the side to the entrance. A discreet plaque on the wall identified it as the Garden Court Cancer Center. "I can't think of a better place for a fugitive to hide, can you?"

Monk was skeptical. "Was she carrying anything? Flowers? A present? A green backpack?"

"Nothing," said Devlin. "I'm pretty sure she didn't make me. But let's wait until we have backup."

A few minutes later, after a dozen other members of the task force had quietly surrounded the center, we walked in as casually as possible; Devlin, Monk, and I. The lieutenant carried a transceiver on her shoulder and a sidearm under her jacket. For once I remembered to bring along my Glock, stuffed into my PBS tote. Devlin showed her police ID at the desk and asked where we might be able to find Ms. Sarabeth Willow.

The guard at reception knew exactly whom she meant. "Mrs. Willow should be in room two-two-eight." We had all heard the word *Mrs.* and had all chosen to ignore it.

The door to room 228 was open, which I suppose saved us some embarrassment. Sarabeth was seated beside the bed, smiling down at a man in his mid-forties. He seemed to be smaller than she, and thin. But it was hard to say how much of that impression was natural and how much was a result of the cancer.

"Adrian," she said, looking up. Her smile evaporated. "What are you . . . Were you following me?"

"Is this the bus man?" Monk asked.

From the doorway, Devlin took a hard look at his face and nodded. She pressed the button on her transceiver. "Stand down. Maintain your positions." The transceiver squawked back.

"You were following me? The police, too?" It sounded like an accusation.

"For your protection," said Monk.

"Adrian, Natalie, Lieutenant Devlin . . ." Sarabeth kept her resentment in check and motioned toward the man in the bed. "I'd like you to meet my husband, Paul. Ex-husband, I should say. Paul, I believe I've told you about Adrian and his friends."

"Sorry if I'm not more energetic," said Paul. His voice was weak and raspy. "I had chemo this morning and it takes a lot out of me."

"Yesterday was a good day." Sarabeth placed a hand on the white bedcover and he grasped it. "We went to the beach at the end of Noriega and had a little picnic." Her eyes fell on the green backpack on a chair by the window. I imagined being able to see grains of sand scattered inside the open zipper.

"Did the picnic involve cranberry-prune juice?" I had to ask. "I noticed some the other day in Sarabeth's refrigerator."

"Guilty," said Paul. "My doctor says fruit juices can help in the recovery time after chemo."

"And was the cranberry-prune a suggestion from Wyatt Noone?"

"It was," said Sarabeth. "Wyatt gave me a few bottles and Paul actually seems to like it."

"But you two can't be married," Monk protested. "You're divorced."

"We are," said Sarabeth. "It was the only way to get Paul covered by Medicaid. We felt we had to safeguard whatever meager assets we have."

Paul nodded. "I don't want Sarabeth paying off doctor bills for the rest of her life."

"It's not a very honorable way," his ex-wife

admitted. "That's why I kept it quiet. I'm sorry if I misled anyone, especially you, Adrian. Do you forgive me?"

Monk grunted and refused to meet her gaze.

During all of this, Devlin was holding up her phone, bringing up the smiling Christmas party photo of Wyatt S. Noone and comparing it to the shrunken, bald man in the bed. Even from memory, I could tell he wasn't the guy.

"Why was this such a secret?" Devlin was frustrated and angry. "Why didn't you say something that first day in the hospital? If I had a loved one, that would be the first thing I'd say. 'Tell my husband—ex-husband—that I'm alive.'"

"I did say that," Sarabeth replied. "I told the hospital staff. One of the nurses let me use her phone so I could call, even though you're not allowed to use phones."

"I'll check that out," said Devlin.

"Please do," said Sarabeth. "I didn't realize my personal life was part of your investigation."

"Everything is part of the investigation," said Monk, "including your being so nice to me multiple times. Under false pretenses."

"Sarabeth's nice to everyone," said Paul. "Men have been known to misinterpret that part of her personality." He smiled forgivingly and she smiled back. "It's one of the things I love about her."

"I can't believe this," muttered Devlin. "This is too much."

It wasn't hard to see what was running through the lieutenant's mind. First the fiasco at the warehouse. Then the mess yesterday, losing a couple of middle-aged fugitives on their way to the beach. And now today, with a dozen officers surrounding a cancer treatment center, expecting to race in and capture a crazed killer . . . In less than a week, her promising career was heading straight down the drain.

We left the Willows holding hands in room 228. Then Devlin left us to go outside and work damage control. That left just the two of us to intercept the first nurse we could find and ask for the doctor in charge of Paul Willow's treatment.

Dr. Simon Rothstein had been making his rounds on the first floor when he answered our page and agreed to meet us in his office. Lucky for us, the man was a true-crime junkie. To him, believe it or not, Adrian was a rock star. Not only could he rattle off a dozen of our most famous cases, but he was also familiar with every detail of the search for Wyatt Noone, at least as much as had been released to the press. If there was any question of doctor-patient confidentiality, it never came up.

"I was thinking you might stop by," said Rothstein as he settled in behind his desk. "Paul was devastated when he heard about the attack. He'd undergone a little operation that morning, to cut out a polyp we hadn't been able to reach before. When he came to, it was all over the news. That was not a fun day, I can tell you."

Lingering in the back of my mind had been the suspicion that, despite his lack of resemblance, Paul Willow was somehow the same man the snipers had had in their scopes. But the doctor's statement put an end to that.

"Is he dying?" Monk asked.

Dr. Rothstein seemed taken aback. "No. There are various options we have now for lymphosarcoma. Unfortunately, some of the more promising ones are still considered experimental. They aren't covered by insurance. But there's still quite a bit we can do here. It's far from over."

"She must love him a lot," said Monk. I'm not sure how much bad karma you get for being jealous of a man who's sick with cancer, but I think Monk was pretty jealous.

By the time Dr. Rothstein returned to his patients and we returned to the Subaru, the police were gone. I could only imagine the lieutenant's mortification as she tried to explain the truth to her team.

"I still think Sarabeth's involved," Monk said as he got into the car and snapped on his seat belt.

"What do you mean, 'still'?" I asked. "An hour ago you refused to consider her at all. Now she's a suspect?"

"She deceived me," Monk said. "It shows a diabolical lack of character."

"She was being nice—and trying not to hurt your feelings."

"No," Monk insisted. "She's involved with Noone. You were right the first time."

"I was not right."

"Don't tell me when you're right. I'll tell you when you're right. You were right."

"You're just angry."

"You're a smart detective, Natalie. You were right."

"I was totally wrong." How did I get myself in this position? "Sarabeth is not involved with Noone. She's made contact with exactly one person, her husband. Meanwhile, Noone is probably a thousand miles away."

Monk didn't hear me. He laughed and shook his head. "Poor Noone. He's going to be so mad when he finds out the woman he did all this for is still in love with her ex."

"Adrian, come on. I know you don't believe that. You're just hurt."

"I may be exaggerating," he conceded. "But not by much. Sarabeth and Noone are in it together. I'm just not sure how."

# 23

## MR. MONK AND THE FACEBOOK FRIEND

Nothing much happened in the next two days. Monk and I drove into work together on Tuesday and walked on Wednesday when the weather was nice enough. He was okay with this kind of spontaneity as long as I gave him twenty-four hours' notice, which I did after checking the AccuWeather forecast.

On Tuesday the police commissioner announced a review board to look into what they called the department's "botched response to the Wyatt Noone case." I found it amusing that everyone continued to call him Noone, even though a handful of us knew this was a made-up name.

Tuesday had also been a slow day for Amy Devlin. The department had taken her off the task force, pending the results of the review board, and she'd been given a choice between desk time and investigating small crimes. She, of course, chose to be out in the field, no matter how menial the work. Tuesday's big case was a break-in at a City Smart Furniture store in the Richmond district. The alarm bells had done their primary job, which was to discourage a burglar from hanging around. Nothing had been stolen or even ransacked. That was how exciting her Tuesday was.

Stottlemeyer was no longer actively going after Fat Tony. For all of his talk about the police commissioner wanting an arrest, it had just been a ploy to get Monk away from Sarabeth's side. The captain was now in charge of the task force. But that investigation had disintegrated into a series of dead ends, following up on phone tips and nationwide sightings that were leading nowhere.

Tuesday night, Julie called to chat. She started out talking about her friend Calista who was all excited about going to Harvard Law. They had been planning to go together. But now Julie thought it was the totally wrong choice and that Calista was bound to be overworked and disappointed. I could hear the envy in Julie's voice, but I didn't point this out. I let her have her coping mechanism and agreed that the eastern Ivy League schools were overrated.

Toward the end of the conversation, she once again brought up an internship at Monk and Teeger. Instead of saying, "Let me think about it" (*No!*), I said, "We'll see" (*Maybe*). Who knows, I thought. If she got to help us on a big case, it might look good on her next law school application. A mother can always hope.

Wednesday night, Monk and I had another

dinner with Takumi Ito. This time we dined at Rassigio's, Monk's only restaurant of choice. A month or so ago, we solved a mysterious little case involving Tony Rassigio, Jr. Ever since, Monk has been treated like a king. The owners dust off their fake AAA rating card from the board of health, post it in the window just for Monk's benefit, and never present us with a bill.

Ito looked haggard that evening and barely ate. Despite his protests, Sarabeth had come back to work that morning. "She's recovering well," he said, "and, to be honest, I'm grateful. She knows everything about that office. What a treasure."

Monk bit his tongue. He literally bit it. And the painful annoyance of a bit tongue kept him from even hinting at his own disappointment and suspicions.

By Thursday morning, I was bored. I tried my best to be a responsible business owner. I sent out an e-mail blast to my list of defense lawyers and security companies. I called a few other private investigators and turned on the Teeger charm, schmoozing and trying to get a lead. It turned out no one was having a busy week.

Meanwhile, Monk alternated between cleaning the office, reading old issues of the trade publication, *PI Magazine*, and touring our little strip mall with a broom and a pad of Post-it Notes that he used to write up polite suggestions and stick them to the doors of our neighbors—ways to make their businesses more symmetrical and tidier. An hour later he would have to go out with the broom again to sweep up the crumpled, discarded notes, which he would soon replace with new notes.

I was at my desk, deciding whether to eat my last doughnut from the shop two doors down. I was also checking Facebook and thinking about putting up the Closed sign and bagging it for the day. That was when Daniela Grace walked in. This time, she didn't bother with the niceties. "Why didn't you return my call?" she asked, her fists cocked on her hips.

"I'm so sorry," I said, standing up and brushing a few sugary crumbs from my blouse. "We've been swamped." To tell the truth, I'd forgotten. She had left a message that morning asking for a progress report and I'd put off calling back until it completely slipped my mind. When I don't have progress, I often postpone the progress reports.

"Am I to assume you've made no progress at all?"

"Not at the moment," I said. "But Adrian's giving your case a lot of thought."

Monk heard his name and glanced up from the January issue. "What am I doing?"

"You're deep in thought about the Henry Pickler case." I turned back to Daniela. "That's the way he works. It may look like he's reading a magazine or putting up Post-it Notes or sweeping the parking lot, but what he's really doing is thinking."

"That's what I'm doing," Monk confirmed, then went back to whatever article he was reading.

Daniela pursed her lips and scrunched her forehead as much as the Botox would let her. "So he's thinking, in his own weird way. And what are you doing?" She came around my desk before I could switch screens. "You're on Facebook?"

"Yes," I admitted because I had no choice. "I'm on Facebook."

"And this is how you're working on my case?"

"You can learn a lot on Facebook," I said defensively. "For example, Henry Pickler. I friended him last week but he didn't accept my invitation. That tells me a lot." I was winging it here. "I also friended his wife, Becky. She didn't accept my friendship, either."

"You friended Henry and Becky? Why?"

I actually hadn't friended either one of them. I just needed to give Daniela a reason why I was wasting time during business hours. "Facebook is a useful investigative tool. You can learn a lot about a suspect."

"I suppose," Daniela allowed. "Although I wouldn't take either rejection too seriously. You're not exactly best chums with Henry. And Becky only knows your name because I mentioned it."

"You mentioned me?"

"In an e-mail. I sent her four or five e-mails when Henry was arrested. It wasn't until days later, after he was released, that she got back to me."

"Hmm." Monk looked up from his magazine. "Is that unusual behavior for her?"

"What?" asked Daniela. "Not getting back to me? Yes, it was unusual. Becky is always a good e-mailer. And she's on Facebook at least twice a day."

"But she wasn't on Facebook while her husband was in jail?" Monk said. "I meant to phrase that as a question. Was she on Facebook at all during the time Pickler was in jail?"

"I don't know," said Daniela. "I suppose I could check. Is this important?"

"It could be," said Monk. "Any change in habit can be important, especially when it coincides with one's husband getting thrown in jail."

"Why don't you check?" I said, and offered Daniela my chair. Since I was already on the site, all she had to do was log out with my name and log in with hers. "What were the exact dates when he was in jail?"

Daniela checked the dates on her phone's calendar, then pulled up Becky Pickler's page and scrolled down. "Is this what you mean about Mr. Monk always thinking?" she asked.

"Yes," I said, and left it at that.

"Well, you're right," she said, looking up, both

impressed and puzzled. "Becky was not doing either Facebook or e-mail on the dates Henry was in jail. What does that mean?"

Monk shrugged. "Offhand, I'd say she didn't have access to a computer on those days, or she was too busy."

"Busy doing what?" Daniela asked.

"I don't do Facebook," said Monk, "so I don't know. Is there any way to see her normal pattern of comments?"

"He means her Timeline," I explained. "Sure, Adrian, bring your chair over and look."

Monk doesn't touch computers as a rule. I had placed one on his desk, but that was just to make the office symmetrical. I don't think I even plugged it in. His way of doing online research is to sit in front of my computer and give me verbal commands. "Lower. Higher. Click on that picture. Next page. Why does this ad want me to buy women's shoes?"

Monk took his time going down Becky Pickler's Wall, looking at her friends' responses, examining her posted photos, having me click on her friends' photos. "Where does Becky live?"

"Somewhere in the Seattle area," said Daniela. "She never gave me her address."

"Perhaps she doesn't want Henry finding out where she is," I said. "I know he's Facebook friends with her." And I pointed to his photo on the left, one of Becky's many friends.

"It seems odd she would keep him on," said Monk.

"She probably forgot to unfriend him," said I.

"Most of her other friends are from San Francisco. I don't see any from Seattle. I find that very curious. Go lower," he instructed. "The picture we saw before, with the moon. Go, go."

"I'm going, Adrian," I said. "Keep your pants on." In a few more seconds, I'd scrolled down to the one he'd wanted.

I've described this one before, the one of Becky alone on a rugged coastline and the pine tree and the skinny moon—the shot taken by her new, camera-shy boyfriend from Australia. Monk had me enlarge it, then put his nose almost against the screen. He pulled his nose back and twitched it. "This was not taken on Easter Sunday."

"Of course it was," said Daniela. "It was posted on Easter and Becky says it was Easter."

"Not Easter," Monk insisted. "Easter isn't determined by the calendar. It always falls on the first Sunday after the first full moon in spring. The moon in this shot is just a sliver, at least a week before or after. Therefore this has nothing to do with Easter."

"I don't understand," said Daniela, speaking for me as well. "Why would Becky lie about Easter?"

"Why indeed?" Monk crinkled his nose. "Have you noticed any difference in Becky since she moved away? Does she seem colder or warmer?

More personal? Less personal? What about her sense of humor? Has that changed?"

Daniela shrugged. "Perhaps she's not as fun-loving. Becky used to repost all sorts of videos; funny cats and dogs, funny quotes about drinking, which I don't really appreciate. She doesn't do that anymore."

"And her e-mails? Have they changed?"

"Again, perhaps not as personal and fun-loving. But I think that's understandable."

Monk leaned back in his chair and laced his hands behind his head. He closed his eyes and I could barely make out some movement of his lips. I love it when he does this, I have to admit.

"What's he doing?" Daniela whispered.

"Solving the case," I whispered back.

Monk stayed in this position for about a minute, until his lips stopped mumbling and a smile began curling upward. Then his eyes snapped open and his chair went upright.

# 24

## MR. MONK IS IN THE FIELD

Monk doesn't care for new people. If you remember, it was one of his hundred reasons for not wanting to open Monk and Teeger.

Police officers are one of his least favorite types of new people. They can be rude. It had taken a while to train Stottlemeyer and Devlin and the rest of the major crimes division to accept his way of handling a crime scene. Even stranger is Monk's way of handling the solution to a crime. For example, I doubt the San Mateo County Sheriff's Office would have been happy to stand by the side of the road and watch us illegally take a shovel to the vacant lot behind the Pickler home. But here was Captain Stottlemeyer, waiting patiently and confidently while Monk, Daniela, and I trespassed onto Henry's overgrown lot.

Actually, we weren't taking a shovel to it. We were taking three, all brand-new. They included two identical models and one more expensive, petite version that Daniela had taken a fancy to in the hardware store. Our intent wasn't to dig. It was to rattle Henry and bluff out the truth.

We'd been in the middle of the lot, within easy view of his office and kitchen, for only a minute when he came storming out into his backyard. "What are you doing?" There was a white picket gate in the white picket fence separating his yard from the field, and he used it.

"Hello, Henry," Daniela shouted back sweetly. "How are you today? I hope you don't mind."

"Of course I mind. Get off my property now or I'll call the cops."

"That actually is a cop right there," said Daniela, pointing to the captain by the side of the road. The captain smiled and waved back. "We brought him along."

"We know about Becky," Monk said. By this point, Henry had made his way across the brush and we stopped any pretense of digging.

"What has Becky been telling you? Whatever she's telling you is a lie."

"Nice try," I said. I was dying to say this next part, but I left it to Monk. He'd earned it.

"Where is she buried?" asked Monk.

It was, strictly speaking, a rhetorical question, although it would save us some effort if he pointed out the spot. Monk looked around. "My guess is not far from where Esteban Rivera died."

"Are you saying I killed my wife?" The timid, nervous man looked appalled by the very notion.

"Yes," Monk put it simply. "It's been clawing at the back of my mind. Why would anyone risk being convicted of a murder he didn't commit?

Because it beats being convicted of a murder he did commit."

"What?" Henry tried to laugh it off. "That doesn't make sense."

"Well, then let's start from the beginning," suggested Monk. "Eight months ago you killed your wife. I'm sure you had your reasons. Every murderer does. You buried her in this lot and told everyone she'd left you. Since you're some sort of expert in this Internet fad, you kept Becky alive by continuing her e-mail and her Facebook entries. You took old pictures of her and posted them as new ones. And the only time you stopped answering her e-mails was when you were in jail and didn't have access to a computer."

"At some point you were planning to phase Becky out," I said. "Maybe have her move to Australia with her new boyfriend." I always have to get my two cents in.

Monk nodded. "Everything was on schedule until the Lucarelli family decided to send Carlos Menendez a message by killing one of his drug dealers right outside his girlfriend's house. You saw it and panicked. The last thing you needed was a forensic team combing through your field, maybe with some nosy canine unit in tow."

"That's why you were out there with a shovel," chimed in Daniela. "You needed to bury Mr. Rivera's body. And that's when you got caught."

From the moment the highway patrolmen shined

their beams into the field, Henry had to play it by ear. He couldn't tell the truth. And he couldn't think up a convincing story involving a shovel in his hands. So he said nothing, trusting that he could hire a good lawyer to get him off, which was exactly what happened.

"I imagine Salvatore Lucarelli was curious," Monk ventured. "An innocent witness willing to take the rap for his hit?" Up until this point, Henry Pickler had not admitted a thing.

"They kidnapped me in my own driveway," said Henry, "without letting me even put my car away. With the top down and the garage door open. Animals."

"Mobsters can be like that," I said sympathetically. "Did they torture you?"

"Torture me?" He shivered. "Good God, no. But they roughed me up. I figured it was safe to tell them. I would never rat on them and they would never rat on me."

"So you admit it," I said. "You admit you killed Becky."

"I didn't admit anything."

"Yes, you shouldn't admit anything," Daniela said. "And that's the last advice I'm going to give as your lawyer, Henry. It's been fun."

"You're quitting?" He seemed so hurt. "Daniela, you can't quit."

"I'm quitting. There are plenty of great defense attorneys. I'm sure you can find one who wasn't a friend of the woman you killed. Allegedly killed."

"It's going to be easy getting a court order to dig up this field," Monk pointed out. "Especially when the Seattle police do a little checking on Becky's existence."

"Plus we can verify that her e-mails came from your computer," I said, again with the two cents.

Monk was amazed. "You can do that?"

"Of course they can," Henry said. He looked off at the field, then back at his house. And he sighed. "This is not going to be pleasant."

"That's what you get for killing your wife," said Monk. "And your mother and your father. By the way, Henry, where are they buried?"

I was stunned, but Henry barely twitched. "I didn't kill my parents. It was an accident."

"You killed your parents, too?" Daniela asked. "Henry, Henry, Henry."

"It was an accident," Henry insisted. "Dad always went foraging for wild mushrooms in the fall. I personally don't eat mushrooms. Too earthy and dirty. But Mom and Dad loved going out and picking their own. Back to nature. And now they're really back to nature." He shrugged. "You can tell I'm not fond of cemeteries."

"Under the apple tree?" Monk guessed. He pointed to the gnarled little tree not far from the picket fence. "It's not native to a vacant lot. It caught my eye the first time I paid a visit."

"I planted it as a memorial eight years ago," said Henry. "How did you know?"

"You strike me as a logical person," said Monk. "This lot is the only vacant piece of property in the neighborhood. I thought there might be a reason for never selling it. So while my partner was playing with her e-mails and Facebook, I called the San Mateo County Clerk. They have no record of the death of any Pickler in the past twenty years."

At this point, eight years after, it couldn't be proved one way or the other as to whether Henry had fed them the poisoned mushrooms or it had been an accident. It was bad either way. Like the movie *Psycho*, I thought. The worst part wasn't the murder in the shower; it was Norman Bates keeping his mother stuffed in the basement.

I looked over to Captain Stottlemeyer, gave him a heads-up, and met him halfway across the lot. "How did it go?" he asked. "Is he coming peacefully?"

"I think so," I said. "If the sheriff's office handles him right, they'll be able to get Fat Tony, too."

At the county sheriff's office in Redwood City, Henry made a full confession. As luck would have it, the sheriff had taken the afternoon off to go to his daughter's soccer game, leaving our friend Deputy Sheriff Clayton Jones more than willing to grab the glory.

It was late in the afternoon when two San Mateo County cruisers made their way north into the city, followed by the captain's Buick sedan and my trusty old Subaru. Waiting for us in front of the barbershop in North Beach was an SFPD patrol car. Another one had been stationed in the back alley.

You could tell by the way Deputy Clayton Jones got out of the cruiser, all swagger, that he intended to be in charge. "I appreciate your assistance on this one, Captain, but I'll take the lead."

"It may be your arrest," said Stottlemeyer, "but it's not your case. It's Monk's case. If it was up to you, Pickler would still be at large and the Rivera case would go unsolved."

"Actually, it's not my case," Monk corrected him. "It's Natalie's. She's the boss. She's the one Daniela Grace hired. It's only right that Natalie do the honors."

"Are you serious? Thank you." I was shocked and flattered. "Is this because you don't want to face down Sal Lucarelli?"

"You know better," he said. And it was true. Monk had taken pleasure in taking down plenty of bad guys just as intimidating as Sal. "It's because Sal was rude. He belittled you by calling you pretty. No one should do that."

"Adrian, I don't object to being called pretty."

"Yes, you do. I practically had to drag you away from his throat."

The captain's mustache twitched as he suppressed a smile. "Is that right?"

I nodded. "In a way. Sal and his mob were amused by the idea of a pretty little assistant being Monk's boss. Especially Fat Tony."

"Natalie hates being called pretty," Monk repeated.

"Then I guess it's settled," said Stottlemeyer. "Natalie does the honors."

"Wait a minute," sputtered Deputy Jones. "The murder was in my jurisdiction. Legally . . ."

"You'll still get the collar," said the captain. "And he'll be wearing your cuffs. But this is Natalie's moment. No one likes being called pretty. I know I don't."

"Being pretty is fine," I insisted. "Under other circumstances it's very nice."

"I know," said the captain. "Shall we do it?"

I realize it sounds silly, a bunch of adults in the middle of the street, arguing over who gets to take the lead. Monk is not legally allowed to make an arrest. Neither am I. But you go through a lot when you're pursuing a case. And part of what gets you through is looking forward to seeing the smile get wiped off their faces, to finally look them in the eye and let them know you're the one who's sending them to jail, not some grandstanding deputy who can't find three bodies in a vacant lot.

We didn't wait for Deputy Jones to lodge

another complaint. The captain opened the door to the barbershop. Monk grabbed the broom and swept his way through the hair. I followed, like a star walking down the red carpet. When we came to the back room door, I opened it fearlessly.

They were waiting for us, not looking happy but managing to hide it behind their casual bravado. As usual, Sal was at his rolltop desk. "Natalie, sweetie. A sight for sore eyes, even when you barge in like a truck driver. Captain. Monk. What can I do for you?"

"Don't look at me," said the captain, and waved a hand in my direction.

I did my best to savor it, taking in Sal's wary eyes, the confusion on the faces of the boys around the air hockey table, and Monk's expression, partly proud of me and partly proud of himself for giving the moment to me. The only face missing from this magic moment was Fat Tony's. "Where's your nephew?" I asked.

"I got a lot of nephews," said Sal.

"Anthony Lucarelli," I said.

"What do you want with Tony?"

"I want you to say good-bye to him. He's going away." Pretty good, huh? It came to me on the spur of the moment.

"Tony's not here," said Sal. "He said he was going with his girlfriend to the movies."

Well, that took some of the air out of our sails.

"Damn," said Jones. "I knew we shouldn't have come so late."

"What movie?" said Stottlemeyer. He was reaching for his phone.

But I wasn't about to let my moment slip away. I had seen something in Sal's eyes, the way they darted over to the left. I held up my hand and the room fell silent. Everyone was focused on me, even though I had no idea what I was going to do.

It turned out I didn't need to know. The sound of flushing water erupted from behind the door to Sal's left and ten seconds later, Fat Tony emerged from the bathroom. From the timing, I don't think he'd had time to wash.

He was just zipping up his pants when he caught sight of me. "If it isn't my favorite PI."

"Anthony Lucarelli, you're under arrest for the murder of Esteban Rivera."

Fat Tony just smiled. "I know you'd like that to be true, Natty girl. But I have a dozen witnesses who will swear . . ."

"And we have just one," I said. "Henry Pickler has turned state's evidence."

I love it when their smiles fade. It never gets old.

"Now, if you'll just go back and thoroughly wash your hands, we can put on the cuffs," said Monk. "Safety first."

# 25

## MR. MONK ON THE NEXT REBOUND

Daniela Grace and I celebrated the next morning by attending an AA meeting at the Mission Fellowship Center on Twenty-fourth Street. We toasted each other with cups of black coffee from her thermos and listened to our fellow alcoholics stand up and share. Once again it was an open meeting and I was not required to join in.

Afterward, we strolled over to Boogaloo's, a funky diner built into an old Cut-Rate drugstore. On the front of their menus they have printed the foot-by-foot instructions to doing the boogaloo, a dance I vaguely remember from old episodes of *Soul Train*. I can't tell you exactly what we ordered, but they were both dishes with eggs and cream gravy, which are the two main reasons for having brunch in any diner anywhere in the world.

The night before, I had e-mailed Daniela the final bill for the Pickler case, and this morning she slid an envelope across the table, right after the dregs of our cream gravy had been cleared. I thanked her and stashed it straight into my PBS tote.

"So do you consider this case a win or a loss?"

I asked. "I mean, because of us, Henry's back in jail, probably for a long time."

"A win, definitely," said Daniela. "In spite of all the lawyer jokes, we are officers of the court. Plus, Becky was a friend of sorts. You don't want someone to get away with killing your friends, even if he is a client. It sets a bad tone." She took a linen handkerchief from her Gucci purse and wiped egg from the corners of her mouth.

"This was our first time working for a lawyer." Maybe I shouldn't have said that, but it was true. It's always been the police or the FBI or private clients. "I'm glad it worked out."

"Don't fish for a compliment, dear. It's unbecoming. It worked out very nicely, yes, and I certainly plan to use you again—even if you've been lying to me all this time about being an alcoholic." She waited for a response, looking me square in the eyes. "You're not, are you? An alcoholic."

"I'm not," I confessed. I felt ashamed but also relieved. "In my defense, that's what I've been telling you from the day we met, but you wouldn't listen."

"We met at an AA meeting, Natalie."

"That was totally my fault," I admitted. "But every time I tried to straighten it out, you assumed I was in denial."

"Well, you were very strident about it. What was I to think?"

"What finally convinced you?"

"The fact that you would never share in a meeting. You're a very forthright person, dear. You're certainly not ashamed to go to meetings."

"I find them very comforting and supportive."

"So the only reason I could conceive of is that you don't want to tell an outright lie in front of a group of people who trust you."

"Thank you," I said with feeling. "For being so perceptive and getting me off the hook."

"You're welcome," said Daniela, who was just taking a bottle of hand sanitizer out of her Gucci. "And if I weren't so perceptive? Were you planning to spend the rest of your life going to meetings?"

"Don't they tell us to take life one day at a time? That's what I was going to do."

She chuckled. "You should consider starting your own support group for single mother detectives."

"Not a bad idea."

"By the way, do you know that woman? She's trying to get your attention."

I turned around in my chair and spotted Amy Devlin waiting alone in line by the cash register. I waved back, excused myself, and went over to say hello. "What are you doing here? Is there a break in the case? You should have called."

"I'm not on the case—you know that."

A small table by the window had just opened

up, and Devlin rushed to take it, barely beating out an older woman and a man with a cane. "Are you by yourself?" I asked.

She seemed a little tired and depressed. "I'm working a burglary in the area and I got hungry. I thought some comfort brunch might cheer me up."

"A burglary. That's nice." I couldn't help feeling sorry, a hardwired homicide investigator being reduced to mundane burglaries. Even her spiky hair was looking limp.

"It's the City Smart Furniture store on Guerrero."

"Right." I vaguely recalled. "You were working that a couple of days ago."

"No, that was a different City Smart, over in Richmond. But this case is nearly identical. They broke in, set off the alarm system, and left without taking a thing."

"You mean just like the first one? That's pretty weird."

"I know," she said, feigning a note of enthusiasm. "Maybe it's all part of some big clever scheme run by interior decorators. I can solve it and get my reputation back. Wouldn't that be something?"

"You never know," I said. "Look, Amy, it's great to see you, but I need to get back to my client. We're wrapping up some business."

"The vacant-lot case, right? Leland called last night and told me. Congratulations. Very clever work."

"Thanks. We'll talk soon, okay? I mean it."

"Oh, Natalie." Devlin avoided eye contact and stared at the cover of her menu, as if studying how to do the boogaloo. "Tell Monk I haven't lost faith. I know he can solve this. I really need him to."

"He will," I promised.

When I got back from brunch, I was all set to do a lap around the office, waving the check and perhaps subtly mentioning just how well our new company was doing. Not only had we just made twice what we usually do, but the money had come from the bad guy's account. A total win-win.

But I was stopped in my tracks, before I could even raise the check, by the sight of Monk sitting at my computer, wearing headphones. He raised a finger to keep me from saying anything, then pushed about twenty keys to get whatever he was listening to to pause. I slipped the check back into my tote.

"I couldn't figure out how to plug mine in," he shouted as he took off the headphones. "There are so many places for plugs. Even with yours it took hours."

"Adrian, you can't play on my machine. God only knows what might be screwed up now."

"Hey, I'm not a child."

"No, a child would have been able to connect

up a computer. Please tell me you didn't hit any button that says 'Erase.'"

The last time Monk had been on my computer, the keyboard got accidentally stuck on caps and italics and bold. I couldn't figure how to turn it off for weeks. Every e-mail looked like it had been written by an angry twelve-year-old. *CAPTAIN, I NEED THE AUTOPSY REPORT.*

*Just stay calm,* I thought. *What's done is done.* These were all good lessons learned in my many AA meetings. "So, you were actually listening to a file," I said. "That's great."

"Natalie, a file is something you read. This is an audio recording."

"My mistake," I said. "What is it?" I moved behind him and checked the screen. "The 911 calls during the shooting spree. Devlin sent them to me last week."

"The call from Sarabeth definitely sounds fake. Like she's pretending to be scared and out of breath. Katrina's call, on the other hand . . . Computer, play out loud." He spoke slowly and clearly to the screen. "Play out loud."

"It doesn't work that way."

"It did before. I said, 'Play through head-phones,' and it switched right over as soon as I plugged in the headphones."

"Brilliant. Let me in there." I mime-pushed him out of my chair and settled in. No caps or italics. Good. Within a few seconds I had the first file cued up and playing through my desktop speakers.

Sarabeth's call was about a minute long and it sounded pretty desperate. On my second time through, I listened for other things—the things Monk always hears. Ambient noise, echoes, faint voices, and footsteps from other rooms. "You know the sound experts in the department have been over this a dozen times."

"I haven't come up with anything, either," he admitted. "Except that Sarabeth is definitely faking it. Now listen to the second audio."

I scrolled down to Katrina's call and double-clicked. I have to admit she sounded a lot more panicked than her coworker. "Everyone's being shot. I don't know what's going on. Get the police, please." The 911 dispatcher tried his best to get more information, but you could hear Katrina running now, her voice fading and out. Her last audible words were, "Run. Save yourself, Sarabeth. No!" A second later came a deafening gunshot. A few seconds after that, someone, probably not Katrina, ended the call.

"She said, 'Save yourself, Sarabeth,'" I pointed out. "That must be when Sarabeth ran down the stairs."

"Or she could have been shouting to someone else. 'Save yourself. Sarabeth, no!'"

"Wow. You're taking this rejection hard. Are you saying she's the shooter now?"

"No. Wyatt Noone escaped with the shotgun.

That seems clear. But she might have been an active participant. I know that she lied."

"Lied about having a husband?"

"About what happened that day. When I looked out the third-floor window . . ."

I'd almost forgotten. "Yes, Adrian. What did you see? You never told me."

"It's what I didn't see. I didn't see a southern exposure with light streaming through the window."

"Okay . . ." There had been a time when Monk would have had to explain the whole thing, from Sarabeth's testimony in the ICU to when he looked out the reception-area window. But I was getting a little better. "Sarabeth said that when Wyatt walked in that day, she couldn't see the shotgun in his hands because of the sun. He was backlit."

"An obvious lie," said Monk. "The sun doesn't hit those windows until late afternoon."

"You knew this when you looked out the window. And yet you continued to protest her innocence."

"I thought there might be some innocent explanation," he said. "Like the sun reflecting off the windows across the street."

"The windows across the street don't reflect," I pointed out. "They're tinted. You know that."

"I know that," said Monk, cricking his neck and shrugging his shoulders. "Don't make this harder on me. It's hard enough."

I heard the captain's clunker of a Buick before I saw it pulling into a parking space right out front. Stottlemeyer took his time wandering in. "Just happened to be in the neighborhood?" I asked. "This is becoming a very popular neighborhood."

"Good day to you, too, Natalie. Actually I have a detective sergeant checking out something at the pawnshop, so I thought I'd string along. He's over there now."

"Pawnshop?" I said, trying not to look in Monk's direction. "What's up with the pawnshop?"

The captain grinned. "We got an anonymous tip this morning about stolen property."

"Really, Adrian?" I sighed. "You're going to get us kicked out of our mini-mall."

"It was right in the window, taunting me," Monk said. "A Mickey Mantle rookie baseball card. I knew from the slight wear on the left corner and the old mark of a rubber band. . . ."

"I don't want to hear it," I said. "Sorry, Captain."

"No," said Stottlemeyer. "It's always good to recover stolen property, although your neighbor can't be too happy." He brushed both sides of his mustache and looked around. "I see you're still sharing an office and haven't resorted to killing each other. Good job, Natalie."

"What about me?" asked Monk.

"Good job on staying alive."

Stottlemeyer checked out the window. The

SFPD cruiser was still in front of 24-Hour Holiday Pawn. "As long as we have a minute, we might as well share notes. I'll start." The fact that he didn't take out a notebook seemed to me a bad sign. "No credible leads on Noone," he reported from memory. "But he took a few million dollars with him, so we're trying to follow the money. None

of the victims' spouses—Todd Avery, Helena Lubarsky, even Caleb Smith's roommate—have had any unusual transactions. The one possible exception, and I hate to say this . . ."

"Sarabeth Willow," Monk stated categorically.

The captain raised his eyebrows and lower lip in unison. "I thought you were in her corner."

"Corners change," said Monk. "Is she suddenly spending money? I knew it. You should subpoena her bank."

"Slow down, buddy. I don't know what happened between you and her. Obviously something."

"She dumped me on the rebound for her ex-husband."

"I see." Stottlemeyer reached out a hand to mime-touch Monk's shoulder. "That's tough luck, Monk. I'm sorry. But this woman was shot twice. Her only offense so far is that she's the sole survivor and the bad guy got away."

"You said she's spending money. On what?"

"She's not spending money per se. But her hubby's doctor, Dr. Rothstein, is a fan of yours.

He knows you're interested in her husband's health and he gave us a heads-up to pass along. Next week Paul Willow is flying off to Berne, Switzerland, for some experimental treatments. This has been in the works for some time. I checked, and it's an expensive program. The drugs alone run over a hundred thousand. And it's not covered by any insurance program. I also checked."

"So where's the money coming from?" I asked.

"Sarabeth sent a money order to cover the down payment. That's all we know so far."

"Maybe it was savings," I said, playing devil's advocate. "Or an inheritance. Or maybe they hocked everything they own to pay for it."

"Or maybe it's her payoff for helping Noone get away with murder," said Monk. "That's what I'm thinking."

# 26

## MR. MONK AND THE LAO-SY DINNER

For the second time in two weeks, Monk and I were having dinner at his brother's. Yuki had called me that afternoon and, after some small talk, asked if we could join them and if we could bring along Takumi Ito.

"I know he's busy dealing with his company," she said. "But we had just a great time last week. And I decided to do an evening of Lao food. Japan's not that far from Laos, taste-wise. I think. Please invite him. Otherwise most of the spices will go to waste. Ambrose and Adrian are not fans of anything spicier than a saltine."

I was a bit surprised by Yuki's enthusiasm. "I thought you hated suits," I said, referring to the people, not the outfits.

"Just because I like tattoos and have a few Hells Angels for friends? No, Takumi was a lot of fun. And I'm sure he could use a little distraction."

I accepted her offer at face value and told Monk the news. I've learned over the years that telling him is often better than asking. And anything is better than giving him choices. I once made the mistake of asking him what color I

286

should paint my living room. He was still deciding a week later after the second coat had dried and the furniture was all back in place.

Takumi Ito was also up for another evening with the Monk brothers, although he was swamped with work. How about a little later, he asked. Later was fine. We agreed to pick him up at East Decorative Imports and found ourselves walking out of the elevator at a few minutes after seven, facing the reception desk and the warm, smiling face of Sarabeth Willow.

"Adrian. Natalie. So good to see you."

"Mrs. Willow," said Monk in the tone he usually reserved for cold-blooded killers and people with stains on their shirts.

"No need to be formal," she said as if nothing had happened. She pressed a button on the intercom. "Mr. Ito, they're here."

"Have you been working all day?" I asked. "I thought you weren't coming back until next week."

"I tried to keep her away," said Ito. He was down the hall, putting on his suit jacket as he came toward us. "But Sarabeth insisted, didn't you?"

"You couldn't do without me. Don't even pretend."

"Maybe not. But you have to go home now—right now—or I'm locking you in. I mean it."

Sarabeth agreed reluctantly and gathered her

bag from behind her desk. We ushered her into the elevator.

We kept the small talk going with Ito, who seemed to be in a better mood today. He had hired three new people, he said, who were starting tomorrow, all three with experience in the import trade. And he was thinking of promoting Sarabeth to Wyatt Noone's old job as finance manager. "She has a feeling for numbers," he said. "And she's the only one who knows all the ins and outs."

Right now I wasn't interested in Sarabeth knowing the ins. Just the way out. During our small talk by the elevator door, I kept my eye on the lighted display. It didn't stop on two but proceeded to the ground level. Half a minute later, I glanced out one of the front windows and could see the office assistant crossing the street and walking away.

The three of us arrived at the Monk homestead a few minutes before eight. Adrian and Ambrose had been raised in a Craftsman bungalow, never restored but perfectly maintained. I suppose you could make a comparison between this and the period perfection of the Henry Pickler house, although this one didn't have a vacant lot next door with three buried bodies.

Yuki answered on my first knock. She was just taking off her apron and pulling a lock of hair off her face. If I didn't know this biker chick better,

I'd have thought she was trying to imitate the perfect feminine hostess. "Welcome to our home. May I take your coats?"

"We left our jackets in the car," I pointed out.

"So you did. Well, I hope you're prepared. Ambrose decided to help in the kitchen."

"Oh no," I said. It was an involuntary reflex. I really know nothing of Ambrose's cooking expertise except that he likes to eat tricolor pasta on three separate nights. He also eats alphabet soup in alphabetical order. "That's the whole point of the letters," he would point out. It was hard to argue with that.

"Yuki!" a voice shouted from the kitchen. "The rice is sticky. What do I do?"

"It's supposed to be sticky," she shouted back. "That's why it's called sticky rice."

"I don't think so."

"Ambrose, leave the rice alone." She turned back and gazed up into Takumi Ito's eyes. The man was nearly a foot taller. "I'm so sorry. But I have to go put out some fires. Literally put out some fires."

"No problem," he said. "Is there anything I can do to help?"

"Do you know how to make unsticky rice sticky again?"

"I think you have to start from scratch," said Ito, and followed Yuki into the kitchen.

Nearly an hour later, after several lengthy

battles between Ambrose and rice, dinner was served. Being a good hostess, Yuki sat our guest on her right and made sure he was engaged in the conver-sation. The Monks made the expected schoolboy quips about Lao food being Lao-sy. And Mr. Ito was as gracious a guest as always.

This time, as before, we tried not to discuss business. And as before, the spices were set up in a separate room. At the dinner table, over the shrimp dish, Ito made a casual inquiry about Lao seasoning and Yuki escorted him into the living room to teach him all she knew. "It shouldn't take long," she quipped, then smiled back at the rest of us.

As soon as they were out of earshot, Monk started hissing under his breath. "What is Yuki doing?"

"What do you mean?" asked Ambrose.

"She's smiling and flirting and practically throwing herself at him."

"She is not," said Ambrose. "She's being a consummate hostess."

"Since when is Yuki a hostess? She's an *H-E*–double hockey sticks–*S* Angel. With tattoos."

"No, no." Ambrose waved away his brother's concern. "There's a reason. We just finished writing the assembly instructions for a traditional English tea cart. The manufacturer asked us to add a few paragraphs about tea time etiquette. Yuki's just practicing."

"Maybe," said Monk. "Maybe. But you can't be too careful with women. That's all I'm saying."

"What does that mean exactly? Are you saying I don't have to be too careful with women or that I should be extra careful? The way you phrase it is kind of ambiguous."

"I mean women will seem all sweet and caring, and then they'll fall for the first ex-husband they run into. Believe me, it's true."

"Don't listen to him," I told Ambrose. "Adrian just had a bad week. A bad month."

"Are you sure?" Ambrose's face darkened and he glanced off toward the living room. "She is being extraordinarily servile."

"Don't start," I said. My whisper was fierce but audible. "Yuki has done everything in the world to prove her love for you, Ambrose. Everything. Including putting up with a Monk husband and a Monk brother-in-law. She's not flirting."

"But he is a tall, handsome Japanese fellow. They could be perfect for each other."

"First of all, Yuki is not Japanese. She's more American than I am. Second, Mr. Ito is married with five children. I've seen the pictures. Third, no one in his right mind would take relationship advice from your brother. Sorry, Adrian, that's just the way it is."

"Your opinion is duly noted," said Monk. "But you still can't be too careful."

An unusual, tinkling laugh announced Yuki's

return to the dining room. Instantly, we jerked our heads away from one another and adopted painfully fake smiles. "How are the spices?" Ambrose asked. "Spicy enough for the two of you?"

"You wouldn't like them," said Yuki. "But they're quite tangy in their way."

"Your wife is a treasure," said Takumi Ito with a little bow. "You are a very lucky man."

The rest of the meal felt awkward and stilted, at least to the majority of people seated at the table. The Lao offerings ended with some kind of mango Jell-O cut into perfect squares and served with a side of coconut milk. The Monk brothers ate only the sweet squares.

Since we hadn't arrived exactly on the hour this time, I wasn't sure when Ambrose would choose to usher us out. I was just about to start making some excuse about having an early day tomorrow when my cell phone started calling from the living room. "Excuse me."

It was Amy Devlin. I lowered my voice and crossed to the front door. "Hi. What's up?"

"I don't know. I think I'm going crazy." She didn't sound good.

"Crazy how?"

"Even a simple furniture-store burglary has me stumped. That's how low my self-confidence is."

"The City Smart stores? Are you talking about the first one, or the second, or both?"

"I'm talking about the first, the second, and the third."

"The third?"

"It just happened, an hour after closing time. It's exactly the same as the others."

"Do you want Monk and me to come over?"

"Would you?" Amy gave me the address, in Potrero Hill on the other side of the 101.

I went back into the dining room to make our apologies and drag Monk to another crime scene. "I'm sorry for cutting your evening short, Mr. Ito. Adrian and I can drop you off at your hotel on our way to the scene."

"There's no need to do that," said Yuki. "Takumi can stay as long as he wants."

"What about the three-and-a-half-hour rule?" asked Ambrose.

"There's no rule on how long guests should stay," said Yuki. "It's a suggestion. When Takumi is ready to leave, I'll drive him—if he doesn't mind riding on the back of a Harley."

"I love Harleys," said Ito. "I have one myself, a Dyna Fat Bob. I had to modify it for noise regulations in Tokyo, so I would love to ride a Harley with full sound. That would be a treat."

"Are you sure?" Monk asked. "It's just as easy for us. Natalie's not that bad a driver."

"If it's all the same, I would prefer a ride from Mrs. Monk."

"I have a Street Glide," Yuki bragged. "Upgraded to a hundred and ten horses."

"I want to come along," said Ambrose. "I like Harleys."

Yuki had to laugh. "We can't put three on a motorcycle. Besides, you never leave the house. Maybe another time, sweetie."

"Another time?" Ambrose shuddered. "Are you kidding? I wouldn't be caught dead on that deathtrap."

I felt bad about leaving Ambrose in this situation. But I'd promised Devlin we'd be right over. And I couldn't very well argue with two adults who wanted to share a motorcycle ride back to a hotel. At the end of the day, I trusted Yuki just as much as Ambrose had trusted her before Adrian had gotten into his head.

# 27

## MR. MONK AND THE SPACE-SAVING BUDDHA

City Smart Furniture has three retail outlets in San Francisco. All three had been victims of break-ins. And according to Monk's strict rules about coincidences, it wasn't a coincidence.

I'm not sure how many City Smarts there are. But the store's concept is very urban and wouldn't make much sense in Wyoming or even in the roomy environs of the suburbs. Every item is designed to make the most of your limited living space. There are Murphy beds that fold down from the wall and bookshelves that open up on hinges to reveal hidden closets. They have stackable end tables and tiny kitchen tables that fold down to become free-standing cutting boards. Just being in a City Smart made me grateful for what I've always considered to be my cozy bungalow. Compared to a lot of people, I practically live in a mansion.

I parked my Subaru next to the red Grand Am and met the lieutenant and Chester, the chain's regional manager, just inside the front doors. They led us through a few showrooms to a glass side door that opened onto a side alley. It was labeled

EMERGENCY EXIT, but the only emergency seemed to be a gaping hole in the glass and glistening shards all over the hardwood floor.

"It looks like a single intruder with something like a crowbar," said Devlin, getting us up to speed. "When the alarm was triggered, the security company alerted us. A patrol car responded in under six minutes."

"Is that your typical response time?" asked Monk.

"Pretty typical, with all the one-way streets and traffic."

"So the intruder could count on a comfortable five minutes without being interrupted."

Devlin hemmed. "It's a pretty ballsy move. But if the perp was desperate enough, he could make that gamble."

"Desperate enough for what?" asked Chester. He was a large man in his early thirties who clearly was at the end of his rope. "Nothing was stolen. All my stores the same way. Three shattered doors. I'm saying it's vandalism, pure and simple."

"Can you think of any disgruntled employees?" asked Lieutenant Devlin.

Monk shook his head. "Not vandalism. This guy cased the stores ahead of time. He knew what he was after and how to get to it."

"But he didn't take a thing," said Chester.

Monk didn't argue. Instead, his hands went up and he began framing the scene.

"What's he doing?" asked Chester.

"Shh," I explained.

The three of us followed Monk who, from what I could tell, was following a faint trail of glass, partial footprints, jostled furniture, and impressions on small, modern-style area rugs. In keeping with the theme, the place wasn't as large as most furniture stores, just very well laid out.

When I looked up from the floor myself, I found us in a section featuring artwork—small, generically modern paintings and sculptures and statues that could fit into the odd corner of an apartment. Monk saw it first, of course. But Devlin was the first to comment.

"Oh my God," she said. She let the sight sink in, her mind working a mile a minute, trying to make it all fit together. "Oh my God," she repeated.

I didn't know what to make of it, either. But it was right in front of us, like an old friend. A tin Buddha, one of the quartet that we'd last seen on the second floor of the import warehouse.

"Does this mean . . ." A gleam formed in Amy's eyes. Just when she'd given up. Just when she'd been reassigned to a purgatory of menial work—insignificant break-ins, not even burglaries—suddenly she'd stumbled across her big break.

Monk turned to Chester. "Did this come from East Decorative Imports? Don't bother answering. It did. How does it open?"

"How do you know it opens?" asked Chester.

Monk rolled his eyes. "Everything in this place opens and turns into a bed or a bathroom sink. Tell me if I'm wrong."

Chester smiled. "You're right." He stepped in front of the Buddha, took its head between his palms, and tilted it back on a hinge. Then he reached in to the Buddha's folded hands and pulled out. The statue's front opened like a pair of French doors. "A work of art and a storage space," he said proudly. "We get them from Japan where they've got even smaller apartments."

"My people should have found this." Lieutenant Devlin shook her head. "Is this how he escaped? Please tell me this is how he escaped."

I also wanted to believe it, but . . . "Hardly looks big enough for a grown man."

"When did you receive shipment?" asked Monk.

"A couple of days ago. Monday?" guessed Chester.

"We saw these in the warehouse on Sunday," I said. "Even if a person could fit, it's hard to believe anyone was in here for any length of time."

Monk inspected the empty space. He sniffed, looked for any shreds or residue from its earlier contents, then worked the doors, probably to see if they could be closed from the inside. Finally he stood back and held up both his index fingers, the universal sign for "Shut up—I'm thinking." Every one seemed to understand.

"Are there Buddhas like this in your other two stores?"

"Yeah," said Chester. "Every store gets the same inventory."

"And what happened to the fourth one? The import company shipped out four on the same day. Did you buy them all?"

"I'll check the paperwork. But I'm sure we sold one directly to some garden meditation center. Let me check." Chester took a tablet out of his briefcase and stepped away to the display model of a small desk that folded out into a diaper-changing table.

"So Noone didn't use the Buddha to escape?" Devlin asked under her breath.

Monk shook his head. "Like Natalie said, it would be a hard fit. Plus it doesn't account for all three stores being broken into."

"Do we have a chance at solving this?" asked Devlin. "Come on, Monk. Let's hear one of your patented percentages. What's the percentage? This time I'm paying attention."

"Fifty-fifty," Monk said. "Our bad guy broke into these stores, looking for something in one of the Buddhas. We know he didn't find it in the first or second because he kept looking. We don't know if he found it here. So our chances of it being in the fourth are fifty-fifty. Slightly less."

"Just a minute," announced Chester from the changing table. "Slow Wi-Fi connection."

Devlin was about to ask another question but Monk held up his index fingers again. And then . . . And then he slowly broke into a smile, his "I got it" smile, the most beautiful expression in the world, in my book. Then, unexpectedly, it turned into a frown.

"Adrian, what's the matter? You figured it out, didn't you? What's wrong?"

"What's wrong? It's even worse than I thought."

"But you have it solved."

"I do," he said faintly. "I know who Noone is."

"You know?" said Devlin. "What does that mean? You mean it's a person we already know? In another identity?"

"That's right," said Monk. "Hidden in plain sight."

"How can that be?"

"It be," said Monk. "I mean, it is."

I was just as confused as Devlin. Not to have recognized Noone's alter ego right in front of us? How could we be so incompetent?

"Got it," said Chester, bringing the tablet back for us to look at. "It's the Lilly B. Goldberg-Sanchez Zen Garden. It was delivered this afternoon."

"The Goldberg-Sanchez Zen Garden?" said Devlin, marveling at the name.

"I actually know where that is," I said. "It's a little public-private Japanese garden. A few blocks south of me."

"Let's go," said Monk. "Our fifty percent is going down every second."

"I have the number for the caretaker," said Chester, enlarging a detail on his copy of the shipping bill.

Devlin took the number and started dialing before we even left the store.

# 28

## MR. MONK FINDS NO ONE

The Goldberg-Sanchez Zen Garden occupied a surprisingly large triangle of land, perhaps an acre, just off Castro Street. A year or so ago, some foundation had built a six-foot stone wall and transformed this scruffy patch into an oasis of rock gardens, wooden bridges over bubbling water features, and miniature stone pagodas. Julie and I had gone there once for a picnic lunch.

A caretaker named Jeremy was waiting for us in front of the locked gate. He identified himself as a neighborhood volunteer and seemed nervous about a manic police lieutenant flashing her badge and demanding access. Devlin was even more impatient than usual, which didn't help. "Was a tin Buddha delivered today?"

"Uh, yes," said Jeremy. "We didn't have time to install it. We're planning to use it to store garden tools. Is that all right?"

"Why should I care?" said Devlin. "Where is it?"

"It's by the northeast corner."

"Can you point, sir, or do I need a compass?"

This was where I took over. Being the most personable and charming member of the team, I smiled, introduced myself, and did my best to ease the situation.

Somehow I persuaded Jeremy to give us custody of the key. I input his phone number and address into my phone, politely asked him to leave the premises, and promised I would return the key as soon as we were through. I didn't know quite what to expect in the way of danger, but experience has taught me to get civilians out of the way, even when walking through a Zen garden on a moonlit night. Jeremy watched as we locked the gate behind us and headed off to the northeast corner.

The fourth storage Buddha was just beyond a lily pond, blanket-wrapped and seated on a wooden pallet. Devlin pulled out a key ring, chose her sharpest key, and dove in, attacking the duct tape like an assassin on a mission. When the blanket was cleared enough to get to the doors, she took a breath and stepped aside. "You do the honors, Monk."

"Unfortunately, I know what I'm going to find." Monk reached into his jacket and pulled out three pairs of plastic gloves, a large for himself and two sets of medium for Devlin and me. How he'd foreseen the need for gloves, I don't know. But he had them and we put them on. Then he tipped back the statue's head and pulled apart its folded hands.

I'd been half expecting to find the shotgun,

and I was right. It was in the bottom of the compartment, wrapped in a pair of moving-van blankets similar to the one still half-taped into place around the statue's shoulders. Monk handed it over to Devlin as if he couldn't care less and kept fishing. Next he pulled out a blue sweatshirt covered in dry patches of blood. This, too, he handed to Devlin and kept fishing.

At first glance, it looked like a flesh-colored rubber ball, slightly smaller than a deflated soccer ball. On second glance, I saw it wasn't complete, not entirely round, with a longer tab in the back and what looked like sideburns. "Is that a wig?" I asked. "A bald wig?"

Monk twitched in the affirmative and held it out toward my face. "Natalie, meet Wyatt Noone. Wyatt Noone, Natalie Teeger."

"I don't get it," said Devlin. "Wyatt Noone is someone we know? Someone with hair? Are you saying he carried on two separate lives? Wearing a silly bald cap half the time? I hate to say it, Monk, but this seems far-fetched, even in your world."

"Not so far-fetched. Takumi Ito was right. If only he'd given them the raises they asked for . . ."

Under normal circumstances, this would have been the start of his summation, the time to settle back and let Adrian Monk lay it out, explaining the inexplicable to us inferior mortals who don't feel compelled to wash our hands a hundred times a day. But this time he was interrupted.

If we were in the northeast corner, then the noise was coming from the west, a combination of scrapes and human grunts, but mostly grunts. Monk might have been the first to hear it, but Devlin was the first to raise a hand and signal for silence. "But . . . ," Monk protested in a whisper. He hates being cut off in mid-summation.

The lieutenant kept her hand up and led the way over the stone bridge and the lily pond, around the perfectly raked sand garden and toward the western wall of the triangle. She stopped us behind a pair of flowering dogwoods where we wouldn't be the first things the intruder would see.

The grunts continued, middle-aged and struggling, as Sarabeth Willow knelt on top of the stone wall, her back to us, and began to lower herself to the ground, grabbing at a few outcroppings as she went. The pain from her injuries must have been excruciating but she didn't let it stop her.

She spent almost a minute holding her side and catching her breath. She was just dusting off her jeans and getting her bearings when she saw us. Her first impulse was to run. But there were three of us and we were all inside a wall. We surrounded her in the middle of the sand garden. To Monk's credit, he managed to ignore the chaos of foot-prints marring the raked patterns of sand.

"Adrian," said Sarabeth, her hands dropping to her side. "What a surprise. I . . . I . . ." She tried her best to recover. "I came to check the paper-work on the statue we delivered today. The gate was locked, so I guess I'm legally trespassing. You shouldn't blame Mr. Ito for the paperwork. He's got the invoices all screwed up and—"

"We looked inside the Buddha," Monk inter-rupted. "We know about Wyatt."

"Where's Noone? Is he on the other side of the wall?" asked Devlin. "Is he?"

Sarabeth stood for a moment, then turned on her heel and began shouting. "Police! Run, honey, run."

"Damn," said Devlin, and took off like a sprinter. I could see her vacillating in her stride, calculating which would be quicker, scaling the wall or unlocking the gate and going around. She chose the wall and vanished around the edge of the lily pond. I felt the urge to join her, like a dog chasing another dog chasing a ball. Monk stopped me.

"Don't go. I need you here."

"What about Noone?" I protested.

"Why do you need Natalie here?" asked Sarabeth, all sweetness again. "Do you think I'm going to overpower you or run away?"

"Let's say I don't trust either one of us."

I heard all this but I was too distracted. "What if Noone gets away? He'll be gone for good."

"Natalie, there is no Wyatt Noone. There never was."

"I know that, but . . ."

"I mean never. Not even in the beginning."

"Then who is Devlin chasing?"

"No one. It was all her."

The woman in question placed a heartfelt hand to her chest. "Adrian, Adrian. Even if you believe this crazy theory of yours, whatever it is, it's your word against mine, isn't it?"

"Not quite," said Monk. "Your prints are probably on the shotgun. And I'm sure you left your DNA on the bald wig. Sweat, hair, skin fragments."

"What? No." There were a dozen things I could have said to shoot this down, but the first objection that came to mind . . . "She had her picture taken with Noone at the Christmas party," I said. And my second objection . . . "Everyone in the office knew him."

"Like I said, it was Takumi Ito's fault. Right?"

Sarabeth nodded a reluctant yes. Her shoulders fell. But a gut instinct told me to pull my Glock out of my PBS tote. I made sure she saw it.

Monk continued, his summation back on track. "Business was good for East Decorative Imports. But Mr. Ito kept denying you raises. That had to sting. He gave you permission to hire a financial manager. But you were already doing the financial manager's work. Whose idea was it?"

"It was Mel's," said Sarabeth. "He said it as a joke. 'Let's make up a fake employee and split his paycheck four ways.' Caleb came up with the name. He got the Social Security number and did all the paperwork. Everyone had to keep it absolutely secret. Not even wives or husbands knew. Not even Paul."

"Paul didn't know about it?" asked Monk, a little dubious.

"Of course not," said Sarabeth. "Otherwise it wouldn't work. Everyone opened a little savings account, just to keep it secret. We were protecting them as much as we were protecting ourselves."

"Even Todd Avery?" I asked. "He worked right below you."

"Todd's not a very curious person," said Sarabeth. "And Katrina knew how to manipulate him. Every time someone showed up, we invented some excuse for Wyatt's not being around. If anyone from Tokyo ever deigned to pay a visit, we could pretend Wyatt had just quit and moved away."

"Who did Noone's voice on the phone calls?" asked Monk. "The Southern accent?"

"That was Caleb. The boy fancied himself an actor."

"What about the photos?" I asked.

"We got pretty drunk at the Christmas party," said Sarabeth. "We put Mel in makeup and a bald wig and different clothes. It all added to the realism."

"I told you Wyatt looked like Mel," Monk reminded me.

"You did," I admitted. "I should have taken that seriously."

Monk forgave me with a sideways tilt of his head. "It was all a petty scam, relatively harmless, until Sarabeth got greedy."

"I'm not greedy," she said indignantly. "I have a husband with cancer. There are treatments. Expensive treatments."

"Plenty of people have husbands with cancer," I said. "They don't embezzle millions and . . ." The Glock trembled in my hand as the cold-blooded reality of what she had done suddenly hit me. "And murder three people. Your coworkers, your friends. To walk into the office in that silly disguise and open fire on your friends . . ."

"Friends," Sarabeth scoffed. Her normally soft face hardened. "I was their menial assistant. I did three-quarters of Wyatt's work for one-quarter of the money. And none of them ever made my life easy. When Paul got sick, no one cared. No one came to visit or even sent flowers. The bastards."

Monk was mesmerized by Sarabeth's flinty expression, as if a panda bear had just morphed into a grizzly, which was pretty much the situation.

"I asked for a bigger cut, for Paul's sake. But they didn't care."

"And so you started embezzling," I said. I'm always the one who fills up the dead space in a social conversation. Otherwise things can get uncomfortable. "And when embezzling wasn't bringing in enough, you graduated to sending out copies as originals."

"These were things we could blame on Wyatt," said Sarabeth. "When we found out Mr. Ito was scheduling a visit, that's what I told them. Blame it on Wyatt." She laughed, and both Monk and I winced. "But oh no! They were too high and mighty for that. I'll tell you what they were. Pissed. Pissed that meek little Sarabeth figured out how to make some real money and not them."

"So you were looking at jail time," said Monk, his voice softening. "Just when your husband needed you the most." I could see him trying to rationalize this, but it was an uphill battle.

"It wasn't that big of a step," said Sarabeth. "Mentally at least. From blaming Wyatt for embezzlement to blaming him for murder. I'm a lot smarter than they thought."

Monk seemed to agree. "The clothes in the stairwell. That was very smart. You needed to give the police some theory of how Noone got out of the building. And shooting yourself, Sarabeth . . . That took real guts."

"I was hoping I could give myself a flesh wound. But my hand was shaking. I misjudged."

"Still it took guts. All in all, a smart plan."

Sarabeth's lips curled sadly. She looked human again. "Not quite smart enough. I didn't recover the shotgun and the wig in time. I tried, but . . . Imagine how I felt when I discovered the Buddhas had already been shipped."

"I can imagine," said Monk.

"And, of course, it's always the last place you look. If it had been shipped to any one of the stores, there'd be no evidence now."

"A bad break," said Monk.

"Adrian!" I punched him in the shoulder, just to get his attention. "She murdered three people."

"But she did it for her husband. You've got to give her points for that."

"Points? I can't believe you just said that. She is not getting points."

"You could be nicer about it."

"Don't blame Natalie," Sarabeth said, her sweetness returning. "If you blame anyone, Adrian, blame me. It's my fault."

"Of course it's your fault," I shouted. "You killed three people." And I raised my Glock just for emphasis.

"If things had only been different," Sarabeth almost purred. "I really liked you, Adrian."

"Thanks, Sarabeth."

"It wasn't just for show, if that's any consolation."

*Not to the three people you killed. No consolation to them!* That's what I wanted to say. Instead, I just let them have their moment.

We heard Lieutenant Devlin before we saw her as she opened the gate, swung it shut, and shuffled slowly down one of the gravel paths.

"Damn, damn, damn," she said, panting out each of the words. "Noone got away."

Monk paused before speaking. It must have been hard. "No, he didn't get away."

# 29

# MR. MONK AND
# THE SURPRISE

A week later, I was dropping off the president of East Decorative Imports at San Francisco International.

He'd had a busy week, keeping the company running on both sides of the Pacific while hiring four employees, including a replacement for Sarabeth, who would not be returning to work for the rest of her natural life. He also had to deal with the publicity, which couldn't have been easy. He'd be lucky to make it through security without some lurking news crew trying to get a statement.

I don't know for sure if Takumi Ito felt guilty about helping to create Wyatt Noone. He already blamed himself for making them hire an accountant, so I imagine, yes, he blamed himself. I never asked. As a wise person once said, "You can only be responsible for your own actions." I actually think that was someone speaking at an AA meeting. I'm going to miss those.

I pulled up at the drop-off curb and immediately disobeyed the signs by getting out to say good-bye. Ito didn't hug. I'm quite used to not hugging, given the crowd I hang out with. But he looked like he wanted to say something that couldn't be said. So I hugged him.

He hugged back, respectfully, then lifted the hatch and removed his briefcase and two pieces of luggage. From out of the briefcase came a gift-wrapped bottle that looked suspiciously like champagne. "I know Mr. Monk doesn't drink. But this is for you to celebrate. I wish I could stay an extra day and drink it with you."

"Celebrate what?"

Ito reacted with a blush. "I'm sorry. I wasn't thinking. Please take this as a thank-you. Promise me you'll drink it on a special occasion." I promised.

After the airport, I wasn't in the mood to go back to the office. But Monk needed a ride to do some afternoon errands—he'd reminded me twice—and Luther Washington didn't seem to be available. As I pulled out of the airport and onto the 101, I saw the exit sign for Millbrae, which started me thinking about Henry Pickler and the very first case of Monk and Teeger, Consulting Detectives.

I don't know what I'd been expecting: to spend our first two weeks without customers, watching Monk vacuum the office all day? Or perhaps the other extreme, having a glamorous widow walk in, asking us to find her husband's killer, like some old Humphrey Bogart movie? I have to admit, this had been a great start, and we'd made enough to pay our salaries and expenses for another month or two.

But now what? We'd gone almost a full week just mopping up after the Willow and Pickler cases, making statements for the DA, helping with the evidence, dealing with the media blitz. Monk had taken Sarabeth's arrest pretty well. But at some point, maybe this afternoon, he would rebel again, refusing to come into the office or to take on a new case. I had to expect this, I knew, although expecting never makes it easier.

I was in my own little world as I pulled into our mini-mall. The first thing I noticed was the lack of any parking spaces. The second thing I noticed was the crowd milling around the opening doorway of Monk and Teeger. The third thing—slow-on-the-uptake Natalie—was the red and white banner draped above the windows: GRAND OPENING.

I pulled up, blocking Luther's black Lincoln, Devlin's Grand Am, and Stottlemeyer's Buick. Julie was the first to run outside. "Surprise!" she shouted.

"A surprise grand opening?" I had to laugh.

"It was Adrian's idea. I told him a surprise was exactly the opposite of a grand opening. But he wouldn't listen. He said you'd appreciate it."

"It's perfect," I said, still laughing. Leave it to Monk to organize a surprise publicity event where next to no one shows—just a few invited friends who had probably been warned not to stay too long.

"Surprise!" the mini-throng began shouting as soon as every one recognized the Subaru. They crowded around as I got out, no more than two dozen in total, almost everyone a friend. I reached back in the car for the champagne, suddenly aware of the reason behind Takumi Ito's embarrassed little gift.

In the hour and a half since I'd left the shop, Luther and Julie, under Monk's supervision, had put up the sign, filled up exactly ten white helium balloons, and arranged two symmetrical tables of identical munchies. From a distance I guessed them to be sliced Spam squares on Triscuits. It was as festive an event as possible—for a man who equated the words *festive* and *chaotic*. I was honestly touched.

The captain popped the cork as soon as the bottle was out of my hands and Monk's therapist, Dr. Bell, handed me a full glass from a previously popped bottle. "Congratulations," he said with a rueful smile that told me this party had been the topic of a lot of discussion on his couch.

Looking healthier and happier than she had in a while, Lieutenant Devlin stepped forward and toasted. "To Monk and Teeger." Everyone around me raised a glass and seconded the motion.

"Are you mad at me?" Monk asked. He had been hanging around the rear and only stepped forward after the third toast. "I know you wanted a grand 'grand opening,' but this was the best I could do. I am what I am, Natalie."

"It's wonderful, Adrian. It is. Thank you."

"It's not wonderful."

"Look, have you ever thrown a party for anyone in your life?"

"Not in this lifetime."

"Then it's wonderful. And it's for our business, which makes it extra wonderful."

"Julie told me to do it."

"No, she didn't." I was as sure of that as I was of anything. "It was your idea and I'm grateful. It means a lot."

Monk cricked his head to one side and rolled his shoulders. "No one's eating the Spam. I need to go push the Spam."

It's always a little hard to calm down after being surprised. It took me until my second glass of champagne to start relaxing and getting into the moment. It was the perfect gathering, I decided. No police commissioner or politicians or cameras. Just a handful of friends and coworkers, the people Monk was least uncomfortable with. I did notice one gate-crasher. Mr. Wittingham of 24-Hour Holiday Pawn held a glass of bubbly in each hand, silent and stone-faced as he toured the premises, paying particular attention to the

California State PI license hanging behind my desk.

Even Yuki was there, hard-edged and petite, nibbling at the corner of a Spam Triscuit. "Ambrose sends his best," she said. "He couldn't be here because . . . Well, he's not on his honeymoon and his house isn't on fire."

"Understood."

"So it's just me. Takumi is on his way back to Tokyo?" she asked, sounding just a little too casual.

"He is," I said. "Any regrets?"

She bristled. "Any regrets about what? About what happened between Takumi and me? No, because nothing at all happened that night. I dropped him off at the hotel. Any regrets that things didn't happen between us? No. Any regrets about marrying Ambrose? Absolutely not."

"I didn't mean that," I said. "I'm not sure what I meant, come to think of it. But . . . Well, something seemed to be happening with you two."

"I was practicing being a good hostess," said Yuki. "A little role playing."

"So you really didn't enjoy his company?"

"Just between us?" Yuki took a breath and lowered her voice. "It was tempting, of course. You think about someone handsome and rich and successful, who can actually leave the house and have dinner or see a movie. But Ambrose has done so much for me. He rescued me. We rescued each other."

"That's not a strong basis for a relationship."

Yuki rolled her eyes. "It's not just that and you know it. There's no one else for me. Ambrose and I are damaged in different ways, but in complementary ways, like two jigsaw pieces you force together. They don't fit at first. But each piece gives a bit and soon they fit perfectly. And nothing else can fit in those notches now, even if you break them apart."

"I'm not sure if that's sad or wonderful."

"It's wonderful," she assured me. "Love isn't about having someone who's perfect. It's about having someone who's perfect for you." Her smile seemed genuinely happy as she toasted me with the Triscuit and walked away.

"I brought a little something," came Daniela's voice right behind my ear.

I spun around, with my first instinct to hide my champagne. She saw my reaction and laughed. "It's going to be hard getting used to," I said.

"Me, too. When someone filled your glass, I had to stop myself from yelling."

"Don't be mad if I show up to a few more meetings."

"You're always welcome." She held out a small, flat, wrapped package. "Here. Every office should have one."

"Ah, Daniela, thank you." I tore open the tasteful beige paper to reveal a sterling silver picture frame with a dollar bill centered under the glass.

"I actually underpaid you by a single dollar, just so I could do this. The first dollar made in your new venture. You hang it on your wall and every day you'll be reminded just how far you've come."

I held the framed bill at arm's length. "It's perfect. If worse comes to worst, I can spend the dollar and sell the frame."

"It will never come to that," she warned. "Don't be maudlin."

I was still nursing my second glass, wondering whether to treat myself to a third. Julie was still there, having a laughter-filled conversation about something with Luther. My guess was the two of them were comparing Monk stories, whether it was his behavior in moving vehicles or his supernatural skill. I hoped they weren't sharing Natalie stories, but that was always possible.

My decision about a third glass of champagne was made for me when Amy Devlin walked up and traded my empty for a new one.

"Is everything back to normal?" I asked.

"What do you mean, normal?"

On the morning after the Zen garden, the media had been full of the story, featuring Lieutenant Devlin's arrest of the suspect. The police commissioner's review board was canceled that same morning and Devlin was reinstated to full service as Captain Stottlemeyer's number two. That's what I meant by normal. It seemed a reasonable question.

"It's never normal after something like this," said Devlin. "People all over town, even officers and FBI agents, still think of me as the idiot who let a triple killer escape. You can't change that."

"Yes, you can. People are proved innocent all the time. They redeem themselves."

"But I did nothing wrong. Look, what do you think when I say the name Joan Crawford? Be honest."

"Joan Crawford? The actress?" Honestly, I hadn't thought about Joan Crawford in decades. "I don't know. *Mommie Dearest*?"

"You see?" I guess I'd proven her point. "Here's a woman who made maybe a hundred films. She won an Oscar. And the first thing anyone thinks about is a scandalous book written by her adopted daughter that may or may not be true. No wire hangers!"

"That's a pretty great line," I had to admit. "They still show the movie on TV."

"That's what I'm saying. *Mommie Dearest* is the first thing people think of with Joan Crawford. With Amy Devlin, they think about that news video. Me standing dim-witted outside an empty warehouse. I tell you, Natalie, it's got me thinking about quitting the force."

"Quitting?" I was shocked. "Amy, you can't be serious."

"I'm not un-serious. If I wouldn't be letting the captain down, and letting you down and Monk . . ."

She lowered her voice even more. "I have family on the Boston force. They're always looking for tough, experienced minority officers."

"Minority?"

"I'm a woman."

"Right. Sorry."

"Anyway, I didn't mean to go off. You asked if things were back to normal, so I guess the simple answer is no, not quite."

By the time Luther and Julie finally left, all traces of the party had been removed. They'd taken the Grand Opening sign with them, along with the last of the guests. The champagne bottles were in the recycling, and the majority of the Spam Triscuits were in double-wrapped plastic bags at the curb, waiting for tomorrow morning's pickup.

As expected, Monk was vacuuming the office floor. I was leaning back at my desk, feeling good from the whole experience and idly trying to think of a way to break his vacuuming cycle. If I didn't, he might go on all night.

"Why do they call it a vacuum cleaner?" I asked, just loud enough to be heard.

"What?" He switched it off.

"It's not really a vacuum," I pointed out. "It's just a fan that pulls air and dirt into a bag. The air comes out the other side, so there's no vacuum being created at all. They should call it a fan cleaner instead."

"A fan cleaner? That's ridiculous."

"No, it's not."

"It's always been called a vacuum. Always. Ever since before the Civil War."

"They had vacuums in the Civil War?"

"I know that's surprising, considering that it was such a dirty war."

"Well, maybe the machines operated on a vacuum system back then, but not now."

"Natalie!" He pulled the plug from the wall and started wrapping the cord. "You just managed to ruin the whole experience for me. I hope you're happy."

It should always be so easy.

I watched as he put the fan cleaner back in the closet and waited for him to settle into the desk on his side of the room. I laced my hands behind my head and was pleased when he did the same, leaning back in his perfectly adjusted, ergonomically designed chair. "This is nice," he said, without any coaxing from me.

"Very nice," I said. "We're partners now with our own office and money in the bank and two big cases under our belts."

"Actually, they were pretty much the same case," he mused.

"No, they weren't."

"Deductively, yes. They hinged on the same deduction. Sarabeth fooled us with a person who didn't exist. So did Henry. I mean his wife used to exist. But we couldn't solve either case until we realized that both of these unseen people were made up."

"I like the way you say *we*."

"Did I say *we?*"

"You did."

"I don't think so."

My cell phone rang. Otherwise I might have pursued the point. "Randy. I'm so glad you called." I threw Monk a single thumbs-up. He threw back a symmetrical two.

"Hey, Natalie." It was Randy Disher, of course. "Just wanted to congratulate you on your surprise grand opening."

"Thanks so much. How did you find out?"

"Your new intern told me."

"Whoa. Is that what she said? Julie is not our intern." I was going to have to have another talk with that young woman.

"Sorry. Future intern." I could hear another voice in the background. "Sharona sends her best. We wish we could have been there."

"I understand. A police chief's job is never done."

"That's true," he said, and the words sounded heartfelt.

I suddenly realized that I hadn't spoken to Randy since Monk had solved the case with the Summit chefs. "So, how's it going? Is everything back to normal?"

"It depends what you mean by normal."

Augh. When will I learn not to ask that question?

"It's not normal," I could hear Sharona shouting in the background. "Believe me."

"She's right," said Randy. "It's very not-normal when you're a police chief and mistakenly arrest the mayor for murder."

"But that's all fixed," I said. "Monk arrested Ellen's brother and the mayor was let go."

"It's not really fixed." Randy sighed. "This is a small town. The mayor hates my guts and everyone else is treating me like a piranha."

"I think you mean pariah."

"Sorry, pariah. You know, one of those man-eating fish everybody steers clear of."

"No, that's a piranha."

"That's what I said. Anyway, the town's not going to forget it. Last week, I was in the Founders' Day parade down Springfield Avenue. Some kids snuck up and spray-painted clown balloons all over my car."

"Oh no. Did you at least catch them?"

"Uh, no. It's still an open case. I tell you, Natalie, this is going to be with me forever."

"No, it's not," I told him. "You've been doing a great job."

"Maybe in the past. Now they're second-guessing everything I do. Even my officers are. If I ever have to arrest the mayor again, I'm going to lose all credibility. It's just like Pee-wee Herman."

"Pee-wee Herman?"

"You know, the guy with the TV kids' show. Years of great entertainment, a couple of big movies. And all people remember is that he got busted doing things in a porn movie theater."

"You are not Pee-wee Herman."

"Yes, I am. I'm Pee-wee. One mistake and Summit is never going to take me seriously again. To be honest, I'm thinking about quitting. Just leaving."

"They don't deserve you," shouted Sharona in the background.

"What? No." Why was everybody suddenly thinking about quitting? "Randy, you can't quit. You've put too much work into this. What will you do if you quit?"

"I don't know, but anything's better than this. I could come back to San Francisco. At least I have family there."

"What is it?" Monk asked. "What's wrong with Randy? What?"

I covered the phone and took a deep breath. In the background, I could hear Randy going on about Pee-wee Herman and credibility and how maybe he wasn't meant to be the guy in charge.

"Adrian, hold your horses. I'll tell you later."

**Center Point Large Print**
600 Brooks Road / PO Box 1
Thorndike, ME 04986-0001 USA

**(207) 568-3717**

**US & Canada:**
**1 800 929-9108**
www.centerpointlargeprint.com